About the Author

Dawn Treadway is the author of the award winning flash fiction story "The Prisoner". Presently she can be found in beautiful coastal California, with her exceptional children, Cooper and Waylon, and two orange feline beasts. Dawn holds a Bachelor's of Science in Nursing and works in Mental Health. When not actively enjoying dark dreams, she is otherwise cultivating her love of everything dark, gothic and sexy as Hell.

Aaron Speca is an "accidental author" who fell into creative writing at the age of 39, joining a writing group at the behest of his wife and her friends. Since then, he has published two short stories with writing partner Patricia Laffoon, and is co-author with Dawn Treadway on the novel Dark Dreams: Progeny of Sin. He currently resides in Virginia with his wife, three children, and a precocious Boston terrier.

Dark Dreams

Progeny of Sin

DAWN TREADWAY & AARON SPECA

Harper*Impulse* an imprint of
HarperCollins*Publishers* Ltd
1 London Bridge Street
London SE1 9GF

www.harpercollins.co.uk

A Paperback Original 2015

First published in Great Britain in ebook format by Harper*Impulse* 2015

A catalogue record for this book is
available from the British Library

ISBN: 978-0-00-812285-0

This novel is entirely a work of fiction.
The names, characters and incidents portrayed in it are
the work of the author's imagination. Any resemblance to
actual persons, living or dead, events or localities is
entirely coincidental.

Automatically produced by Atomik ePublisher from Easypress

Dawn:

Dedicated to my father, Dr. Gerald Treadway, who instilled in me the belief that I could achieve absolutely anything, if I did the work.

Aaron:

For Wendy, my true partner

Chapter 1

Jade Shear could feel the spark of emotion ignite; like a caged electrical storm it slithered up her skin and spread throughout her body. "No, damn it, not again," she cursed into the air. Jade's eyes strained shut as her long, French-manicured fingernails drew into fists.

Opening her stinging eyes she watched her customers begin to twitch and look around nervously. It was as if, suddenly, something ominous had just descended. She felt a wave of anxiety sweeping through their emotions even before the patrons themselves were aware of it. She let out an audible sigh and began trying to suppress the assault on her senses.

The patron's responses were varied. Some began to look lost; others, more strongly affected, looked almost angry.

Jade opened her fists and tried to stabilize herself inside the circular wooden countertop forming the epicenter of her store. The emotion around her relentlessly crawled through her body, like a horde of ants on a mass exodus through the inside of her spine and limbs. She leaned forward and steadied herself, inhaling deeply. She closed her eyes, grabbing a thick, red curl between her fingers and began to twist. Fixating her mind she began deflecting the patrons' feelings, pushing them away. *Get out of my head!*

Her eyes opened and Jade swore she saw a man-sized shadow

move behind one of the crowded bookshelves in her peripheral vision. It disappeared so quickly she thought, for sure, it was her imagination.

"Hey, gorgeous, thought it was your day off!" Matt lilted accusatorily and sauntered toward the register. Nothing ever seemed to ruin his good mood. It was one reason she could stand to be around him. The other was that he was one of the few men she could be near and not read lascivious feelings about her pouring off of him. "You all right, sweets? You look like you need a drink." His perfectly arched brows rose slightly for a moment. "And a hairbrush." He chuckled and tried to tame her hair.

"Can you please not start with me?" Jade tried to shake out the last bits of the obtrusive emotions around her. She actually loved when Matt "started" with her.

"Now, darlin', what in the world would be fun about that?" He moved his hand like a wand through the air when he spoke, a gesture he always seemed to make appropriate. Whether recapping a bad date he'd been on, appraising someone's outfit, or generally talking trash about another of Jade's employees, there was always "the hand" emphasizing his dramatic points.

He continued, without waiting for a response. "Girl, you need to stop with the workaholic spinster act." He gave her a cursory disapproving glance from her disheveled hair down to her beautifully attired feet. She saw a small smile escape when he eyed her footwear. "Get out of here, go dig up a life, girl, get laid, fall down drunk somewhere." He let loose with yet another wave of his hand around the store. "You know this place is fine. I've got the wheel. I make a fabulous captain." Matt laughed; the man certainly loved to amuse himself.

"I just need a book or two, then I'm out. I won't stay," Jade swore, even as she scanned the shop for other things she could be working on.

"Okay, mama, but I'm watching you." The characteristic hand wave ended with an accusatory finger pointed at her.

A gust of hot air blew up from the floor behind her. It seemed to come from nowhere. Jade inhaled as the fragrance of dark sandalwood and a dirty masculinity wafted into her nostrils. Her eyes closed and as she breathed in, her mind was abruptly flooded with the image of all the sex she wasn't having.

Matt's lowered voice invaded the darkness of her shut eyelids. "Oh, my Lord, no, I am not looking at you, not anymore, now I'm watching that!" She opened her eyes and saw the look in Matt's eyes glaze over slightly as he motioned to something, or someone, behind her that had now consumed his attentions.

"Do not turn around quickly, but girl, turn the hell around. Slowly, I said, do not startle it and make it run away," Matt hissed as he placed a hand on her shoulder.

"What are you talking about now? Is there some kind of animal in my shop?" Jade turned and not twenty feet away, he stood.

Legs crossed, a gorgeous man leaned against a bookshelf, his cocked head resting against it in a lazy pose. A long stream of dark, almost black, hair fell below his extremely well-built shoulders, contrasting with the lighter red of the cherry wood. This man was making no attempt to hide the fact he was staring right at her, assessing her. She felt some disdain for his audacity, but honestly his stare caused her to catch her breath, and then consciously begin breathing again. Rather than turn away, she stole another peek. Jade's eyes met his and they seemed to grab and pull her in. His eyes contained darkness, but she saw that they were actually an intense gold laced by black lashes. As she trailed down his body, large muscled arms exploded out of the sleeves of his black t-shirt.

His emotion came upon her unbidden and she felt a sudden wave of lust crash over her. She unintentionally released a breathy sigh and clenched her teeth as the pure animal nature of him surrounded her in an all-encompassing cloud of arousal. Between this force and her body stood only a flimsy white tank and it apparently was going to provide her no protection. Her breasts and nipples tightened and became overly sensitive to even the slightest movements she made. The lower regions of her body went moist and warm and she crossed her legs; the clenching, however, made the feeling even stronger.

"Holy cow," fell softly out of her mouth.

And Matt concurred, "Yes, ho-oly cow, girl." Her mouth had apparently remained open because, keeping his gaze stuck on the tall hunk of man before them, Matt put his hand under her chin and popped it closed.

Trying to shake off the lusty arousal, she turned and tried to take on the look of the professional establishment owner she was, and took a tentative step in his direction.

Of course, that didn't work out; instead she tripped on the edge of the Turkish rug beneath her, twisting her foot and breaking the heel off her favorite Jimmy Choo knee-high boots.

"Damn it," she said under her breath, "I saved for months to buy those." As she bent down to pick up the broken heel, she tried to take a step backward and stabilize her still sexually stunned body against the wooden counter.

Naturally, being that she was Jade, her hand landed at the base of a stack of returned books, sending them and herself tumbling to the floor. She was now red-cheeked, with hair strewn across her face and in her mouth, on her hands and knees. She lifted her head to wait for the typical Matt-like wisecrack, which surprisingly never came.

The mysterious man flashed a condescending grin the Cheshire cat himself would have been proud of and slowly turned and sauntered toward her front doors. Then he seemed to disappear. But that couldn't be right, could it? He must have simply walked out the door and she had missed it.

"What the fuck was that?" Jade gaped at the space the dark-haired man had occupied, as she sat back onto her heels and shook her head to clear it.

Matt only raised his brows and looked down to her. His mind was obviously still more focused on the gorgeous stranger than his boss. As her clumsiness was pretty much constant, he looked at her with only a slight smirk. "That, my dear, was sex; pure, walking, fabulous sex. And not the weak-ass, watered-down kind. That man was fully loaded," he chuckled, "and I would love some." Matt furrowed his brow and bent down to help her.

"Okay, Jade, tell me right now," Matt demanded, tapping his fingers on the patterned rug beside her sore knees. "What was that hot slice of man feeling? I have to know."

Jade looked at Matt, past his crisp blue jeans and perfect orange polo shirt, the look in his eyes full of anticipation. He was one of the only people she trusted with the knowledge of what she could do. Well, actually, the only one, because she was reasonably sure he was the only one who didn't ever want something from her. "I hate my curse, you know that. When I make a conscious decision to take advantage of the annoying thing, I am ashamed of myself. Please don't make me go there."

Unfortunately, most of the time her ability crept in without her inviting it. Even now, all around them she could sense the crowd's slow change back to their previous mix of emotions. *Curious,* she thought, *that man appears as a sudden shift in emotion consumes the store and knocks me on my ass and, blam, he walks out, and it all goes back to normal?*

"Come on, Jade, you're not going to tell me anything?" He gave her his sweetest puppy-dog eyes.

"Sorry, dude, but I didn't even try," she lied; this was the easiest way out of the conversation. Jade hated using her blasted mental capabilities to read emotions, almost as much as she detested her ability to change those feelings, and she had absolutely no intention of discussing them or the sexual barrage that strange man had given her. The memory made her body release a shiver from head to toe, which unfortunately came to rest in a warm, aching pool deep down in the lower regions of her stomach.

Why did this have to happen to me? Jade asked herself for the millionth time.

A swirl of wind formed in the discarded trash and debris on the dirty sidewalk, out from under Nias's black combat boots as he transcended outside to the not-so-fresh air of New York City streets.

He usually didn't take such a risk. Humans seeing a tall, dark stranger appear from out of nowhere tended to become alarmed. He had simply wanted to remove himself from within the vicinity of the human female immediately.

When Nias first saw the backside of the statuesque redhead twirling a single curl and lounging on her forearms at the book counter his body began to boil. He knew right away he was staring at trouble. She was stunning. Watching the girl in plain, low-rise jeans and a white tank top … there was definitely something different about her. He could tell immediately that there was a force within her, the power they needed. But there was something else as well, something insisting his gaze remain on her, and not stray.

When she turned around with her friend to look at him he could feel her immediate pull on him. All he had wanted to do was remove the space between them. Slip a hand around the curve of her hip to the small of her back and pull her body flush against him, for a long, slow kiss.

The few moments after he had seen her were bad enough, but when she turned to look in his direction, the effect he had on her became abundantly clear. He began to mentally undress the beauty and, in detail, strip her down and find ways to make her react to him. His loins began to swell as his brain began to get more descriptive. It was only when she tumbled and their eyes broke contact that he was able to snap out of the apparent spell she had put him under. He had no other recourse for the moment but to get out of there before he walked up, took her by the hand, and transcended her straight back to his bedroom.

He silently cursed Jibreel and the other Goddesses for asking him to locate Jade Shear. Oh yeah, that girl would definitely be trouble.

A slight queasy ache swelled from the pits of his stomach. He straightened his bearing back to that of the warrior he was, returning to his now-comfortable state of numbness.

Nias turned to survey the street. Humans, with their matching white paper coffee cups, sat a little nervously now, lounging and taking in the sun. An ordinary blond couple opened the wooden and glass door and moved into Jade's establishment. Resting his hands in the front pockets of his faded jeans, he found peace in his old habit of surveillance, and slowly the feelings began to subside.

None of the scattered few had noticed him appear. No wide, stricken eyes or signs of panic were visible. Only the common human reaction of shifting as an anxious tension swept through them. But it always did when a strong high-caste Daemon was near.

His memory shifted to the last image he had of her as he exited the store. She was kneeling on the ground, a disheveled mass of books surrounding her, on her hands and knees in the middle of it. She was a beautiful disaster.

This was the female that was supposed to help him traverse Sheol and rescue his brother?

"Unbelievable," he grumbled.

He had spent ages, millennia even, in Sheol. He didn't need assistance. Arousing or not, that clumsy human was going to get them both killed. She couldn't even manage to stand on her legs; how the hell was he supposed to traverse Sheol with her? Much less kill multiple caste-leveled Shaitan in blazing underworld heat. And he was there to seek *her* help? The woman on her hands and knees, knocking things over and tumbling to the ground – *she was supposed to be able to protect him from the Shaitan?* He realized his teeth were grinding.

Nias had a flash, a sudden, intense desire to leave her, to never see this female again. *This is a really stupid plan. People are going to die; this girl is going to die.*

Now he had to return to Jibreel and her sisters and tell them he had found her. This day just kept getting better and better.

"I am fucked," he said to himself and transcended out.

Chapter 2

Nias opened the immense white door and stepped through for the second time in a scant few hours, taking long strides over the cloudlike path toward the Goddesses. Bathed in a bright light, the area consumed him in a powdery whiteness. He kept his head down, raising a hand to his brow and using the front sheet of his hair like a shield against its radiance.

Djinn were rarely asked to meet with the Goddesses, and almost never here, at the Temple. And so, when he received the summons that morning, curiosity got the better of him, and he transcended immediately to the place of worship. Now he returned with a pit in his stomach to tell them the "good" news.

Three of the High Goddesses stood facing him, the edges of their figures wavering against the light that Daemon could barely gaze upon. "Eternally beautiful, eternally dark, it has always been curious how he made your kind. If he were capable of love, or even remote affection, I would say it was used during your creation." The center Goddess tilted her head of glimmering white hair to the side, using her hands to trace his outline when she spoke to him.

"Thank you, Goddess, your compliments honor me, as always." Nias, although playing the subservient to their vanity, couldn't help but curl the side of his mouth in a flirty smirk, his golden eyes flashing with a hint of mischief. He continued walking, moving close to her and leaning in toward her ear when he spoke next. Lowering his tone to something just north of a whisper, "Jibreel, thank you for inviting me back into your home." He couldn't help but tease them. They were without true male companionship in Arcadia.

She sighed and then noticed the other two Goddesses looking at him as well and stood up straight to regain an authoritative posture. "Our creatures in the Unseen tell us Joss is being held by the Empusa; this is good news for you. It gives you plenty of time to train the girl and prepare her for your journey into Sheol."

"Train the girl for our journey into Sheol? You have to realize what you're saying is absurd."

The ethereal blonde to his left immediately became more animated. "Djinn! You will not speak this way to Jibreel! With a wave of my hand I could end your life. It would, in fact, be a pleasure. I do not share Jibreel's affection for creatures like you. Whether above ground or below, I would end you all. I see how dangerous you all are. And you, specifically, Nias."

I dare you to try, he thought, but made sure not to show his feelings about her threats openly. He spoke to them with a deep, composed voice. "You know as well as I, no living human belongs in Sheol." He inwardly shuddered at the memories of his time there … of what he was tasked to do. "I can certainly handle anything they can throw at me. What possible good can come from me training her?"

"You are the most capable warrior available. You know why Phaeton cannot go; he needs to retain his position as Sovereign of the Djinn Sentry. To leave the humans unguarded would bring chaos. We require your help, and your brother needs you."

The Goddess Eeia had intentionally used Phaeton's new title to gauge Nias's reaction, he knew, and was sure she was not disappointed as he bristled at the sound of it. "Unquestionably I will go for Joss, but the woman, I don't need her. I won't take her." *Do not order me to take her, come on, girls, do not make me take the beautiful trouble,* Nias silently pleaded.

"If she has retained the Gifts she will ease your passage. For your brother, for the balance, you will take her. Are her powers legitimate? Could you feel her?" Oh yeah, he was feeling her all right, way too much, in fact.

"Yes, yes, she has powers." He knew then he had lost this argument. For his brother he would take the girl. "She is stronger than I have ever felt from a human. The empathic Gifts granted to Jade are definitely potent." Speaking of the girl brought on a reaction in him he didn't know what to do with. He found himself shifting from one cloud-covered combat boot to the other. *I do not shift uncomfortably,* he thought. He corrected himself once again, retaking his typical firm, masculine stance. Gritting his teeth, Nias lowered his head slightly and exhaled, resigned to the course the Goddesses had set him on.

Damn.

Jade figured she must have blacked out, because one moment she was walking home from the bookstore after staying, despite Matt's protests, and the next she was inside what looked to be a large amazing loft space. She was inside someone's home. She dropped to her knees, hitting a cold, hard floor, and then she fell into a kind of shock.

She started muttering to herself, "Okay, this is too weird. I was just outside, and the sky was dark. Now I'm in somebody's loft, where I can plainly see out that window," she pointed a dizzy finger toward the floor-to-ceiling casement, "the sun isn't even down; it is clearly twilight out there." She was talking to herself out loud, to hear her own voice more than anything. She turned her body to figure out exactly where she was, and her chin ran smack into the denim-covered legs and steel-toed combat boots of the man who was responsible. And she screamed as loud as she could.

Nias fell to his knees and put his hand over her mouth.

"Woman, you are obviously upset, and at this point I can

understand that, but if you would stop with the screeching and remain calm, I can explain everything."

That was good because she wanted some answers. "Where am I? How did I get here? Did I pass out? Did you give me drugs? Are you some kind of kidnapper? If you are, I will let you know now you definitely have the wrong girl. I haven't a dime in the world, so you might as well just save yourself the trouble and let me go!" Her words came out rapid-fire, a battering tempest of chatter that she could see nearly overwhelmed him.

In response to her questioning this large dark-haired man merely began to laugh out loud.

"I'm sorry, did I amuse you?" She squinted up at him.

"No, hellion, I just find your way of communication different, that's all, and no I am not a kidnapper, I have not given you drugs, you did not pass out, and you are in California; San Francisco to be precise. As for the way you got here, I transcended us."

"You what?"

"I transcended us – a process Daemons use to move around."

"Daemons?" She looked up to take a real, solid look at this maniac…and ran smack into the eyes of the gorgeous man from the physical disturbance this morning in her bookstore. *Criminy, I have been abducted by the hottest lunatic ever.* Jade looked around her, trying to assess the likelihood that she could escape and outrun him. She saw an open window and on the opposite side of what seemed to be a living room, the front door. *Door is further, but I probably won't break a leg if I go for the door. Door it is.* She shoved him away and was up and running!

Before she took three steps, he was in front of her, a giant wall of muscle. She turned on the tips of her replacement stilettos and bolted for the window. This time he gave her five steps. He was in front of her again. Mr. Tall, Dark, and Broody gently picked her up with one of his arms behind her back, swung her legs up and over his other arm and carried her to the divan, where he smoothly sat her down and smiled.

"Can I continue? Or would you like to take another turn about the room? If it's exercise you're looking for I can think of much better ways to expend your energy." He folded his arms, as if daring her to make another run for it. His golden eyes flickered with unmistakable amusement.

"Oh, for crying out loud, fine. I will listen to what you have to say. Only because you outweigh me by at least a hundred pounds, are way quicker than I am, and clearly you are willing to use force to have your way." She was waving her index finger in the air, much like Matt did when he got excited. "But stop grinning at me; I am a hostage, not a plaything."

"Pity." His eyes did a swift head-to-toe assessment of her body. "I can assure you I wish this could be done any other way. Unfortunately the circumstances at hand have forced me into your life."

"That I can see," she hissed.

"Jade, I'm afraid our time together has just begun," he said, squinting his eyes a bit. "I, or rather my family and I, require your assistance, and your gifts. We know you have the ability to sense emotion; we also know you can, in various degrees, affect emotions around you. Also your ability to tell if beings are lying may come in handy as well."

"How in the world could you *know* that? Or my name? Who the hell are you?" If it were possible, this conversation was starting to freak her out even more than what had already happened.

"My name is Nias, and let's just say I have it on the best authority."

"Well, then, Nias, do you know where this curse came from? Can you tell me?" She wasn't sure why it had come out as a question and not a demand; maybe it was fear at finally having an answer. What she did know was even discussing its origin made her recall all the pain and sadness it had brought into her life. If there were a way to find out where it came from, possibly there would be a way to get rid of it. She would do almost anything to accomplish that.

"That, I cannot do. I am not at liberty to inform you of any more than you have to know in order to help us."

"Why am I even having this conversation, then? For all I know, you found out somehow, got Matt drunk, maybe, I don't know."

Then it hit her. The strangest thing about this situation was she could tell *he* wasn't lying. She always got a feeling when someone lied to her. Almost like a sharpness at the back of her neck and behind her eyes, like a fierce headache was coming on, and she wasn't getting it from him. So there were only two possible conclusions; one, he believed what he was saying so strongly that it didn't come out at her as a lie, which meant her half-sarcastic comment was correct and he was insane. Or two, he was being truthful. Surprisingly to her, it wasn't the possibility of the former, complete insanity, worrying her the most; it was the possibility of the latter, that his story could reflect the truth, causing the bubble of nervousness and trepidation to rise up from her gut.

"Well, can you get rid of it? I want to get it out of me; it is awful, to tell you the truth. You are looking at this thing as a gift, but it isn't. This thing has made me a freak. My own parents couldn't handle it. Or I guess it was me who found it hard to tolerate their loathing of my oddity. It wasn't just them; try making friends when you know their every feeling and lie. It crashes into my head, and did I mention it hurts? Can you, they, who, whatever, make it go away?"

Nias was not completely surprised to see the look of pain in her eyes, but it had an effect on him he did not expect. He had an overwhelming need to make that look, the causes of that look, go away, but he knew it was impossible. He needed the part of her causing that pain.

"No, I can't. I was asked to find you, explain the situation, and obtain your help. And to be honest, I doubt they would be willing to take away something they find useful." He couldn't help but place his hand on her forearm, to touch her, to soothe her. And then, as quickly as he had placed it, and felt the warmth of her skin, her eyes flickered straight towards his own, and he yanked his hand away.

He would not do this. This human would not affect him. He pulled himself together and got back to the business at hand.

"My brother has been kidnapped by some very bad individuals."

"I feel his pain, as I seem to be in the same situation." He appreciated her sharp wit and snappy comeback, and smirked despite himself.

"Trust me, Jade, you are not in the same situation. I will not hurt you. If you try to run, I will bring you back. But I will not ever hurt you." And he suddenly realized he meant every word of it.

Again Jade could feel he wasn't lying. He meant what he said, and strangely she didn't feel like she was in any immediate danger.

"I need to get to him, and I need you to use the abilities you possess to help me do it. The place I have to take you is evil beyond your reasoning; it will be like nothing you have ever seen or imagined," he continued to explain.

Jade shuddered at the sincerity and seriousness in his voice. "Where is this place and who are these people?"

"I cannot give you any more information right now, but we need to start with your training immediately, if I ever expect to see my brother alive again."

"Why in the world would I get involved with this? It sounds extremely dangerous, and I'm sorry to be harsh, but it just isn't my problem." Even as she spoke the words, she thought of the one and only thing that could possibly make her do something so crazy; to actually have a normal life, to be rid of this blasted curse. This man might not know where the curse came from, but even if there was an infinitesimal chance she could find its origin and maybe, just maybe, find out a way to make it stop, she wanted to try.

"Unfortunately, Jade, the moment you came into contact with me you started being watched and it became your problem. The Shaitan have eyes everywhere. They have, no doubt, seen you by now, so you are involved already. You're just not safe without me or one of the Djinn beside you anymore." Nias looked into her eyes and she thought she saw a tiny glimmer of regret. Then she experienced a flash of anger that he had put her in this position. If what he said was true, he had already endangered her life.

All thoughts of agreeing to this madness had flown out of her mind. She clenched her teeth as she responded.

"I appreciate you want to retrieve your brother, but I don't know anything about these … these Shaitan, or Djinn, or Daemons, or whatever they are called. I have a business to run, I have a life!" *A sad and pathetic life; one where I cannot keep a relationship intact, prevent my head from erupting into spontaneous bursts of pain or even manage to stay out of dreamland long enough to cope with the madness.* But right now she didn't care, she needed some air to breathe not full of super-hot "I'm a Daemon" guy. She needed to get away and think, time to sort through this mess.

She continued her tirade getting up and taking a step toward him. The tension in the room was palpable. "I am going to go, please do not stop me, do not contact me, do not drug me or drag me across the country anymore!"

She paused for a time, looking at him, and when he made no move to stop her, she stormed past him and out the door. To her surprise, he let her go.

As Jade walked out of the flat, she wondered what kind of fiendishness was truly involved in getting her there. She had been to San Francisco before, and as she looked around she realized quickly he was telling the truth on that count. Did he take her across the country, unconscious on a plane? Surely not a public one. How long was she out? She had not felt herself go under or come out of a blackout. What she did know was she needed to find a way home.

Luckily she was a credit-card-in-the-pocket, and not a purse kind of a girl, because she was going to need a cab ride and a plane ticket before that hot but vexatious man came looking for her. She was not sure why he had let her walk out, and right now she did not give two shits about the why's, she just wanted as far away from here as she could get.

Unfortunately, as far away as she could get was two blocks, when something metal slammed into her stomach and then hit her over the head, and this time everything did go black.

Chapter 3

When she came to, it wasn't in a lovely flat with a gorgeous alpha male. Instead, she was in some kind of an abandoned warehouse-looking place. It was so dark she could only see by the thin cracks of light coming through what she assumed were doors, which extended from the floor to incredibly high ceilings. Her head was pounding and a foul odor smacked her in the face. She had no idea what it was, but it was a smell one could only imagine in a nightmare. A stewed thickness wafted of feces and other body fluids. She had never smelled decaying flesh, but she could imagine it smelled exactly like this.

She tried to move and realized she was chained to a beam, which connected to the ceiling. Terrified, she struggled, but the chains did not merely shackle her wrists and ankles; she felt them wrapped around her body, rendering her practically paralyzed. She began screaming from the depths of her soul, fear producing a sound she never imagined could come out of her. As she cried out she swung her head around, violently at first, but that made her pounding headache turn into an explosion of agony. She continued screaming and crying until snot and tears mingled and dripped from her face. No one responded, and she couldn't see anyone else there. She finally passed out, most likely from the combination of fear and pain.

Next thing she knew, someone slapped her across the face so hard it split her lip and flung the other side of her face into the beam. She would have registered immense pain, except what was in front of her stole every bit of her attention. She sensed the emotions coming off of the person joining her in the cavernous space. If pure evil were a feeling, this would be it; hatred, jealousy, rage, loathing, greed, mistrust hit her all at once, and then she tried to shut them out. She pushed against it with her mind, despite the throbbing in her head. She had minimal success, making it slightly less overwhelming. She could make out a shadow of someone hunchbacked. From what little she could make out, it looked like he, or she, had been born with some hideous deformities. It seemed lopsided. One arm appeared to be longer than the other. Its breath smelled like putrid sewage … no that wasn't it; it smelled of death. She could also hear the voices of several others behind her, but they weren't speaking a language she understood.

Then a high, whiny voice spoke in English. "How is it you know Nias, what business does he have with you, human?"

Fuck, fuck, fuck, did it just say human like it wasn't one? She only wanted to go back home. She wanted to wake up from this whole nightmare. She began crying again, and she couldn't breathe right. The chains were too tight and she couldn't calm herself.

She was screaming again!

"Stop!" It slapped her, hard. "What is your business with Nias? Answer me or I will not continue to be so kind," it whined in a macabre, singsong manner.

Although fearful, she felt compelled to lie. "I don't know who that is! I have no idea who…what do you want from me?" she managed to choke out through the blood running from her mouth.

It tore through her shirt with a razor-sharp claw, drawing down her chest, diagonally over her breast, across the chains, ripping across her stomach. She cried out and then bit her bleeding lip. The nails made a scratching noise as they pulled over the last of her bindings. Sharp pains were now emanating from her torso in concert with the continued pulsing in the back of her skull.

"Do not lie to me, I saw you transcend in with him! You were in his home; I saw you converse. What did you discuss?"

Her vision was hazy and she wasn't sure what she should say. She didn't want to make it angrier, but she had the feeling giving it too much information was definitely a bad idea. Actually, she couldn't think of a good idea at all.

"Speak!" It ran one of its razors slowly down her arm.

It was horrifying, but the feeling of being trapped and powerless over the situation was starting to make her angry, despite her terror. She clenched her teeth and began to struggle again, but this time with fury. She shoved aside the pain and pushed back at it with her mind, grabbing the emotions within its head and twisting them. She attached herself to the darkness within it and it consumed her; she knew it would, but she also knew it would only last until she gained control.

When attempting to alter someone's emotional state, she used the opposite emotion to push it out. Her success varied. It depended a lot on how in touch with the opposing emotion she could get, and how strong the target was. Although the utter darkness and pure hatred was heavy and difficult to move, she found its self-doubt and the creature allowed her manipulate it; at least, she hoped, enough to get it to stop injuring her. She tried her best to channel pleasure until she could feel its hate dissipate, if only slightly. Unfortunately, she was finding it a little difficult to find any pleasant images to pull from. She only wished hate could move hate. She was feeling plenty of that and channeling it could have knocked the fucking thing on its putrid ass.

Jade thought she would try to trick it into letting her go. She tried to speak evenly. "I was taken by the man you're referring to, but I'm not sure how." The best lies were always the ones that contain at least minimal truth. "I have no idea what he wanted from me. What is it *you* want from me?" Her anger and pain were starting to make her breathless.

"I need to know what the Djinn are planning. They are a bad lot. They hurt people, did you know this?" It continued in its high-pitched, unholy melody. She could sense immediately it was lying to her but decided to play along.

"I didn't, but I knew when he abducted me that he had bad intentions. I was afraid for my life." *Yeah, does this stupid thing not get that I am afraid for my life now?*

"Yesss," it hissed, "you were right to fear for your safety, you are much safer now."

Really? Did it really just rip its claws through my body and tell me I was safe? She had to get out of here. The pain in her head was abating, but it was starting to swim now, probably from blood loss.

"I really can't breathe right," she pretended to hyperventilate; "can you loosen … the chains?"

It made a discontented grunting sound, and called out for someone else to come and do the chore. And *something* else arrived, but she couldn't see it. Its breath was rapid and short. It sounded as if it only used its mouth to breathe. Whatever it was she could feel its hand come from lower than a man's hands would be. It seemed to be the size of a small child. It unlocked the chains to give them slack, but as it did so there was a moment it let them give a little more than it needed to, and she felt the chains fall below her knees. Jade was by no means a fighter, but the adrenaline pumping through her body made her fear and anger override her pain. Before she even knew what she was doing she had stepped out of her bondage.

With both arms straight she clasped her hands together and, using them like a bat, she swung at the hunchbacked creature, knocking it to the ground. The child-sized thing hissed at her and clutched at her legs. She punched at it, and then grabbed at the shadow, ripping at its skin with her fingernails. Thank God for her long fake nails. She could tell she had wounded it and torn at its flesh, which is exactly what she had wanted to do to any one of them since they had flayed her own skin. She began running blindly, staggering for the light coming through the walls, hoping she had been right and it was a door of some sort. The floor was damp or slimy, maybe, and she could feel her feet almost slide out from under her several times as she ran.

When she actually made it to the wall she crashed into it as hard as she could, trying to use her body like a battering ram. She didn't look behind her, but she could hear multiple shuffling footsteps rushing toward her. The wall didn't budge. As she felt up and around the sides of her prison, panic began to take over again. She heard herself starting to breathe too quickly as she became hysterical. Then they caught up with her. The first one grabbed her by her hair and ripped her backwards to the ground. She managed to get her hands behind her before her head hit the floor, but her arms burned with the impact. It began dragging her back across the slick floor. It was speaking fiercely in that bizarre language again, stopping suddenly to kick her in the ribs and yell something at her. She started to break a little. If they started in on her again …

And then she heard a deeper voice boom through the darkness; it was right above them and it seemed to speak the same language, but with a much deeper tone. She turned in the dimness to see a figure towering over the beast, grabbing it by its neck and twisting, producing a horrible cracking noise. She could hear the sound of other monsters scatter and then pained, high-pitched moaning. Another force seemed to be beating them down.

Jade still lay on the floor in a state of alarm and shock, turning over and trying to crawl away without being noticed, pain wracking every part of her body. She couldn't even force herself to her feet, but still, escape was the only thing she could fathom. Then a large thing that felt warm and solid and smelled like a familiar musk picked her up in its arms and held her close. As she began to struggle, still panic-stricken and feeling the pain of the gashes that other thing had ripped into her body, it spoke.

"Jade, it's okay." He, and it was most definitely *he*, the he she had run from, pulled her face toward his so she could see who he was. "I've come to get you out of here. The things are dead, I've got you." Even in her shock she knew that beautiful face and his voice soothed her. She immediately sensed inside his mind; he was hyper-alert, aware and concerned; he emanated calm safety. And involuntarily, she curled in tightly to him.

"Get me the fuck out of here, please!" she said breathlessly.

He began walking with her toward the other side of the warehouse, as he shouted in that unusual dialect to some others she couldn't make out in the darkness. She suspected he was calling out orders at them about going after the fleeing creatures. It sounded like there were four or five other men. But she had no intention of lifting her head to find out. She felt safe curled in her current state, buried beneath his long, dark hair, which spilled over her. He even smelled like safety. A warm rich musk mixed with sweat, a dirty masculinity. She could feel the hard muscles in his arms and the thickness of his chest, and for right now she wasn't moving a muscle of her own.

Damn it, why did I let her go?

Right after she had left, Nias had taken the three flights from his flat down the cramped stairwell two at a time. He slammed open the heavy door at the bottom with all the ferocity and frustration the situation had caused to fester inside him. The thick carved wood tore from its top hinges, dangled and then careened to the sidewalk.

Nias stalked past one streetlight to the next, one block after another. The scent of Chinese food and stale beer sickened him as he searched for what he needed. Threatened and fearful humans moved quickly out of his path, as gusts of wind swirled like dervishes around his menacing stomp, projecting dirt, discarded trash and anything underfoot. Lightning crashed in the deep-blue sky as his emotion became even darker and his self-loathing for letting this happen meshed with a determined vengeance within him.

Now because of his fuck-up, Jade was gone and he was one step further from retrieving Joss. Nias inhaled and through the sweat of strippers, cheap cologne and myriad smells of the dirty San Francisco night, he caught the scent of what he was searching for, and what he was hoping not to – the smell of Shaitan, and Jade's fear. And he knew they had taken her.

Nias had then transcended directly to the Djinn Sentry. Phaeton, being the current Sovereign, had ownership and control of the compound, their base of operations, for the Cause. Nias walked in and started ordering Daemons to locations throughout the city. He would cover them all. The more guards he had out, the faster they could find her. They always found the Nests in these mass deployments. All Djinn had a potent sense of smell. When they got within a few blocks of a Shaitan Nest, they would know.

It had taken the Sentry about an hour to locate the Nest. When they did, Nias had transcended directly inside with a small group consisting of whomever he could immediately muster. The girl had been badly injured, but he could also see she had put up a fight they would have not suspected her capable of.

He could see she had escaped the bonds they had put her in, but not before she had been cut up. The beautiful redhead was being dragged across the blood-splattered floor of the dirty warehouse, and he was consumed with a burning rage toward the beast that had dared to touch her. That it did so sent a shuddering hatred through him he did not expect. He grasped its neck with the blind fury of a man who had been personally violated. After he picked it up and finished it, he was flooded with disappointment that he had not drawn out the vile creation's pain.

Nias took Jade into his arms and held her shivering body tightly to his chest, wanting to absorb her panic within him. He ordered the extinction of the rest of the pack, calling out to the Djinn to spare no violence; tear their heads from their bodies if they wished, he would welcome it. Dispose of the rot when they were through. The Sentry would take the dead creatures back to the incinerator in their compound.

He didn't realize Hamartia had witnessed his bloodlust and emotion until he stood with the unconscious girl in his arms and she appeared suddenly before them.

"Hello, my delicious pet." Her voice scraped through the darkness like nails on a chalkboard, giving him chills penetrating to his very spine.

He growled, "Hamartia, I so do not miss your hideous whine. What could possibly draw you out of Sheol? I can't imagine anything worth you missing even a minute of your enjoyment of the suffering and torture of the damned." He watched her tall shadow approach him in the dimness of the room. She had long black, dreadlocked hair, which fell around an ugly scarred face. Her body was diseased from her conception and had continued to slowly rot for millennia. Wetness from her open sores shone through the encrusted dark fabric of her ancient, worn, floor-length gown.

Iblis had once taken her as a lover simply to amuse himself with something vile. It had been during a time when he had a sick fetish for fucking things that disgusted him. After centuries of finding pleasure in those who didn't consent to his advances, he sought a distraction with a different kind of depravity.

When he was through with using Hamartia for his lasciviousness he took immense pleasure in telling her all about his experiment with the filthy and nauseating, letting her know she actually managed to make even the most depraved beast ever in creation, himself, sick. Some believed she had developed affection for him, if she could even conjure such a feeling. Spurned, she fell into a blood-hungry rage that continued to consume her existence. She had never left Sheol before, to Nias's knowledge. Head Mistress of Pain; dominance and humiliation were all that gave her pleasure now. But, yet, here she was.

Unfortunately, she had also always had a lust for Nias. His

physical beauty, strength, and power were an attraction she had been fixated on even before the humiliation Iblis caused her.

"Maybe it is just that I missed gazing at you. Why do you hold the human that way, Nias?" The she-beast drew out his name like she was playing with it on her tongue, and tilted her head in query. "She is beautiful, but have her quickly and discard her, like the other women you take to your bed. It looked to me from watching you end Rin that you almost felt something for her, but she will never hold your attentions like I could."

He could hear her jealousy and it made him fear for Jade's wellbeing. He knew Jade could no longer leave his side, at least until this conflict was resolved. If she lived, they would have to find a way to remove her from the attention of the Shaitan.

"No, Hamartia, she never could. The disgust I feel for you will never be the kind of attention I would give Jade."

"You use her given name?" She pulled a hiss in though her teeth. "Why did you transcend her to your residence, Nias? We saw you converse with her and block her exit. It looked to be more than bedding."

"She is nothing to me, Hamartia. You have no reason to concern yourself with this girl." He did not want to give her any hint that Jade could be the key to his saving Joss.

"Your reaction to her miniscule injuries was extreme; I would very much like to take her home with me." She took another step towards him as if to relieve him of his burden.

He bristled at Hamartia's description of what her compatriots had done to her. Jade made a tiny moaning sound, and Nias realized both her clothing and his had become more saturated with blood as he held her. He needed to get her somewhere safe and tend to her wounds now.

He glared at the monstrosity before him, disgusted with both her inner and outer self. "This one will be discarded quickly; your perception of the events is obviously skewed. I hope our next encounter will not be soon, if ever." And he transcended himself and the girl out before Hamartia could get in another word.

Chapter 4

Jade abruptly found herself in a dark room, once again being held by her beautiful kidnapper. Although the room was only lit by the glow the moon and stars sent through the large windows, the fullness of the moon allowed her to see the essence of it. The furnishings were extremely nice, but different from the flat she had been in earlier. This was a huge bedroom, well appointed, even more moneyed. The change in the time of day implied she was in yet another time zone.

Her arms were wrapped around his neck, and she was still trembling and bleeding badly through what was left of her shredded clothing. She couldn't feel animosity right now; hell, she couldn't feel much of anything except pain mixed with some level of gratitude. The pain was worst from the front of her body and her arm, where the grotesque fiend had ripped her open. But Nias's firm grip on her was calming and soothing and in his arms she got the sense she would be all right, which was completely insane since he was the one who had got her into this mess in the first place.

Nias walked over to a dark wooden four-poster bed with a dark-blue duvet and a pile of brighter-blue pillows. He turned his head toward the fireplace and under his glare the fire suddenly ignited and rose to warm the room. When he bent down to place her on the bed, she didn't want to let go. She felt so confused, shaken, and hurt she wasn't sure whether she needed his strength around her for a little while longer, or whether she should demand to be taken to a hospital. The latter seemed the right thing to do, but that wasn't what her body, as badly injured as it was, wanted to do.

He looked into her eyes and she felt a pang of fear coupled with a need for him. He lowered her gently onto the bed and sat down next to her. She heard a thump and then another, which must have been his boots hitting the floor, because the next thing she knew he was stretching his expansive chest and long legs, clad in faded jeans and an old black t-shirt, out next to her. He leaned on one elbow, his long, shiny black and dark-brown hair falling and folding on to the bed.

Damn, he was something to see; she almost forgot about the pain. Then it shot back at her and he put one of his hands flat on her stomach, as if to comfort her. Even with the pain, she noticed his heavily muscled bicep shift when he moved.

She couldn't help but read him; she was freaked, badly injured and in a strange place. She wanted to trust him, but the darkness in him she felt earlier was prevalent, like a pervasive hum, an unholy deadly enigma. Right alongside the darkness was his concern. She decided he was most likely her best bet right now. She certainly wasn't going to try to run off and get taken by more of those things, even if she were capable of that kind of movement.

"Where am I?" she managed to croak out. He put one finger on her lips to quiet her.

"Be still, Jade. As I told you before, you are safe with me." The matter-of-fact manner in which he said it, the gentle way in which he was now touching her after the rough manner of their initial meeting, it felt almost surreal how soothing it was. She reached up to take his hand. It was warm and she gripped it with both of hers. She looked toward his beautiful face. His bright gold eyes were looking into hers and they didn't look cocky or sarcastic. For the moment, he seemed to be actively trying to calm her. She would even say he looked kind.

"I know you're in pain. I can make the pain and the wounds go away, but you will have to trust me."

"Honestly, that worries me, but I really want the pain to stop." She gave him a half-hearted attempt at a smile, trying in vain not to cry. "Okay, what can you do?"

"Just close your eyes, Jade. You're safe with me."

"I heard you the first time, but, before I trust you, which I can't promise I'll be able to do, how about you tell me your name. Your full name." Her voice was hoarse, but she was trying her hardest not to sound defenseless.

He gave her a smirk of sorts and chuckled softly. "Very well. My name is Nias Hu'dor."

"Okay, Nias Hu'dor, I'm going to do my best to close my eyes and trust you here. I suppose if you are going to kill me I'm kind of screwed anyway," she rasped. He smiled kindly at her attempt at humor, and it made her feel calm enough to lean back on to the pillows behind her and tighten her grip on his hand as the pain continued to sear her flesh. "Although trusting you for more than your warmth and monster-killing rescue seems a very risky prospect." She closed her eyes.

Next thing she knew she felt his fingers take hold of her tank top and the sensation was followed by the sound of ripping material.

Jades eyes flew back open. Her tank lay on either side of her body exposing her cut flesh and barely covered breasts. Nias was astride her and was moving the inner crook of his elbow toward his mouth, where he licked and then calmly used his teeth to rip a hole in his own lower arm. His teeth sank in and tore at the soft flesh, causing his blood to begin a dense, steady drip. She started to panic and tried to sit up; Nias gave a searing glare as he looked straight into her eyes and pressed her back down. Moving his bleeding arm over her, the blood bubbled out and flowed on to her chest and belly. Again she squirmed and he held her in place. Using the hand that wasn't bleeding to hold her by the collarbone, he began to cover her wounds with the warm red fluid. She struggled violently beneath him, frightened at this display, but couldn't escape; it was as though his grasp were made of solid metal.

"Jade, look at me," and she did, but it had to have been with fear in her eyes. "I will not hurt you, I promise. Trust me, you are safe now."

He continued to repeat that mantra of safety as he threw her tank to the floor and unbuttoned her jeans. He began smearing the thick drops down her chest, smoothing them out over her cuts with his palm.

He started at the base of her neck, his flat hand and fingers swerving down her body. Then went back up to her bra, which had been cut slightly, his hand wandered inside and he let his fingers linger by her taut nipple longer than necessary. He grazed the hardened bud slightly as his fingers flowed so tantalizingly off of her breast, and continued down her body. His eyes connected with hers and she gave him no sign she wanted him to stop.

Her whole body convulsed and caused a wet heat between her legs. He stuck four sticky fingers below the top of her open jeans, barely sweeping them over the top of her tight curls to make sure the sliced skin was covered to its end. Again she shuddered involuntarily, and gave a tiny sigh of acquiescence. He finished by squishing more blood from his vein to the long gash on her arm and firmly sliding his hand down and off of her wrist.

She couldn't help it as his touch sent a tremor through her and she began shaking. She was completely aroused, covered in this man's blood; he had his hand practically at her throat and she wanted more. More of all of him, cocky bastard that he was. He had taken her full circle, from being attacked and nearly killed to a state of euphoria. And now she was face to face with a man, a seriously erotic one, who looked even better than the ones she loved to dream up and thought were perfection, and she looked like she'd just been murdered. It was a lot to take in all in the same day, much less in an hour.

"Thank you?" She asked it as a question in a breathy voice. Her wounds did feel better and she glanced down, seeing some of them miraculously starting to close. She had definitely lost control of herself and the situation.

"You're welcome," he said looking dreamily and directly into her eyes.

"Criminy, that was the sexiest 'you're welcome' I've ever heard." The words fell from her mouth before she could stop them. His voice was soft and deep. But the tone ... the tone managed to stroke her entire body all over again. The electricity was palpable between them.

Then she thought back to his previous behavior; what an arrogant ass he'd been and how she had detested him. She thought about getting up and walking out, since she wasn't having the sharp pain anymore. But her body seriously objected; it had gone to the dark side and it was staying.

She drank him in; this was much closer than she had been to him before. He had a chiseled strong, square jaw and full, kissable lips, but they were completely outdone by the intensity of his exotic golden eyes. She took in the entire length of him again; he had an energy emanating from his body and demanding attention. He somehow managed to be sleek, long, intensely muscular and amazingly masculine all at the same time; like a panther, a big sexy cat, staring with his intense yellowish gaze.

"Are you warm enough?" he inquired in a deep, sexy drawl; he had a hint of an accent she hadn't noticed before. She couldn't place it, but the sound of it slithered out, wrapped around her, and slowly whispered "sex".

Her mind betrayed her next as she thought about her books and her dreams. *What usually happens at this point? Should I begin running my fingers through his hair, do I stroke him? Should I ...* and then he leaned in and kissed her.

His hand was back to her belly, and he turned in and lightly brushed his lips against hers. She had wanted this so badly in her dreams and now she felt horribly nervous. With all of her wishing and dreaming and hoping, and even with the aroused state she was in, the fact that she had no practical experience at being intimate, and barely any at kissing, was all she could think of right then, and her body tensed. She began to tremble and wonder what came next, as the fear, excitement, anxiousness, and desire all came to her at once.

Nias could not believe how out of control this human girl was making him. He hadn't had any intention of getting twisted up in bed with her. He had only gone after her to correct his mistake; he should have never let her go. But when he found her being dragged across the floor, her body torn open by that lowlife Shaitan, he felt a protective surge come over him. The need to safeguard someone had never before made him feel so hostile.

He had to pull her close. Seeing that she had put up such a fight even when outnumbered and surrounded by Daemons had made her nearly irresistible. She was courageous and feisty. It made him want to own her, to keep her, and he generally had no patience for humans.

He had brought her back to Phaeton's knowing it was the safest place for her. He told himself he was only keeping her safe because they needed her. But the truth, he knew, was that he wanted her as well. She had a sass women didn't normally have around him. They typically threw themselves at him. She was scared and injured and he still wanted her. Seeing her lying on the bed, her fire-colored curls spread over the blue of the sheets, made him crazy; and then to explore her body as he fixed her wounds with his blood brought him to a fervor and thirst stronger than he could have imagined. Her full, round breasts, her tiny waist, her heavenly ass; he wanted to fix her quickly so he could play with her. Her lack of knowledge in these activities, the innocence he never suspected, it just got better and better.

It made his cock thicken even more to think about being the

one to show her the way to complete pleasure.

Nias eased his free hand up under her chin and lifted her face to take her in. She was so close to him, he could feel her warm, sensual breath. She smelled like ripe, sweet plums and warm sunlight. *Innocent, feisty, naughty girl.*

"Don't worry, Jade, just listen to my words." His pants were constricting as he felt himself harden even more with the thought of how she might taste. And it wasn't the blood running through her veins that had his taste buds watering. He suppressed the growl threatening at the back of his throat.

He stroked her hair back from her face, ran his fingers through its length and placed it behind her ear and up, cascading upon the pillow behind her head. Then he moved his hand to the back of her neck and pulled her up, as he changed his mind and decided to dispense with any verbalization.

His mouth took hers; his tongue pushed its way through her inexperience, showing her the way. And she began to follow his lead. Her pouty lips were claimed as his as he began to move his tongue within them. He leaned back to look at her and ran two bloody fingers across her bottom lip, pulling it to the side, smearing his blood across her face and making her lip swell.

He felt predatory, he wanted to be rough with her; he felt like strapping her down and owning her. Yet something pulled him back from the primal urge that normally claimed him. There was something different here, something on the edge of his consciousness that he couldn't get his head around.

He wrapped a hand around her waist and easily scooped her forward until their bodies were flush. His hand went around to her exquisite ass, grabbing her firm roundness and pushing it in even closer; his hips rocked forward, and he pressed and ground his engorged shaft against her blood-soaked body. She melted into him, wrapping her hands though his hair and around his neck. A soft moan came out of her beautiful mouth, as they resumed the intense intertwining of tongues. The kiss was scorching as his tongue ravaged her mouth, cruel and demanding. There was an intense rush of heat, and he reached his hand up to fist her hair, pulling at it and biting her bottom lip, then slowly releasing it with his teeth. She languorously closed her eyes and moaned while she shuddered beneath him.

He shoved her, a little more violently than he intended, flattening her back to the bed. As she turned her head to face him, she was a perfect blend of innocence and vixen. She may have been inexperienced, but that wasn't stopping her from enjoying everything he was giving. She gave him a coy smile, wiggled beneath him and her body began to purr. He could feel his pulse racing and his breath became short. It made him almost angry to be thrown off so much by this human.

He stopped to take her in and a moment of confusion washed over him; he hadn't felt this kind of passion in so long. There was something about this girl he couldn't get enough of, even in their short time together. His whole body felt alive and seething. He smashed his lips against hers. He knew he was being too rough but couldn't help himself. He was drowning and she was his breath.

Growling at her, he grabbed both her hands and yanked them up over her head, holding them in place. He slid a knee between her thighs and eased her legs apart and moved his body between them. He crushed the seam of her jeans up into her pleasure point, grinding gently. This time her moan was not as soft, it was far more wild and severe. He went in for more of her and again their tongues coiled in an erotic dance. The inside of her mouth was so succulent he had to taste the rest of her. Backing up, he lowered his hand deep into her open jeans, his fingers found her slickness, and he pushed them inside as her muscles clenched around him.

He found she was untouched; she had never been intimate with a man. Blissfully he thought of all the things he could teach her; he wanted nothing more in that moment than to give her a thorough education in all the carnal pleasures. Inch by delicious inch he would take each soft, sweet fold of her body into his hands and into his mouth. He would show her sweet innocence what it was like to have him deep inside her. He knew how to bring her over to a darker side of sexual feeling than she could imagine. He would own her, his possession.

Between her legs was so warm and inviting, a momentary impatience wanted to remove his fingers and thrust his achy cock inside, but not yet, he told himself. His fingers plunged and curled inside of her. She ground her hips against his hand. Arching her back she moved her hips in time with his strokes. She was perfect. Her desires matched his own. And he wanted to ruin her for all other men so she would always need to come to him to be satisfied.

He felt raw as he shifted the top of her jeans lower, exposing the milky perfection of her thighs beneath.

"No, I can't," she protested, her voice breathy and weak, her eyes still closed.

Keeping a firm grip on her wrists, he traced her moist heat with his fingertips. "That was hardly a refusal, more like an invitation. Should I listen to your words? Or would you rather I hear their intention? Which I believe was to tease and coerce me into giving you real pleasure?" He taunted her as he continued to outline her sensual essence with the tips of his fingers.

"Yes," was all she managed. Her body undulated beneath him, her breath panting. He laughed softly and resumed removing her jeans. Unzipping her boots with his wandering hand, he tossed them to the floor, then slipped the jeans over her ankles and into the air with one swift movement.

"Yes" Jade heard herself say. *Wait! That wasn't what I meant.* But she couldn't even fool herself with the weak protest. His body was heaven; his fingers were fire inside her. An ache of pleasure was forming in her lower body. It was growing, consuming her. Her nipples ached and she thought she might explode.

And he pulled away.

"No," she managed through her haze.

"Kitten, I thought it was yes. You will make up your mind, won't you?"

When she opened her eyes to protest further he reached around and unsnapped her bra, removed it and replaced it with his tongue.

"Aah," she inhaled sharply and suddenly.

He grinned at her with amused, cat-like eyes. "Did you have something else you wanted to discuss? Should I stop?" He lifted his head just a touch to inquire.

She could only speak in barely whispered breaths. "No, don't stop, it's okay, I really don't want you to," she purred, despite her conflicted opinion of him. He was arrogant, conceited, talented, delicious, warm… and then he was licking her, lapping her tight bud, pinching and kneading the other. She began to rock as one of her hands ran through his long hair, involuntarily holding him there. Although inexperienced, her body seemed to know what to do, what it wanted.

His mouth left her breast, leaving one set of dirty fingers behind, and he began licking down her belly… past her tight curls… until he was between her thighs. With a roguish look in his eyes, he smoothly picked up one of her legs at a time and placed them on his shoulders; then he slid his belly to the sheets, wrapped his arms around her hips, focused his gaze elsewhere and pulled her to his mouth. Her moan escaped, still louder than before, and she could hear his chuckle in response. But right now, she thought the phrase "couldn't have cared less" had never been more appropriate, or true.

He took long, lazy, controlled strokes with his tongue. Spreading her with his fingertips, she came completely undone; any vestiges of her feigned control were lost. Her hips bucked softly and her back arched. Again the pressure began to rise in her, right at the point where he laved her. His mouth expertly drove her to places her dreams had not even brought her, sucking and nipping at her pleasure point until the pressure drew to an explosion and she convulsed. Bliss ran through her in waves for what seemed like an eternity. But this bad boy apparently liked to see her lose control because he didn't stop. He continued at his leisure until her body bucked and shook underneath his ministrations again and again and again for him.

Her mind was collapsing into a thousand random shards of rainbow-colored light as she croaked out, "no … please … oh God …" As she pitched, as if to get away, her nerves overloaded by the stimulation he was giving her, he pulled her legs back down off of his shoulders and pinned her ankles to the bed. Raspy, her voice cracked, "Yes … God yes …" as she succumbed completely, her hips undulating beneath his lips, the smell of sex filling the air. Drops of sweat pooled on her toned belly as a beaded mist coated her forehead and ran down into her dampened hair. Any remaining thoughts of the pain she had been through that night fled against the assault on her senses, until ultimately she mentally and emotionally exploded, crying out and crashing into the mattress underneath her, trembling.

Finally, writhing, she begged him to stop. Jade lay exhausted, dreamy, and sated as she dissolved into the bed. She looked up at his face as he moved up her body, and she could see the arrogance beneath his visage; a completely justified pride, power, strength of soul and body, a never-wavering confidence … and motherfucking gorgeous to boot. *He is a primary being, a god, a deliciously evil dessert.* Her thoughts ran rampant through her brain as the blitzkrieg on her senses abated.

He pulled his shirt off over his head. *How could he drive me to such places without even removing his clothes?* He kneeled there for a moment and licked his lips before ripping the duvet from underneath her, sliding up to her side, and pulling her into his warm arms, covering them both. She melted into his body, feeling warm, smooth, soft, hard, safe, and dreamy all at the same time.

Chapter 5

Jade was lying curled in his arms, molded to his body, her long red curls tumbling over the blue cover; and Nias didn't want to be anywhere else. Knowing he brought her to peak gave him more pleasure than he knew possible. Could a human woman be making him feel this way? *Not possible*, he insisted. He was merely having a deep, intense lust for her, which in and of itself was a pretty unusual feeling for him to have toward a human. He deeply enjoyed sex with human women, even more so with Daemon, but this was stronger than that, like somehow she fit with him. There was a force which propelled him toward her, and held him there. He lay watching her in her languor; beautiful pink lips, the high, soft bone structure, her high-arched brows the only physical manifestation of her incredulous defenses toward the world. She was a fiery one; the flames of her hair suited her perfectly. And even though he normally would have had his own way with her, then cast her aside, a good hour passed while he placed kiss after kiss on her.

"You are amazingly beautiful," Nias said, placing his head on his hand and leaning on one arm. He watched her lie against the pillows and accept his kisses, her eyes only half open from the pleasure he had given her.

"I'm not sure what you are, but I or, um, my body, seems to

really like it." She smiled a wide grin at him.

She reached up, taking a piece of his shiny dark hair in her fingers and began to twirl the end, something he had seen her do to her own hair and it made him feel a touch vulnerable. Letting someone give him contentment was something he rarely allowed, especially a human woman. Typically he would cast her aside, but instead, he felt the need to reach for her. Trying to end the overly intimate contact, he took her hand in his and kissed it.

He watched her fade to sleep, listening to her breath. Despite her mild protesting he could see she felt safe with him, and he was delighted. He finally fell asleep with this human curled in his arms, hesitant about how much her safety comforted him. He was so pleased by what she had done, such a tiny act and enormous at the same time.

And that was what scared him to death.

When she woke she was a little hazy and still completely enveloped in him. It took her a few seconds to remember where she was, and then it flooded back to her: met hottest man she'd ever seen; kidnapped; out cold, maybe; fought with hottest man she'd ever seen; kidnapped AGAIN; tortured and nearly gutted; definitely out cold; miraculously healed; got obscene with the hottest man she'd ever seen; drowsy, sleepy, safe, out cold; NO kidnap; and wake up still snuggled tightly to hottest man she'd ever seen, still covered in their blood. Yep, that about covered it.

Leaving her eyes closed, she felt the soft sheets beneath her bare body, and heard only the near silence of the early-morning breeze. But she could also feel his body against her, his powerful presence and masculine smell permeated her very being. She shifted involuntarily against him as her hand went to his hips (*still clothed!*) and sighed deeply.

She looked up, realizing he was already awake and gazing at her. She had a sudden vision of their encounter and was struck with self-consciousness. The reality of her situation invaded the fantasy, and she blushed beet red, looking away. *Deviant sexual behavior is so not like me. But that sure as hell didn't feel deviant!* She shook her head. What the hell had she been thinking? She barely knew this man. And yet she lay there cozied up and secure in his body. He was sex on a stick; it oozed out of him, the way his massive arms unavoidably flexed whenever he shifted. It was only one of the highlights of his impeccable body. The arrogant smile he gave, which always accompanied the soft, dark, sexually charged laugh, raised her ire.

"What is it, Kitten?" She jumped slightly; his deep, seductive voice startled her.

She could have screamed. She could have lashed out at him. She could have gotten up, demanded some clothes and gotten the hell out of there. Maybe she should have done any one of those things. But after everything that had happened … "I was reflecting on the absurdity of the situation. I could be crippled by fear, ashamed at myself, or throw my hands in the air and confess I'm just not in Kansas anymore. I guess that's what I've decided to do." Again she chuckled at her own humor.

"I don't understand, what does this day have to do with a Middle American state?"

God, has he never even seen "Wizard of Oz"? Where was he from, anyway? "Never mind, I have a really strange habit of making myself laugh when things are too … overwhelming."

"I understand you feel undone. But, I believe I have discovered a way to calm you a little. Shall I apply my findings again?" He flashed another wicked grin.

"No!" *God no,* she thought, even though her protest came a little more sharply than she intended. "Please keep your *findings* to yourself for a while. I have never done anything like that before. I am a little humiliated with my actions. What I'm trying to say is I should have stopped that from happening and I didn't and I'm not sure why. Okay, I am going to shut up now." And her face turned bright red again as she managed to dam up the words tumbling out of her mouth faster than she could think about them. He continued smiling wickedly at her. "What, why are you grinning at me like a cat with a mouse trapped under its paw?"

"You do realize, my Kitten, you said, 'for a while' don't you? You asked that I keep my so-called 'findings' to myself 'for a while,'" he stated with a big sardonic grin.

"Oh, well that's not what I meant," she choked out, as if she didn't even believe it herself. *Weak, Jade, truly weak.* "Anyway, now that I'm not being ripped apart by monsters, or smeared with blood – which reminds me I would really like a shower – or molested, I have a whole lot of questions for you."

"First of all, 'molested' implies you did not consent and I'm pretty sure I remember every stroke, moan and wiggle, and Kitten, you heartily consented; and second, we can take a shower any time you wish."

"Okay, molested may have been the wrong word, and I did not mean take a shower together. Smugness isn't going to get you anywhere."

"On the contrary, I think it already has." He arched his brow.

"Stop it." Now she was grinning and thinking about that co-ed shower. *Stop it yourself, Jade!*

"How about I show you where you can get cleaned up and then I'll answer all the questions you have?"

"Alone."

"If you insist."

"I insist." *Shut up brain, I do not want to hear it.*

"I'll call down to have someone bring up fresh things for you to wear. I imagine you are hungry as well?"

God, there are others here? She flushed again, wondering if her cries might have been heard. "Yes, I am a little, thank you. I know you said you would answer all my questions later, but, where are we? Why are there people who have *things* for me? This doesn't look or seem to be the place we were earlier. I thought that was maybe where you lived."

"This is my brother's home; he has several people who work for him here, and they will bring you clothes and food. You were in my home earlier."

He picked up a phone on a side table next to the bed and told whoever it was on the other end of the phone what he would need, "jeans size 6, tank top medium, jacket black, and something comforting for a human to eat, and breakfast for me as well." The last part struck her; she realized this meant he must eat something different. Scary. What the hell would that be? Did she even want to know?

He got up to show her to a large, beautiful bathroom. She pulled a sheet off the bed and flipped it toga-style around her bloody, naked body and did the walk of shame to the bathroom. It had dark granite countertops and bronze fixtures. The tub and sinks were black, and the floors a natural deep-brown travertine. She loved fixtures and granite and flooring; she took a lot of time decorating her book store and small flat. But this place obviously had a bigger budget than had been available to her, which was barely enough to scour flea markets and resale shops.

The bathroom fit nicely with the bedroom; they were both, lovely, dark, large and cozy at the same time. *Um, that sounds just like Nias – lovely, dark, large and cozy.* She cursed herself for thinking crazy. She didn't know where she was, who was after her, who the hell the man she'd just had sexual relations (*for the first time ever!*) with was, or what exactly he was. Now she was going to shower and eat dinner with him like they'd known each other for ages. *Yep, Jade and the Daemon having a little food together, I feel like I've seen this movie.* This whole damn day was surreal and it wasn't going to be getting any closer to any reality she had ever known anytime in her foreseeable future. *And, for God's sake, Jade,* she scolded herself, *stop touching him, purring at him, staring at him and lusting after him. First of all, it is wildly inappropriate for the danger of the situation, and second the cocky bastard is loving it! But so am I,* she snickered to herself.

As she removed the sheet she noticed herself while passing in front of one of the mirrors. *Oh my God!* Dried blood was smeared all the way down the front of her body. She moved closer. The blood on her body covered what remained of the long cuts that thing had sliced into her. There was a gap in the scars and she remembered it had scratched over the chains that had bound her. She felt a wave of terror run through her as she remembered being there. Nias HAD calmed her down. In fact, he had taken those gruesome memories completely away for a while. It was truly insane how comfortable she felt with him. He *had* kidnapped her, but it was like it had never happened when she was with him. She enjoyed him that much? That quickly? As Sherlock would say "something is afoot". She could conjure no explanations for the moment, so she looked back at herself. Blood had seeped into her hair when it spread around her neck from his application, and mortification struck her again as she noticed the remnants of bloody handprints on the backs of her knees and between her legs. *Shower, Jade, get in the shower*. She was feeling dirty for several reasons now. Another walk of shame commenced as she moved to the shower, waited for the water to warm, and got in.

After soaping every part of her body twice, she washed her long hair, rinsed, and exited the shower. When she got out there were fresh towels and clothing laid out on the countertop. She hadn't even heard anyone come in, which bothered her a little. Being deep in an escapist dreamland would do that. Her mind had checked out, like it often did in moments of stress. Except this time it wasn't visions of some random creation. This time her mind hovered on Nias and herself. New possibilities had come to mind. Never in her romantic visions had she imagined dark, gothic scenes, complete with blood and tearing flesh. Her knight errant had always rescued her from some historical complication, Jane Austen-style. Someone wasn't acting a gentleman or she had been humiliated in front of a room filled with The Ton, so he married her and they lived happily ever after. Not monsters, never Daemons in jeans and boots with long, shiny, dark hair.

She combed through her hair, left it to dry on its own, and got dressed. Clean and fresh-faced, she re-entered the bedroom. While she had been in the bathroom with her endlessly rambling thoughts, it seemed Nias had cleaned up as well and finished eating. Whatever it had been, he'd eaten it extremely rare and used a knife to cut through it. The plate and silverware looked almost as bloody as her skin was before she had cleansed it. What did he eat? *God! Hopefully not humans!*

But she dismissed that thought and joined him on a cozy sofa to get some far more important answers. The minute she sat down on the end of the couch he moved toward her.

Nias had eaten, but simply being around the girl made him ravenous.

"You look lovely clean and wet." He did enjoy her covered in his blood and couldn't wait to dirty her up again. He could think of several ways of accomplishing this goal, and, contemplating it, his arousal started to thicken. There would be plenty of time for that. He wasn't letting her leave any time soon, if ever. There was a long, nasty road in front of them; he still needed to prepare her if they had any chance of staying alive. But if they did survive, he just might keep her permanently.

He mentally shook his head to center himself again; she had him off-kilter. He needed to focus on the task at hand. Their journey would begin soon enough.

"Okay, I'm listening. I know you have questions."

"What the fuck were those things that abducted and hurt me? Why did they do it? What happened with your blood? I can tell it made my cuts feel better, but why? And is it my imagination or are they almost healed? Where exactly are we? What are you exactly? Although I'm not sure I want to know because I really don't want to get any more involved? When you keep saying I have to train, what could that possibly mean? When I leave, will they come after me again? And why the hell do you keep calling me Kitten?"

"Hum, where to begin, let's start with Kitten. I call you," he leaned forward without thinking and placed his mouth to her full, pink lips, his tongue slowly licking the seam between them, "… Kitten, because you are soft and beautiful." He leaned in again to taste her opening slightly during the connection and giving her mouth the brilliant idea to do the same, allowing him to slide through and drink her in a bit. She let out a tiny raspy moan, which caused an immediate pulsing at his groin. He connected to her eyes and continued, "And when I touch you, you purr." This time when he kissed her his mouth opened fully and his tongue found its way back in. He allowed his hair to fall forward over his shoulder enfold her into him. She closed her eyes, beginning to enjoy the feel of him again, and then he heard the sound that made him lose control, purrrr.

Chapter 6

"Hey," she protested in more of a whisper rather than the shout she had intended. "Hey." The same whisper forming only slightly louder this time. Fighting her own seemingly unstoppable need, she unclasped herself from his warm, full lips. His eyes caught hers again and those amazing lips formed a quirk, shooting a flame of desire through her. *Push though this Jade*, she said to herself, *you need to get some answers and find a way to get back home.*

"Don't try to distract me. I want answers and I intend on having them." As much as it pained her, she finally did move away from him. Being the fiend he was he dropped his fingertips to the skin of her arm and ran his nails down her bicep, over the sensitive, easily aroused softness of her inner elbow, and scraped it off the end of her hand and fingers. Goose bumps exploded across her arms and legs which made her shiver and feel a bit dizzy.

Shaking her head, she pressed forward, trying to get her frustration to the forefront. "Kitten, huh? That is real cute; you gave me a pet name. One of an actual pet. Why is it I feel that is completely appropriate? You stroke me and I unconditionally respond. Do I even have free will here or is this some kind of sexual trance thing?"

"My siblings and I have a strong sexual force about us, this is true. But it is not who I am, it is what you want," he grinned flashing perfect straight white teeth. "I'm not using any magic on you."

Magic now? But then how else to explain what I've seen, unless I'm completely hallucinating. "I'm not sure what to make of that answer. I'm going to consider it, and get back to you with my opinion."

"I'm quite sure you will," he chuckled with amusement, in that infernal sardonic tone.

"For now, I would appreciate it if you took your sexual force to the opposite end of the couch. So I can concentrate. Yes, I said for now; let it go, Smiley." Jade crossed her arms, letting out an exasperated huff.

He moved his hands to the couch and pushed his gorgeous body away from her, stretching his legs up on the coffee table in front of him.

"Next question?"

The intoxicating human sat up straighter, her breasts heaving forward during the movement, making him stifle a growl. Then she crossed her legs underneath her on the sofa. He was still staring when her hand went up into her mane of red curls and took a lock between her fingers, twirling the strand the same way he had seen her do it at the bookstore.

"Why are we at your brother's house and not yours?" It was ridiculous, the woman had him staring and losing his concentration. *I am a warrior, not an adolescent chasing my first little girl.* He looked at her and answered her question.

"Phaeton is the current Sovereign; this place is more of a compound than anything. He is in charge of the Djinn Sentry. Many of them live on this property. Because of their presence, and some other magic surrounding it, we are safe here. We will also conduct your training here." He was now fully intent on getting down to business, having pushed aside the stirring within him.

"Okay, what is the training and what would I be training for?" Her gaze followed him back and forth, taking in the change in his demeanor.

"Maybe you would like to eat before we continue, your food

is cooling and this answer may be extensive. I wouldn't want to burden you with it on an empty stomach."

He removed his feet from the coffee table and walked across the room to bring a covered tray and water to her. She found a hearty beef soup and fresh bread.

"I had it made for you while you were in the shower."

"That was really nice, actually." He was pleased he had done something right. For some reason he cared what she thought. He placed a glass of water in front of her as well. "You don't drink water? You don't eat either, do you? I know you pretend when you're with me, but you never really eat anything. Do you eat regular food?"

He gave her a droll, blank stare like he had no intention of answering, which made her even more curious.

"No, really, are you like a vampire? Do you drink blood but you don't want to freak me out?" She needed to have this conversation. It was scary to her that she didn't even know what the hell the man, whom she had just let cover her in blood, ate. "Do you eat flesh, bloody flesh? Your plate looks a little gooey." She wanted to close her ears and not get this answer; this might be the perfect time for her "ignorance is bliss" theory. But she had already asked and it looked like he might answer.

"I eat uncooked food. I am a strict carnivore." He lifted his hand to her before she could react. "No not human flesh, I protect humans. As for the other question you asked the answer is yes. I can get as much strength and far more pleasure from blood as from meats. And as for the next question you are going to ask, yes, I could and would love to drink from you; and I can be quite creative in where I choose to drink from." He gave her a wicked smile that made her legs cross and squeeze together at the top, and her areolas tighten in response. He was male perfection, even in the middle of this nightmare. He continued in that delicious, melodic tone only he possessed, "You my sweet, dirty girl, would love it. I have an extremely potent sense of smell and your blood smells divine." He ran his nails up the inside of her tightly squeezed and blessedly covered thigh. Jade inhaled deeply and thought about how demented she had become, because she considered how much she might enjoy it.

She got up in order to sit on the coffee table, keeping herself out of his reach. As she buried herself in her food, not trusting herself to even speak to him at the moment, he watched her in silence.

As she was eating, he tried to explain what he was to her. If he wanted to move forward with Jade's help he felt she deserved a few answers. He could, at least, give her that. He suddenly thought about risking her life and he realized he no longer felt so eager to do it. This woman he had known for a day seemed a little more important to him than she should.

"I am a Daemon, one of two kinds; my kind is called the Djinn. The monsters that abducted and harmed you earlier are Shaitan. You were extremely lucky, because they enjoy inflicting pain. The fact it only scratched you means they were after something and needed you coherent to get it. I won't go on. Hopefully you will never learn the full extent of their depravity."

He could see goose bumps form on her flesh and then watched her shudder.

She changed direction on him with her next question. "Okay, I'll focus on you for now, you've been blinking me around the country; your blood stops my pain. What other powers or abilities, or whatever, do you have?"

"We call 'blinking', as you say, transcending; we can move anywhere instantly, we only need to know where it is we want to go and we arrive, anywhere above ground. Also we can control fire and weather and have acute smell and hearing, which we used to find you earlier." He purposely left out the part on how their emotions could sometimes affect both fire and weather without their conscious thought – there was no need to add that to her apprehension. "However, none of this works in Sheol, which is why we have to move in on foot."

"Where is this Sheol? I heard you mention it to that woman, if that's what she was. Your brother is being kept there, right? By the Shaitan? Are you sure he's still alive? I'm so sorry to ask you, but from what you're telling me they seem more than a little dangerous."

He paused, his face darkening. She had asked something he didn't want to consider at all. "No, I'm not absolutely positive he's still alive." He said it that way because he refused to believe anything different.

"But they took him for a reason. He isn't directly connected with the Sentry. He is a free spirit. Joss lives his life separately from us, like I was trying to do before he was taken. Until they let us know their intentions we are confident they won't end him. But they are sure to damage him physically and psychologically over time, so we need to train you and move in as quickly as possible. Iblis, the father and Lord of Sheol, is given the souls of the worst of human life. He punishes them in ways I do not wish to speak of. Your murderers, pedophiles, those who torture and cause pain to others during their time above ground, also those who decide to take their own lives; they all end up there." He could feel the pain of this last answer and the memories it dredged up, and wanted to move away from it quickly.

"Centuries ago, Djinn and Shaitan inhabited Sheol together. But we saw how the Shaitan had begun to trick humans and lead them to slaughter, forcing them to the Unseen. So we left to try to protect them …"

Jade practically flew off the table, obviously stunned, and began to completely come undone.

"You mean Hell don't you? Because you're a Daemon and you come from freaking Hell, right? You are telling me you used to live in Hell and then you and some of the others, after hundreds of years, millennia, possibly; you and the other Djinn finally decided it wasn't okay that the Shaitan, the monsters that abducted me, are minions of an even more evil *thing*, this Iblis. That they abduct innocent humans and torture them, in ways I can't even fathom, for eternity. Call it what you will. But you want me to go with you into the pits of HELL and get your brother. Am I getting all this straight? This is your plan? And you really think it will work? With me? I am the one to help YOU get through Hell? I think I'll just take my chances with the Shaitan above ground if that's okay with you; well even if it isn't, I'm fucking out."

He was a little speechless. Nias could not remember another time in his life when he actually was at a loss for words. But here he sat. He watched her head for the door, which led to the hallway, tracking her as she stalked across the room. She was attempting to leave. He knew there was no way she could get out of the house, much less the compound, without him, so he let her go for now, to give her some time to cool off. Then he would go find her and start again. Eventually she would either begin to accept her circumstances or she wouldn't. Either way he would get her to cooperate.

As Jade walked swiftly to the door of the bedroom she had expected Nias to grab her and stop her at any moment, but he hadn't. She walked into the hallway and then broke into more of a run when she realized the possibility of getting free. Her mind was moving even faster than her body. *I can't believe I let myself get taken in by him! He wants to take me to Hell! Why in the world would he think I would ever even consider that? He was just using me! That's it. Just another asshole who treats women like something they can own, possess, control.*

As her mind railed and she searched for a way out, her breathing became heavy. The hallways seemed to go on forever! She passed door after door. Through the open ones she saw bedrooms, bathrooms, rooms that she had no idea what their use was. She tried a few of the closed ones. Some were locked, but those that weren't simply revealed more of the same. No way out! She tried to regain her composure; she needed to calm down. Eventually she came to a stairway, which led both up and down. She headed down, hoping to find a door, any door, out of this gigantic house.

When she reached the bottom of the next flight she had to choose left or right. She could see some kind of light coming from the end of the hall to her left and so she went in that direction. As she approached she could hear multiple voices coming from the end of the hall. If she got close enough, she would be able to take a read of their emotions. Sometimes, when there weren't too many people in a room, she could even tell before she entered how many there were in it by the emotions running through them.

She got a little closer, and she could feel four or five distinct personalities. She went further down toward the room and saw a large armoire with glass shelving. She crouched down behind it, and in doing so was able to see the whole room through the glass. Unless they knew to look for her, they wouldn't see her sitting there. They weren't shouting, but there was an atmosphere of seriousness in the room and voices were being raised; a heavy debate was taking place.

The room was very Goth socialite – a little bit rustic Rococo. It smacked of monsters with money. Furnished with heavy wooden antiques and expensive-looking paintings of fleshy pale nudes, the room had a color scheme of dark reds, deep blues, and gold. Rich burgundy tapestries hung around windows, which stretched upwards two full stories and were surrounded by intricately carved walls. Somehow the furniture managed to look oversized and cozy, a neat trick for the old French and Italian theme. Jade had an image in her mind, due to the expanse of the place and the interior furnishing, that at least a few flying buttresses held the whole building up and stone goblins stood guard outside.

There were actually five of them in the room – one woman and four men. Two of the males stood behind the couches. Most of the heaviness seemed to be coming from a huge, amazingly hot, dark-haired male. He looked similar enough to Nias that Jade knew this must be one of the siblings he had spoken of, but this guy looked more rugged, more muscular. While Nias was tall, with heavy arms and shoulders, he managed to be sleek; he always came off like the predatory cat she had first seen. This man was still tall and lean but more pure warrior. She could see him in the old country with a dirk or present-day muddy on a rugby field with torn clothing and a mass of injuries that didn't bother him a bit. The second man, who seemed to be doing his best to negotiate between Big and Rugged and the girl, was about six feet tall and blond. Much softer-looking and softer-spoken, he seemed far more reasonable than the others. The two men standing were both between six two and six four, still gorgeous, but not so much as the others. They stood silent, almost to attention, and seemed to be waiting for orders.

The girl was dwarfed by the men. She seemed to be around five four. But even with her small stature, she was holding her own. She had long dark hair pulled back tight in a low ponytail. Jade could see the familial gold eyes shine out of her beautiful, almost perfect, features. She wore black combat boots, black jeans and a tight fitting black t-shirt. She wasn't made up, but she carried herself like she knew she didn't need it, and didn't seem the kind of girl to care that much anyway.

"We need to figure out what is going on and we need to do it now before it gets worse!" the largest male boomed.

"I agree, Phaeton, but don't go out there on a killing spree before we have a chance to find the source of the chaos," the girl countered, and went on. "The Shaitan never do anything without being told to do it. We need to know what Iblis is planning. Why would Hamartia be above ground? I can hardly believe that sick bitch could walk away from her closest companions – bloodshed, pain, and misery – for even a day."

"Ella is right. We should find out how we can stop the whole, not kill the few. Hamartia's presence signifies something completely different is happening. We have to find out what." The blond simply stated things matter-of-factly, without elevating his voice at all.

The girl, who obviously was named Ella, continued, "Don't get me wrong, Phaeton, we will stop them from doing harm, with the same force we always use. I don't want them to suspect anything is different in the way we are approaching this latest assault. I will lead the Sentry to the streets, as I always have. I wouldn't want to let a day go by without our usual body count. But I will not simply injure the body of the beast and allow the head to grow again."

"I will join you on the street. My abilities will speed the process of finding the Shaitan and learning about their plans; besides I haven't had the opportunity to end nearly as many of the scaly low lives as I would like recently." Phaeton smiled.

"We would be honored to have you with us. We could benefit from your tracking, they could be anywhere in the world by now. If you can get us to the right city, we can easily flush them out by scent and sound." This was spoken by one of the standing men, one whom Jade assumed to be part of the Sentry they spoke of.

"If Nias is successful at bringing Joss out, or when we find this mission has failed, the Sentry will move in force into the Unseen. We will fight until we achieve our purpose or Iblis finally takes us down for good. We begin tomorrow scouring the streets for the information you believe is necessary, Ella. Start with all the major cities; if you smell and hear nothing in twenty-four hours move to your next location. You lead your Southern group through Europe; I will take the North Corps and start in Asia. Do not let the humans see you transcend, as always. Let one Sentry settle first, find an appropriate location and then the rest can settle safely. Locke, you are home base for now. I believe Nias has persuaded the girl into helping us and will begin training her soon."

Jade was a little shocked at Phaeton's assuredness. She had definitely decided *not* to help. Or had she? If so, why wasn't she trying to escape? Instead of moving and trying to find a door, she was crouching here listening to them plan their assaults, and finding herself wondering if these beings could indeed help her find a key to reversing her curse.

Then she felt a familiar heat come up behind her.

Chapter 7

"Hello Kitten … learn anything of value?" He could smell plums and almost taste her in his mouth again when he came up behind her.

Jade screamed and jumped at the same time. Everyone in the room turned to look at her. Her face became completely red as it was apparent she had been spying.

"Damn it, Nias!" She turned to scowl at him.

He began to laugh, as he found her delightful. Even caught spying on a room full of royal military Djinn, she had the courage to scold him. He actually enjoyed her bravery.

"Nias, how nice of you to come out of your room and join us, we've been letting your friend here in on some of our plans for tomorrow," Phaeton announced.

"What, you knew I was there and you didn't say anything?" *I am so humiliated.* With a beet-red face she turned, gave Nias one more dirty look, and introduced herself to the others. "Hi, I'm Jade Shear."

"Yes, I figured as much when I first heard you sit down, and could smell human. I am Phaeton, Sovereign of the Djinn, and Leader of the Sentry." Nias had to roll his eyes at his introduction. Even though Nias had stepped down because he no longer wanted to be Sovereign, he and Phaeton continued to have a potent sibling rivalry; an endless struggle of power and ego. He thought back to their last conflict before they finally left Sheol under Nias's leadership and the memory made him tense.

Phaeton continued, "I thought I heard you come in last night, Nias, but I didn't know if you had brought our guest. I am pleased to have both of you staying with us. Will you be here long? I know the two of you have a lot to get accomplished in the next few days. That is if Miss Shear has agreed to help us." Phaeton looked to Jade to see what her answer to his query would be. Nias looked to her for the same reason, having no idea what she would say. He was curious to see how she would handle the situation. If nothing else, it would be amusing. "But before you respond to such a question let me introduce our family, this is our sister, Ella."

Nias saw the look in his sister's eyes as she responded and said hello, albeit in a snarling, disapproving tone. "Ella! You will treat Jade with respect; she has been through hell in the past twenty-four hours!" Nias was shocked at his own outburst and reaction, as Ella looked a little stunned and Phaeton raised an eyebrow. One of the other men cleared his throat to break the silence.

"I'm Locke. Not sure what my position is in this family. One day I realized, much to my consternation, that I had been adopted, or taken prisoner, much like yourself. I'm still not sure which. I've tried to escape, but they always manage to pull me back in somehow. I guess someday I'll learn to tell them no, but it's been several thousand years and I haven't seemed to do it yet." Locke stated all of this in his usual irascible tone. Nias smiled at him. They had been best friends for centuries. Locke was friendlier and much less guarded than the members of his own family. "I see Nias hasn't managed to completely scare you off yet? His personality is a little abrasive. He seems to believe he is the one and only cat, and the rest of us are merely his toys."

"Locke, it is good to see you too. I've missed your lovely sense of humor," Nias said with a good-natured needling.

"Nias, I shouldn't expect you to remember as you were only

semiconscious at the time, but I saw you yesterday. So I can't imagine you've missed me too much."

"Yes, my friend, I believe it's been way too long." And Nias gave his best friend a slight push at his shoulder.

"I'm sorry for them, Jade. They have been best friends for so long they no longer feel it is necessary to treat each other civilly," said Phaeton.

"What do you mean by 'she's been through hell in the last twenty-four hours'?" Ella had recovered from her surprise and wanted to get back down to business. She was a no-nonsense kind of girl. She always did what she wanted, which at this point was command an entire division of the Sentry under Phaeton. Nias and Phaeton had a soft spot where their sister was concerned. It didn't matter what she did, how many fiends she could kill in a night, how controlling and demanding her disposition, even the numbers of men, both human and Daemon, she took advantage of, made fall in love with her and cruelly disregarded. They would always treat her like their little sister, always be on her side in any disagreement. Anyone who dealt with the family knew this. No one messed with Ella; she messed with them.

Although in this moment Nias felt the need to protect Jade, and this was getting to be an annoying habit of his. He wanted her to feel safe, always. He wanted her to be comfortable even with his enigmatic and derisive family. The hellion would prob-ably try to run for the door any minute now and he would be the one responsible for bringing her back, but he had started to like having her around. Of course, there was always the lust. There was no way he was letting her go before he had taken her. Long and slow, she would spend several nights, or even weeks, in his bed, willingly, before he was letting her go anywhere.

He also knew the family needed her to help him traverse Sheol. His feelings were starting to make him lose sight of the objective. He should sleep with her soon, he thought, so he could get his mind back to where it ought to be. She was somehow confusing his thoughts.

"Hey, Nias, we would like to be informed of the past twenty-four hours, please," Ella repeated, snapping him out of his thoughts.

"Well, as it will probably clarify her answer to Phaeton's question regarding whether she has agreed to help us, I would love to explain."

"Oh, no please, allow me," Jade said forcefully. His family and friends looked a little shocked at how Jade seemed to treat Nias as an equal; they had never seen a woman he hadn't won over and dominated immediately.

"I was actually on a walk when I was kidnapped by pretty boy here." Surprised glares came from all. "Not sure I have to even explain to you all my shock at the whole Daemon thing, so I tried to escape, got captured and sliced up by monsters, at which point Nias showed up, broke one of their necks with as much effort as it takes to break a pencil and sent others to kill the rest. I was torn up and, well, and then brought here." Nias noticed her look at her feet and grab a curl between her twirling fingers as her voice faded a little at the end.

"Excellent work on your kill, Nias, I had gotten a report of the extinction of a San Francisco nest earlier. What did you see of Hamartia? We are all concerned about her appearance here."

Jade had seen the looks on all their faces when she said he brought her here and then, after listening to them talk about the killing, Jade spun on her heel. Nias saw his beautiful red-headed spitfire become enraged and attempt to escape the room.

"Kitten, please do not leave us," he stated, with as little sarcasm as he could muster, as she turned her back on them and started to walk away.

"Ahh! For the love of God, stop it with Kitten. I am leaving, no, I do not want to help. I have had all I can handle, really." And she stomped out of the room, heading down the hallway.

Nias transcended in front of her halfway down the hall. She stopped when he appeared.

"Why do I even try to get out? You 'ask' for my help, but in reality I am a prisoner and have no choices here." She said this, putting air quotes around the word "ask", in a tone he knew she meant as angry; but he could see she was truly upset, scared, and overwhelmed. He was struck by his need to soothe her. He took a step toward her until he was able to feel her sweet breath and he wanted to taste her again. He wanted to crush his mouth to her plump lips until she couldn't remember she was upset. He inhaled sharply, as he watched her look up at him quickly and begin to chew her bottom lip for a moment. The action made her lower lip swell a bit and she looked even sexier because of it.

"Jade, I know you want to go home and I can see you are upset, but it really isn't your option to leave. You're right, we asked you, but we know you don't have any choices left to make. Come back to the sitting room with us and we will discuss what must be done." He moved his hand, as if to touch her.

She took a step back. "No. I mean, yes. Yes, I will go back and discuss my options. But, no, please do not touch me, Nias. You will not touch me anymore. I am not one of your cat toys; I will not be touched by you again." She turned and went back to rejoin the discussion.

Surprisingly, Nias understood how she must feel. He was hoping she would change her mind soon, particularly about the touching.

"So glad you have rejoined us," Phaeton said, standing up from his position on an overstuffed bright-blue sofa. He began walking toward her.

"Nias has reminded me that my options have become rather limited." She scowled.

When Phaeton arrived at her side he reached out and touched one of the ends of her hair, pulling down slightly on a couple of the curls. It was a flirty gesture and Nias had to suppress a growl.

"I understand your frustrations. We are grateful for your presence here, Jade. As Nias has already explained, I'm sure, we are extremely worried about our brother Joss. Time is certainly crucial," Phaeton said, still fondling her hair. Nias tried to tell himself that just because he wished to sleep with her didn't mean he should actually feel jealous. He and Phaeton, after all, had been sharing women for centuries. It was nothing for them to have slept with the same woman. He had seen both his brothers flirt with his ex-bedmates as they had seen him do with theirs. This was more of the same; a beautiful woman was just that, beautiful. They should all have a chance to enjoy such, and the woman should have a chance at all of the Hu'dor brothers as well. They always seemed pleased to have been "acquired" by the family.

Phaeton moved his hand down to her arm. Before he even realized it, Nias found himself in between them. He thought it was actually a subtle movement. He walked across the room as if to join their conversation, slid between them, and gently moved her out of Phaeton's reach. His brother would no longer touch her. Nias decided that until he had been with her he would not share. And that was final.

"Jade, we are having a little get-together this weekend. We often come together to relax, myself, Nias, Ella and many of the Sentry who live on property. We would love to have you join us. I believe you will enjoy yourself." He grinned at her. *Did she just smile back at him?*

"Nias always does, that is, if he can remember it. He hasn't missed a party of any sort since he stepped down from Sovereign," Locke added from across the room.

"You can say that again," Ella concurred.

"We would love to, but no." They looked at Nias as if they knew he was up to something. "Jade and I, as you all know, have much to accomplish; our priority is with Joss. I think it is best we don't indulge right now." He actually believed himself when he said it. "Jade, we will go to our room and begin planning for your training."

"Phaeton, speaking of *our* room." She looked right at Nias while she spoke, as if intending to rile him. "I was wondering, the house seems quite large, is it possible for me to have my own room."

Hellion, Nias thought.

"Of course, Jade, I will have my people make up a room for you right away."

And on that sour note, Nias took her forcefully by her elbow and directed her back to their, plural, rooms.

Chapter 8

The room they had provided for her had been decorated much like the rest of the house. It was huge, had dark wood floors and a strangely homey Rococo feel to it. A huge, intricately carved four-poster bed with a brown and cream damask print spread on top stood on a far wall with a French dresser on either side. A few overstuffed chairs sat facing a gorgeous fireplace with an oversized mantle, and this one actually *did* have a few of those creepy old goblins on either side of the flames. *Some brethren from days gone by, maybe?*

She was able to sense Nias couldn't stand having lost "control" of her. He obviously wasn't going to let her make a move in this house or anywhere else without him knowing about it. She knew this by the Sentry he had placed outside her door. Well, at least she had gotten her own room.

This was the first time since this whole ordeal began that she had a moment to sit by herself and think about her situation. It seemed obvious at this point that she was going to have to do what Nias and his family wanted her to do, at least for now. That was actually the nicest family of hostage-taking killers she had ever met. Well, besides the sister who seemed a little bitter about her being here? Not sure what that was about. Had that tiny, beautiful girl actually complimented her brother on his kills? Yes, yes she had. But Phaeton and Locke had been lovely, even as they planned to force her into accompanying Nias into the depths of Hell, and spoke of slaughtering soul-stealing Shaitan.

So, Jade, you actually do have a choice here. Crumble and whimper, which isn't going to get you anywhere, or try to run again and be killed either by the Shaitan or by the Djinn themselves. Refusing to help them and knowing they exist couldn't possibly bode well for her continued survival. They obviously had no problem with killing in general and it seemed, on some level, they enjoyed it. So although she found herself in a completely surreal situation, she refused to fall apart, and wasn't willing to die, certainly not before she'd lost her virginity. She picked unvoiced choice number three, to be an impregnable force and not be defeated, by either her own fear or the bad guys. Or the "good" guys, for that matter. Despite being scared out of her mind, she would be strong and get through this, *no matter what!*

Her life had never been normal. She had never trusted anyone. She was going in to this shellproof and confident, not like some whimpering, helpless female. She had never let herself be helpless and she wasn't going to start now. *Bring it on, Nias, you arrogant fuck. I am ready!*

She had a plan to get her needs met as well. If this was going to happen, she would find a way out of this curse. They had magic and she had need of it. And, she had another plan as well. She smiled, just considering it. As far as their touching each other anymore, she was through. Yes, she was attracted to him. She would love to roll around in his sheets with him, maybe have a chance to get her hands on that unbelievable long, muscular body. But he was using her; he was going to take her to Hell! This was definitely not the beginning of the trustworthy relationship she had always wanted. This was a Daemon, for God's sake, one who didn't care whether she lived or died. He was going to put her life at risk without blinking. She would keep her hands to herself, and try to survive.

Okay, pep talk done… check that off the list!

When Nias knocked ten minutes later she opened the door to assault him with demands. He leaned his hulking six foot four-inch body against the door frame; his long silky hair hung to the side as he cocked his head, slightly amused at her new fortitude as she spoke.

"Okay, I'll do your stupid training, although I'm sorry to inform you I'm about as coordinated as a giraffe, so good luck with that. But there is a stipulation. I can't train day and night. I will *train*," she sputtered as if the very word was ridiculous, "although I still don't have a clue what that entails, during the days with you and you will do anything I want in the evening." Although she was feeling passionate, she managed to keep her voice relatively calm; she thought she sounded menacing, for once, and she liked it.

For the second time since she met him, Nias threw his head back and laughed. His eyes sparkled. "Oh, Kitten, I thought you were going to at least try to hold out on me. Although I could tell by our earlier play time you wanted me, I didn't think you were as aware. Not that I'm complaining. I haven't wanted anyone so badly in decades." He took a step toward her, and she took a step back, afraid he might spring on her. "I just thought you were going to be different. I really didn't think you were going to want me so soon, or this badly. This is a very welcome pleasure; the evenings will most definitely be yours." He smiled at her with all of his straight pearly-white teeth shining; but he managed only to look like a vicious lion who had finally captured its prey, teeth bared, about to rip a giant piece of tasty flesh off her.

"My God, you are sure of yourself. I believe it might be my turn to throw my stupid, conceited head back and cackle at you." She stared him down, wry smile in place, although drawn towards him. "What I want is more like foreplay."

"Umm, very well, then," he drawled, like she was something yummy.

"Yeah, not so fast, big boy, I want a friend. I want a companion. I want a super freaking hot piece of alpha male ass, to do all the girl stuff I never got to do, with anyone. I did them alone. Because your lame Goddess, or whatever she was, cursed me with knowing what deceitful, lying, irascible, insouciant dickheads people are. I have had to steer clear, or been kicked out of, any kind of meaningful bond with anyone, ever. And you, my friend, *are* going to be that super freaking hot piece of alpha male ass, who is going to make up for all of it. That is, if you really want my help."

After all those tough words and a look a professional poker player would have been proud of, she began having a bit of apprehension that he would say no. Too bad! He would do what she wanted, or she would simply refuse to help him until he changed his mind. *Kiss my ass, Nias.*

There was a part of her that saw him as arrogant, a part that knew he was a Daemon and a killer and a hostage-taker; but despite all of it there was a part of her that still wanted to be back in his arms, back in his bed with the fire and the calm he seemed to bring to her. Not to mention his proclivity toward licking her. It was different from any other relationship she had ever experienced. He didn't lie to her. He was tall and sexy as hell and he was a conceited, overconfident ass, but he made her feel good and she liked that. And although they would probably never play house together, she wanted to steal some time with him. Jade felt he owed her after living with this curse and the torture it had given her, although she was starting to wonder whether she had given people the chance they deserved. After growing up with incompetent parents, maybe she had simply picked the wrong friends – and definitely the wrong boyfriends. She was a prisoner in this house and yet she liked these people. It was baffling.

"Fine. I'll do it. The nights will be yours; we will do what you wish. But here are *my* demands, Jade." *Yay,* she thought. However it worried her slightly that he had used her real name instead of "Kitten", and he also looked kind of serious; that smirk he always wore had subsided.

"I want you to stop trying to run, stop acting like a brat, and take this training as seriously as you can. Because when I tell you my brother is with some very dangerous beings in a horrible place and he means the world to me, and my family, I mean it, and that is not a joke. Soon we go to Sheol." He didn't look or sound angry, he looked and sounded concerned, really concerned.

"I understand and I'm sorry. I can feel you're worried about him. I intend to take this seriously, and I'll do my best to follow your instruction." And, yes, she could truly feel his worry. For a moment, when her eyes met his intense golden gaze there was no hostility. They were two people on the same team; she felt like it was the most intimate moment they had shared. Maybe it was possible they could actually function like friends, if only for a while. *That would be nice.*

Chapter 9

Nias had asked Locke to bring her what he referred to as "training clothes". They consisted of some black stretch yoga pants that went a little past her knees and a tight, black tank top, which barely contained her extra-large D-cups. By how snugly they fit, she assumed they had to be Ella's. Otherwise Nias had purposely ordered them too small to add to his personal visual pleasure. She knew he was taking this training seriously; she believed him when he said it. But by the look of these clothes he wouldn't be passing up the opportunity of seeing her figure to his best advantage. She definitely wasn't putting it past him.

Locke, who was the blond introduced earlier as Nias's best friend, and in the employ of the family in some way, came to supply her with this apparel. Jade was interested in the opportunity to get to spend some time with any man who would claim Nias as best friend. His shaggy yellow hair was several inches above his shoulders and he, like the rest of the Daemons, was beyond handsome, but in a lighter and kinder way; more like the tall, perfectly built, dirty-blond yoga teacher you want to run away with. Despite his great looks, he didn't have the instant pull over her that she always felt around Nias. It was a relief. She was glad to have a chance to converse with anyone besides Nias at this point.

She met him in the corridor outside her room. She was following him down to whatever room it was that she would "train" in.

"You must be pretty overwhelmed with all this." He looked to her as they began walking.

"Locke, right?" He nodded, and waited for her reply. "I cannot even begin to answer that question because I am so overwhelmed by this situation." He chuckled lightly, but continued to walk.

"You are a funny girl, Jade. Although you find yourself in this position, you're still managing to keep your sense of humor, and if I'm not totally off-base, you're still a little upbeat."

"Well, what are you gonna do, really? Ignorance is bliss. I guess you know I have certain abilities?" He nodded again. "Well, I've never taken the opportunity to play ignorant about things, but I'm taking full advantage now. Nias says there are bad things involved. He told me we were going to some evil place. But as far as I'm concerned I have put my hands on my ears like a small child and I'm over here going 'la, la, la, la, la. I am not listening to Nias, even though he continues talking.'" She sighed and continued. "I don't know what this Unseen World, Sheol, looks like, don't know what those monsters look like, and I am doing my very best to ignore what they've already done. I intend to train, whatever the hell that means, and not think past it. I'm not thinking past the foot in front of me."

He laughed, "I love it! Finally someone else around here with my fucked-up outlook on life. Nias appreciates it, but the man has two feet firmly planted in reality and action. Well, at least he used to. Considering he was that way for thousands of years, I'm hoping he'll bounce back."

She gave him a curious look. "That comment is almost enough to get me to ask questions. Nice try, but nope, I'm simply not biting today. Nias, whoever that man is, will have to be his own problem. Because there's the foot in front of me and 'la, la, la, la, la.'" She covered her ears.

They traveled down two flights of stairs into what looked to be the basement, or if she wasn't wrong, an old torture chamber, converted to a gym of sorts. There were windows, which ran horizontal to the floor. They were high up on the grey stone-block walls, and close to the ceiling, which made her think this place was partially subterranean. The floors were black and padded, wall to wall. The room itself was huge. It could have easily housed two Olympic-sized pools.

No one was there when she arrived. So when Locke left her alone, she decided to look around until Nias chose to join her. She walked towards what looked like a metal stand full of equipment across the room, but its contents took her by surprise. What she found where weapons, medieval weapons. She owned a book store; she had books on pretty much anything you could think of. And she had seen several with pictures of these weapons. A seven-foot double-edged battle axe, and a set of knives in various sinister shapes. One had a three-sided blade shaped like a triangle, which she knew was infamous for creating wounds that were nearly impossible to close and heal because of the unique damage it created. Another had a jagged edge, like a band saw, which looked a lot like shark teeth. Several were longer blades, which looked extremely sharp, and another set of shorter knives appeared destined to be inserted into some nearby wrist sheaths. These she knew were worn for easy access in a fight. A large wall of swords from ancient Chinese to medieval Scottish to what she could only figure was English pirate were set to the side. Each was set on its own pair of prongs and was arranged, longest to shortest, from the floor to ten feet high.

The other weapon, among the virtual plethora, was a ball and mace – a shaft or pole of metal, which connected with a chain to a steel ball covered in spikes. The worst part of this last item was the dried hunks of bloody flesh stuck between the spikes. *Ahh! Who didn't wash blood chunks off their weapon? Who had weapons like these covered in blood in the first place? Daemons, who took pleasure in killing did, that's who Jade!* Even if they were killing monsters, it was still killing. Even the idea of killing a worm for tackle freaked her out. Extinguishing the life of anything was difficult to think about. She wasn't squeamish; she could do it. But it wasn't something she would ever say she would enjoy like these beings seemed to.

She saw a familiar shadow move through her peripheral vision and knew her trainer had arrived. Here was the man that she, in one moment, wanted to cozy up to but in the next wanted to run screaming from. The one who owned medieval weapons covered with dried blood, come to teach her how to fight. This was going to be good.

"I see you have received your training gear. I thought it might suit you. Looks as though I was right," he said, staring at her boobs and then actually licking his lips, and circling behind her to check her out from all angles. She knew this should have made her angry, but she'd seen that look before. It had come from a pair of hooded gold eyes staring up at her from between her thighs. Merely thinking about that look managed to give her that dewy, tight feeling between her legs.

Nias was wearing long black sweats with black stripes up the sides. They were slung low on his hips, leaving a slice of skin between them and the black t-shirt he was wearing. It was that perfect strip of man-flesh right under his abs and above his pubic region. The fine beginnings of a dark strip of hair ran equidistant between those delicious creases perfectly built men get, the ones running from their hips at the sides of their abdomen and slanting down into their pants. It was like God was trying to put arrows towards the good stuff. Jade loved those creases. His feet were bare. The vulnerability of his skin made her pause. Something about his bare feet made her feel comfortable around him, like he was letting loose a little.

When she stopped dreaming of that lusty look of his, getting wet thinking about him in general and staring at his delicious man creases, she looked up. He was stalking around her as if gauging her vulnerable points. She couldn't imagine she had a point which wasn't vulnerable to him.

He had to be at least ninety pounds heavier than she was and almost a foot taller. Not to mention he was covered in all that sleek, yummy muscle. And then he stopped. He turned to face her, head on, and arched a brow, cocked just the side of his mouth, locking his eyes to her own.

"I said I would take this seriously, and I will," she blurted.

"Looks as though you're taking something seriously."

"Nice weapons. You plan on teaching me to kick some ass?" she said, trying to change the subject away from the fact she was caught checking him out, again.

"Yes," he said dryly.

Nias had been about ten paces away, circling her like the predatory animal he was as they stared at each other. But suddenly, he stopped and walked toward her with a blank, emotionless stare. This may have been the scariest face she'd seen on him. Quickly she tried to read him to see what was going on, but before she had a chance he was on her. He grabbed both her hands, pulled them inward slightly, and she was pulled forward. He ducked his head underneath her and she flipped right over him, landing on her back.

"Ow," she groaned. "I guess this training isn't going to consist of some laps and a few jumping jacks, huh?"

"No, it isn't." He had gone into some kind of commander-of-the-army mode. He was focused and ready, it seemed, to put her through the paces. "We can start there. If you can get one of the Shaitan to their back, I can teach you to break their neck pretty easily."

Nias had no intention of making this easy on her. His job was to turn her into a killing machine, in a week. Originally he had planned on teaching her some basic self-defense and a little mind control, and off they would go. He knew she would be injured.

He suspected she might even be killed. But if she could use the talents Jibreel had given her to help him walk right through the Shaitan and retrieve his brother, then one less human in the world would have been no real loss. He had been done caring for them, especially as individuals. They were too fragile to get attached to.

Until he met Jade, all his well-placed defense systems were protecting him, keeping the nightmares at bay. But his need to protect this human was growing despite his efforts to quash them. He had begun to feel concerned about her going into Sheol. He would not have believed he would ever care for another human at all, but this was something much stronger than even simple caring. He wanted to keep her. He wanted to continue to banter with the girl; he wanted her in his bed, all the time, and more than anything, he didn't want to see her get hurt. It was everything he had been trying to avoid. His self-imposed numbness consisting of a steady stream of hard alcohol and sex with consenting strangers was supposed to keep this from happening, and it had been adequate up until now. Yet here he was, face to face with a human who seemed to be able to tear his heart open and wriggle her way in. He wavered between his desire to run and his need to stay.

But for now he needed to teach her to kill the Shaitan, and there were only three ways to do it.

He stood above her as she lay on her back with an irritated look on her beautiful face. He was doing his best to act nonchalant, even though it was far from what he felt. He would simply have to keep her too busy to think about getting a grip on a real read of his feelings.

"You can kill the Shaitan by breaking the neck, removing the heart, or decapitating them. Seeing as I doubt you will ever get close enough or have the physical ability to remove a heart, you've got two options left. And you will learn them." He stuck out a hand to her and pulled her up to her feet, making sure not to make eye contact. "They are strong, most of them, not as strong as Djinn, but far stronger than a human. You will need to move quickly and catch them off-guard. Which should be easy, the catching them off-guard part, because they will never expect you to attack first."

"It seems absolutely crazy to me as well, Sensei, but I told you I will give this my best, so how in the world would you like me to accomplish that?"

"Come toward me. I am a Shaitan. You will throw me down to my back, just like I did to you. When I get close enough, you will grab my wrists like this," and he grabbed hers from the outside, "you will twist the beast inward, avoiding the claws. The momentum will pull them down; then you get under them quickly, flipping them over onto their backs as quickly as I did to you. It has nothing to do with strength, it is all technique."

He could tell there wasn't an ounce of her that believed what he was saying, but he could also see from the look in Jade's eyes that she would give every ounce of energy in her to learn. They did this move together over and over until she had a rudimentary grasp, as he continued to focus on the training and not her.

"Now the easy part. Learn to break my neck." He loved the feel of her in his hands and the vulnerable position he kept putting her in was taxing every bit of his will power to not rip her clothes to shreds and take her right here. The tiny moan she was making every time he flipped her was not helping, but he set his mind to the task. Taking her by one arm, he threw her to her back again. *Focus Nias*, he demanded of himself.

"You will come up to it when it falls in this position and place a foot on its neck right below its chin; push upwards and to the side and listen for the crack." He demonstrated on her neck.

"Holy cow, really?" She raised her eyebrows and looked a little shocked and reluctant, but he also saw a growing excitement in her as he moved his foot, releasing her face from the floor where he had it smashed. Every time he taught her something and she grasped it, he could see her confidence was building.

"Really. It will be you or it, Jade, you must strike quickly." He glowered at her, but was still heartened by her attention to everything he said. Her patience and ability to learn was impressive. He spent the next hour showing her how to position and twist her foot at just the right angle to break a neck. He found he was proud when she got it. He would not be proud; he didn't want to be proud. He tried to focus on anger, but he wasn't feeling it. He tried to focus on irritation and impatience, but she was giving every bit of energy to learn how to fight. She was learning how to kill Shaitan because she had no other options but to accompany him to Sheol, because he hadn't given her any. She could have refused to train at all, and yet here she was; she might even learn to keep herself alive, it was lovely. Fuck, she was amazingly lovely.

Across the room and unknown to the two of them, Locke watched the interaction. He saw his friend's face vacillate between the old, caring Nias, who gave his heart to everyone around him, the one who would die to save the humans he protected while he had been Sovereign; to the one he had turned into after the events of last year. Immediately after the tragedy he had expected his old friend to recover the strength he had always had, to return with more force and fervor than ever, but he hadn't. He had turned into someone Locke would have never expected; someone cold and without feeling at all. Locke would have expected too much anger or too much violence; too much emotion in any form would seem like Nias, Nias grieving. But void of feeling? Never in a million years would he have seen it coming.

Locke had known Nias well. He had always known the heart of his best friend teetered on the edge of caring too much for those around him. It was his nature. He had always been meaner and fiercer and stronger than everyone around him, but the other side of that extreme emotion was its alter ego, the side of Nias that he never showed. The side he hid with everything he had. And he thought they had all believed it. Nias seemed to actually believe Phaeton and Ella and Joss and Locke himself couldn't see him for both extremes, but he constantly betrayed himself. When he looked in the eyes of any one of them, his caring side spilled out; at least it used to,

…until Rachel.

Now Locke was watching him fight, for the first time in a year, to keep his emotion toward someone inside. And that someone was this human girl.

Nias hadn't truly shown any emotion until now, until Jade was forced into his life and split a tiny crack in the bastion Nias had built. Locke was hoping this human could break through the façade and bring his friend back. He smiled broadly and hopefully as he exited the room.

Chapter 10

Jade didn't know what to think anymore. Although she could tell that Nias was trying to conceal his emotions from her, instead he was *blasting* her with them! She was doing her best to focus on the lessons he was giving her, and she felt like she was pulling it off. But the whole time she was focused on Nias and the raging conflict he was having with himself, he was back and forth from concern, to anger, to arousal, to pride, to fear and even for moments to pleasure. It was making her dizzy.

She *really* didn't want to speculate on what he was thinking. She knew a lot of women at the store, not well, but it didn't take much for a woman to start going on about their boyfriend or husband or even last date. It was always, "what do you think he meant by…" or "can you believe he did that, what do you think he meant?" ad infinitum, *gross*. Jade had been forced to listen to girls go on and on trying to decipher what some man was thinking or feeling, based on his latest word, or gesture, or some stupid scenario. And the women always seemed to have it wrong. *I'm not going there. Okay, I'm going to try really, really hard, not to go there. Holy cow, I want to know!* Every time that tall, silky-haired, sleekly muscled, golden-eyed beast touched her, she was losing it more and more. Every time he let her throw him to the ground, she had another inappropriate thought.

So she tried to think about her dream men. They were kind to her; they treated her with love and respect. They didn't kill, although the fact she was training to do that now probably negated killing as something she could hold against him. Her dream men might be only that, dreams, but they had all the qualities she wanted in a man. Nias was hot, it was true, and she would definitely have been looking forward to spending time with him at the house, not in Sheol. But what she knew about how he treated women was not good. He had kidnapped her. He had smeared her with blood, albeit to heal her wounds, but still blood had been involved. He had, well, had oral sex with her, when they didn't even know each other. Even though it took two and it might be hypocritical for her to feel this way, nevertheless this led her to believe he did this a lot with women, and random acts of sex must be a regular thing in his life. *Look at him; it can't be that difficult for him to find a partner.* Damn, she knew it was ridiculous, but she wished it wasn't that way for him.

"Hey, do you have sex with women you don't know all the time?" Never one to mince words and not wanting to be one of those women who wondered and never asked, she blurted it out while they were taking a small breather between learning two methods of killing a demonic creature. He froze and then turned to stare.

"That would depend on what you define as 'don't know' and 'all the time.'" He turned and grinned at her from the weapons rack, where he was picking out something sharp for her to decapitate monsters with.

"I'm going to take that as a yes." The words came out more sharply than planned, and despite herself she felt jealous. Suddenly she could see herself using her new killing techniques on anything female that got near him. *Lalalalala. Damn!* She had no right to feel possessive over him. She wasn't going to check what he was feeling. It didn't matter. Damn it, she tried her best to get a read on him again, a glutton for punishment.

But found this time she couldn't.

"Are you blocking me?"

"Blocking you from what?" He turned to stare at her.

"From reading you, how you feel."

"Are you curious to know how I feel, Kitten?" He smirked.

"I was just trying to see exactly how callous you are, to see if you would leave me in the middle of Sheol to fend for myself. I was curious if that's the reason you were training me so hard," she lied.

"Really, is that the reason you asked me who I sleep with and what my motivations for doing so are?"

"Well, yeah." She realized how half-hearted her denial was and looked down.

"I can't read you like you can read people, but I can definitely read you right now. And you are lying." He left the weapons rack, and now he was walking toward her. "Kitten, are you trying to see if I am interested in more than sex and achieving our goals together?" He was looking into her eyes like he had when he'd been in bed with her, hungrily…mischievously ravenous, like he might even lick his feline chops.

"No," she managed to squeak out, only kind of lying now, "I am actually concerned that I can't read you. It has rarely ever happened to me, and considering my fighting skills, or lack thereof, I was sort of relying on it to keep me alive." She looked back at him, into his exotic golden glare. She gave him her best, 'see I'm not hiding anything' innocent look.

He gently put a hand on either side of her face and brushed his lips across hers. His proximity began to absorb her. She tried to object, but it was useless. Having him so close all day long was too much for an ordinary human girl. It was divine. His arms went around her waist and pulled her in, his tongue parted her lips and dove in. She could feel his hardness swelling against her.

It had been almost eight hours since he had kissed her, and her body was not so subtly informing her that it had been way too long. She melted into him; her arms swung up around his neck, and without conscious thought from her she could feel one of her feet bend at the knee and slowly lift from the floor. Butterflies began to flutter in her tummy. Whatever it was about him that made her feel this way, the Daemon, the "energy" the Hu'dors had, she didn't really know or care. She wanted more. She leaned into him with full acquiescence.

Her eyes were still closed when he backed up, holding her shoulders, and looked at her. He wasn't smiling.

"Well?" he said flatly.

"Well what?" she answered breathlessly, slowly opening her eyes, to see he was actually waiting for an answer.

"Could you read me? Surely there was an emotion there you could decipher."

"No, nothing," she said, and she would have loved to know his emotions right now, dammit. Regardless of his ridiculous plan to use her to move through Sheol, it would have been great to know what emotion that kiss had produced in him. In her gut, she knew he needed her for a reason. Only minutes before, he had admitted having sex with women he didn't care for, and earlier he said that all the Hu'dor siblings had this effect on women. So maybe it was a good thing she couldn't read him.

In the past the only time the curse had subsided was with her mother. One time, when she was eleven she had cut her foot and her mother had been so kind to her; Jade had believed the woman had truly loved her. Her mother had cleaned and bandaged her foot and Jade felt an overwhelming love for her, and had lost her ability to read her mother. It had come back when it became apparent that the moment between them was fleeting. Thinking her mother capable of actually loving her was a joke, and she had pushed the woman away emotionally, completely, after that. Subsequently the ability returned.

Nias was simply going about his sexual quid pro quo with another of his random female admirers – with her. So it was truly odd that her ability would fail her at this moment. Unless it had nothing to do with the other person's feelings and was based solely on her own misplaced, delusional attachments. But whether it had been just her mother or a complete loss of the curse, she had no idea.

"Jade, this is not a good time for your gift to fail."

She glowered back at him. "So sorry to be broken when you need me to perform," she said with venomous sarcasm. Despite having agreed not to be bratty, she was finding that an impossible task right now. Her thoughts and emotions seemed to be taking on a life of their own.

"Maybe it is something wrong with me. I need to find someone else to see what is happening with you." He put his hand around her arm and practically dragged her out of the training room.

Nias was a mess. The whole training day had wreaked havoc on him. Being with Jade and witnessing her focus, her sharp, dry sense of humor, and her spectacular body in those extra-tight clothes had almost been too much. Tomorrow he was switching her to sweats. He was barely … barely … able to control himself through their kiss. But now the apparent loss of her gifts was of primary concern.

He needed to find another person in the house to check and see if her abilities had truly gone. They traveled to the kitchen together and found one of the humans employed for cooking.

"Can you read him, Jade?"

"Yes, he is worried, probably because we're staring at him and probing his brain." The human did look rather taken aback, both by their urgency and in being the subject of their discussion.

"Thank the Gods, let us find a Sentry and make sure it isn't all Daemon you can't read." He ran her out of the kitchen and down two flights of stairs to the front door.

"There's the door! If I could have only found it earlier today, I would be out of this mess and on an airplane right now."

Taking the brass handle of the great wooden and metal door Nias swung it wide and pulled her through and onto the front surroundings.

"Holy cow, this place is beautiful. I knew it would resemble some old gothic castle, but I never would have expected such amazing grounds outside. This place is Notre Dame and the Gardens of Versailles all wrapped into one Daemon-infested prison. If your neighbors only knew," she chided as he continued to drag her along.

Nias only glared back in her direction. He didn't have the patience for her chatter right now. All he wanted to do was make sure the girl still worked and then get away from her.

Nias found a Sentry standing guard at a gated entrance to the compound.

"Sir!" The guard looked shocked to see Nias in this part of the compound.

"Nellion." Nias nodded as he responded. "This is Jade. She will need to ask you a few questions. It will be helpful to us if you would please answer some with accuracy and others falsely."

"As you wish," Nellion replied. The girl proceeded with her questioning.

Nias had to smile when the human used this moment as a chance to try and learn more about the Djinn. When she began, Nellion answered in truth, but true to the cause he gave no real background or personal information. He *was* speaking to a human.

"How long have you been – what do you guys call it – above ground?"

When Nellion answered that he had lived in San Francisco most of his life Jade grasped the sides of her temples. "Aaagh, okay. I work!"

Nias didn't think, his body just responded to this girl unasked. Before he knew what had happened he had pulled the girl toward himself and held her as the pain in her head subsided. Brushing her disheveled hair back from her face, he tilted her chin upward toward himself. "You okay?" He looked down to her. When the pain, it seemed, was only momentary, he felt himself flush at the over-reaction. "Yes, ugh, he likes living here, he is a Djinn, duh, and he apparently won't be giving me any information I really want. I will not be asking him any more questions."

"Thank you, Jade. It is important to us that you retain your abilities. I am sorry it hurt you for us to acquire this information."

When Nias looked over to thank Nellion for his help, it was apparent that he was taken aback by the fact that Nias was holding the human. Nias released the girl and took a step back. He cleared his throat, took her wrist, and turned toward the house. He quickly returned her to her room, put a Sentry outside her door, and went to have a drink.

Nias found Locke in the library reading in one of the two high-backed, burgundy, velvet chairs, which sat by the hearth. As it was getting dark outside, Locke had the fire going. The room had three walls with dark wood shelving and books to the ceiling. The wall, which held the door, was a rich, deep green and the floors, as throughout the house, were a deep walnut. Nias went directly to the bar on the far end of the room. He gave himself two, no three, fingers of Scotch, slammed it back, and made another.

"All going well with our girl?" Locke smiled facetiously and looked over the top of his book at his friend, who was finally taking the opposite chair next to the fire.

"Please don't ask. I have had a full day of her and need a break. Not a good time to start giving me shit." Sinking back into the chair, Nias ran his free hand through his hair and let out a sigh.

"Really, because when I looked in earlier, I thought I saw her gaining a fairly competent, albeit clumsy, grasp of some effective attacks."

"She has come quite far for one day of training. She catches on quickly. Maybe tomorrow I'll let her have a go at *you*, if you won't let it rest."

"If it isn't the training causing you to drown out the day, what is the problem you're trying to eviscerate now? Same as usual? Or do I detect there is even more weighing on you tonight? You know, when I saw you this afternoon you almost looked …" he gave a mock gasp … "happy."

"I am not drowning or eviscerating anything. Can I not just relax and have a drink after a long, long day?" He decided to ignore Locke's last observation.

"Nias, I spent a few minutes with the girl when I walked her down to you. She is quite amiable."

"She may be amiable, but she is making me crazy! It cannot even be explained," Nias blurted out, then paused and took another deep draught.

"Sure it can. I think she pleases you. You did your best to block out the world. With your brother being in who knows what situation and the girl demanding your attentions your well-built walls are coming down. She is chipping away at those walls. But feel free to try to resurrect them. I've gotten used to dragging your drunken ass around, what's one more night?" Locke was one of the only beings in any world who could get away with talking to Nias like this, and tonight it was getting annoying.

"It isn't just that, she … is different."

"I know." His friend didn't look at him when he said this and Nias knew he didn't need to.

"Locke do you know me so well? I am doing everything I can to separate my head from her and I am losing."

"Stop running, the Gods have put you in this situation for a reason, can't you see? An attraction like I saw you having with her is simply meant to be. You can't save everyone *or* block them out completely. Risk is going to be involved."

"You could see all that just by sticking your head in the door? Locke, she will be injured, you know this as well as I do, and I won't have it. I cannot be the cause of harming another I am responsible for, I just can't." Nias flung back the rest of the scotch, and stared into the fire. *I am a warrior, not this emotional wreck.*

"Then do what you have to, to protect her. Despite what you believe of yourself, you were the greatest Sovereign and protector

any of us have ever known. When the time comes you will know
what to do."

Chapter 11

Jade felt she'd been dispensed with like a trivial annoyance. *Fine. He can make sure I'm still functioning and try to get rid of me, but we had a deal. I trained, now he has to do anything I want for the evening.* The thought of being in charge of Nias made her smile.

When she went to change she found a pair of black, low-rise jeans, which fit her perfectly; it was like the man had taken her measurements while they had been rolling around the bed together. The tank top he gave her this time was white and had a picture that looked like a tribal tattoo drawing of a black panther. *Very cute, Nias,* she thought. He knew it would remind her of him. Arrogant man, he knew how hot and beautiful he was. He was so not ashamed of himself. He was actually funny when he wanted to be.

After she dressed, she left her room to find her partner for the evening. He *would* hold up his end of the bargain. She moved through the beautiful winding corridors until finally she found the stairs again, wandering until she found a staff member tidying up one of the many bedrooms, and asked if she knew where Nias was. There was no way she would be able to find him in this enormous house by herself. She still felt like she was walking through an unsolvable maze. The woman told her he was on the main floor library and gave her directions.

When she found the room she walked in and grinned at Nias and his friend.

"I am all freshened up Nias, ready to push you around for the evening," Jade said when she barged her way into the room. She wasn't sure what was going on in this library between Nias and his friend, Locke, but Locke seemed to think her presence amusing. Nias gave her a sinister look, as if assessing her.

What Nias saw seemed to please him. "Jade, I would love to spend the evening doing whatever you wish; if you would give me twenty minutes to shower I will be back to begin our evening together. I am quite sure Locke could entertain you while I'm gone," he said, aiming his glare. He threw back the remaining alcohol in his glass and disappeared.

Jade walked further into the room and stared into the fire for a moment. The burning wood filled the air with the smell of the forest, something she didn't get much of in the city. She sat in the chair opposite Locke's, folding her legs up on the chair underneath her in a crisscrossed fashion to get comfortable.

"He is the oddest man," she said looking toward Locke, who laughed at her comment.

"Well, in his defense, he hasn't always been so moody. Most of the time I've known him, he has been the pillar of strength the rest of us leaned on."

"I can feel, or at least I could feel the strength coming from him until I lost any sense of his moods today."

"You lost your abilities?" He suddenly looked worried.

"No, apparently, only in reading Nias. Everyone else is still coming in loud and clear. So what is his deal? It seemed like the man is in a constant state of confusion, jumping from emotion to emotion, and today as we worked on weapons together I got so many feelings coming from him, until they fled completely."

"Jade, if he knew I even alluded to any of his past experience he would lose it, but if you're going to go into a place like Sheol with him I think you, and he, would fare better if you had a little background information." Locke stared into the fire. Jade could tell he was considering whether he would be betraying his friend by talking to her.

"You can trust me, Locke, I can't really explain it, but I would never hurt him. I can tell there are pieces splintering inside of him. From the moment I met him I felt safe with him, for no good reason. In fact, our whole relationship makes little sense to me, but he always makes me feel safe. I wish I could do that for him too." Jade could still read Locke's reluctance, but also a strong love for his friend. "It was a woman?" It came out far more sheepishly than she had wanted, and she cursed herself for being selfish; this was about Nias, not her romantic delusions.

"There was a woman involved, yes. Up until last year Nias had been the Sovereign, then he stepped down, leaving Phaeton to pick up the pieces and take over." Locke paused and then left his chair to walk across the room to pour a gold fluid into a crystal glass. "Can I get you something, Jade?"

She ignored his query and continued to press, knowing Nias would be back soon. "Locke, you know he won't tell me himself, please."

Locke sighed and she could feel his mind clicking, as if finally settling on a course of action. "About a year ago he was called to Marseilles. There had been an attack on a human woman, which the Sentry had successfully prevented, but the woman was in a bad state emotionally. He went to see what he could do for her. He always gave too much of himself to the humans. Protecting them had become more than redemption to him, as it was for the rest of the Djinn; it was more of an obsession. I think when he learned he could, he took it upon himself to save humans before the Shaitan could turn and take them. Rachel had come from abuse and had the potential for harming herself. The Shaitan love this kind of human. The Shaitan find it easy to use half-truths to convince them to end their own existence, which would condemn them to Sheol and place them in the 'care' of the Shaitan."

"Nias brought her back to the compound and cared for her, fixing this girl became everything to him. As if this one success would make the difference. He believed that a breakthrough with Rachel could change the future of human destiny. He tried every-thing to help her, to turn her self-loathing, before…well, there were complications he did not foresee; in the end he was unsuccessful. It ended badly." He stopped and took a sip of his drink. Locke had been jovial every time Jade had seen him before. To see him solemn said a lot about the serious nature of the situation. "He had always taken care of everyone around himself. He was an exemplary ruler, and cared a little too much. But this was different. Jade, I just wanted you to know he is more fragile than you think."

"So I hear you telling me to tread lightly. He may be a little wounded." She did her best to sound nonchalant, but damn, why did it have to be another woman? The thought of him with another woman had already blocked her powers over him during training when she had asked him about his sexual relations. She would simply have to get over it; they weren't dating, for God's sake. He wasn't hers.

Nias reappeared as Jade was finishing her discussion with Locke. He tilted a single brow and asked her, "Where to, my Kitten?"

She wanted them to eat together, so he transcended them into the kitchen, where they spent the next two hours preparing dinner.

The kitchen was a perfect mix of modern amenities and strange antique beauty. The walls were cream with a beaded line of metal rivets moving throughout in a formless shape. The countertops were dark-brown soapstone with the same rivets surrounding the giant washtub sink, which was copper, as were all the fixtures in the room. The sink, island, and stovetop were on enormous individual antique buffets covered with the countertops. A mass of dark shelving was open to the room and displayed the most amazing burnished gold-laced cream china, which must have been hundreds of years old, and Jade didn't even want to know how costly. A heavy antique chair sat next to the island for guests to sit and observe the chef, who would be Nias himself.

Nias, it turned out, cooked far better than she did, which was not at all. She was mostly looking for the company; he actually knew what he was doing.

"What would you like for dinner, my beauty? Name it, you worked so hard today. Your wish is my desire." He did a mock bow. The dichotomy between the way he was during their training and his present demeanor was striking.

"Soup is good, I love soup."

He grinned. "As you wish."

She watched as he pulled spices and vegetables and who knew what else from drawers and cabinets. *This is amazing*, she inwardly giggled, *hot man, cooks hot food, life is good.*

Before she knew it he was pulling her into the process.

"You don't just have to sit there. Come on, I'll show you what I'm doing," he smiled.

He extended a hand and took hers in it, pulling her down from the counter, where she had been perched for the best view, *and what a friggin' view he made.*

He stood, pressed warmly up against her backside, while they both held a ladle in a large cast-iron pot; as they moved the wooden spoon around its edges, his hips pressed more firmly against her. When she felt him harden and his hair fell forward over her shoulder, she had to bite her bottom lip to keep from purring.

"How is it that a Daemon learns to cook?" she said in a shaky voice. His proximity was intoxicating. Jade reached to place her hand on the counter and brace herself in a manner she figured would look nonchalant. Unfortunately, what she actually did was catch her baby finger on the edge of a bowl of tomato sauce. The damn bowl flipped and leapt to the floor, splattering the front of her shirt and jeans on its way, making a huge blotchy red mess of her. Nonchalant, it was not.

"How is it you can't cook at all? I'm wondering how you ever fed yourself," he chided, as that beautiful mouth quirked to the side and he picked up a kitchen towel to begin blotting her.

"Ha ha, make fun of the clumsy girl," she said as she tried to turn her reddened face away.

He took the side of her jaw into his fingers and tilted her face back toward him. He gave her one of those looks that says it all; it said "in my eyes you are fantastic". And then as quickly as he had placed that large warm hand, he removed it and averted his gaze.

Nias was doing exactly what she had wished would transpire.

He listened to Jade talk about growing up with the curse as they tooled about the kitchen together, the loneliness she felt when she had finally decided close bonds were more painful than prosperous. Amazingly, he was being nice to her. He was actually sweet when he wanted to be.

They sat together at one end of a giant table in a dining room fit for a medieval castle. The table would seat twenty if needed. There was a huge bronze chandelier above them. It was a sump-tuous room. And completely silent, or maybe it was that she had tuned everything else out except for him.

Nias picked up a spoon and raised it to her lips.

"Are you really going to hand-feed me now?"

"I simply don't want either of us to be in danger of having any more food flying toward us," he said with complete seriousness, and then grinned.

"Thanks, I guess you'll be teasing me about that endlessly." She parted her lips and accepted the spoon from him.

"Endlessly, yes I would very much like to have the opportunity to tease you endlessly." *Really?*

He placed the spoon on her bottom lip and his eyes were locked on it when he tilted it upward to let the fluid flow into her mouth. It was flirty, the way they were interacting. She was sitting in a giant gothic mansion flirting with a Daemon.

He finished feeding her every last drop in her bowl and placed his hand so close to hers she could feel the heat. No matter that he was calm and domestic and innocently flirty. The sexual energy radiating around him never ceased. It sat there with her like a third guest, like an ever-present dark and delicious fiend, waiting.

"What is it you have planned for me next this evening?"

"I was thinking of reading," she paused and looked up at him, "and you would be there too. You will just keep me company, doing whatever it is you do. Daemony stuff, I guess." She shrugged.

"Kitten, I have been alive for quite a while now," he smiled, "before all these ridiculous modern entertainments. I read, and in fact, I would very much like to read with you."

"Okay, that would be great. We can build a fire, or I guess you will just make one pop on, and we can relax and read. I am so sore after all the faux monster slaughter."

She was thrilled someone would simply be there, a warm body enjoying the same thing she did. Not a solitary space-out, a way to escape, but sitting down to read because she felt like it. With someone else who felt like it. Maybe it was that she couldn't read his moods anymore, but having him around and all his attention was making her believe that maybe she hadn't given people the chance they deserved. Maybe some of them would have wanted to hang like he did.

After growing up with her parents and knowing they didn't want her around; finding it out because they thought it, not because they were straight with her. Although there couldn't be a great way to find out that you irritated your parents and they wished they'd never had you. This had been the basis on which she had judged people throughout her life, and people had thought a lot of nasty things; it had seemed better to steer clear.

But the limited time she had spent with Nias was almost enough for her to believe a life with this beautiful, dominant, arrogant, erotic Daemon could be as good as dreaming. A life with him, yeah right; now she was definitely dreaming.

"Hello, my Kitten, where did you go?" he said, lightly moving that warm hand back and forth over the top of her knuckles.

"Nowhere, sorry." She smiled and looked up at him a little when she noticed him touching her.

"I was actually thinking I could read to you, not next to you." He sat still in his chair and looked at her as if this comment was run of the mill, a little afterthought.

But she accidentally let her mouth hang open a bit and let out a deep sigh, because this most beautiful, masculine alpha male had not only cooked for her and then fed her, but now he was going to read to her. She tried to pull it back together, but nope, nope … it wasn't happening.

"Um, okay." He took her hand and stood, then helped her up as well, then put his hands on her dirty, tomato-stained waist and in a flash…

… she found herself positioned on the couch in his temporary bedroom. This would be the same one they had conversed about Hell on for the first time. The very one where he had told her he intended to drag her to Hell and risk her life to save another. And this had been after the blood and the best kissing she could have ever, ever … ever dreamed of. She wouldn't think of that conversation right now. And so she mentally covered her ears and in her head said to herself, *Lalalalala!*

He stretched her legs out and leaned her against the opposite end of the soft, over-stuffed seating from where he sat. He quickly transcended somewhere and brought her back a huge cozy black sweatshirt to put on instead of the dirty tank she was wearing. She threw it over the old shirt and wiggled until her stained tank and bra were off and the sweatshirt remained. He smiled at her. "Well done."

Putting her feet in his lap, he removed her tennis shoes and mindlessly began to run his fingers over the tops of her feet.

"What did you want to hear?" he said, as he looked over at her.

"I was going to read romance, so how about you pick?" Yes, it was a test.

"*Wuthering Heights*? It has something for everyone; an intense romance, a dark handsome and arrogant antihero, who is clever and never succumbs to society's niceties. He wears his jealousy, anger, spite, and love like a coat for all to see and never makes apologies for himself, a man so desperately in love it nearly breaks him completely. All in the name of a love so true it survived through it all, even death." The voice was back, the sweet, melodic, sexy one with the indescribable drawl. Every time Nias used this voice it was like living, breathing seduction. Along with the way he sat with his feet on the ground, angled toward her on the couch, and continued with warm hands on her feet, giving her his complete attention. It was nearly irresistible.

"When you say it like that, it does sound perfect."

Nias disappeared again and came back with the book. After he resumed his place on the couch, he patted his lap, inviting her to put her feet back up, and opened an extremely old-looking version of the story. He began to read from the opening line.

"'I have just returned from a visit to my landlord – the solitary neighbor that I shall be troubled with. This is certainly a beautiful country! In all England, I do not believe that I could have fixed on a situation so removed from the stir of society.' "

His voice took on a honeyed tone, drawing her into the story immediately. His perfect enunciation of every word, the surprising, yet gentle, intensity he added to the reading … she felt herself being sucked into a downward spiral of newfound intellectual desire for him that intertwined and coupled with the physical. Adding this level of intimacy would be her ruination, and she had asked for it. All the while, when he glanced up, those erotic eyes took her in, and his crooked little grin melted her. *Pull it together, Jade,* she told herself, *you are headed for a heartbreak the likes of which you can't even imagine.*

Continuing to read, he looked up briefly and gave a small nod of his head, and winked. And in that little moment, she was lost.

Chapter 12

The next week progressed similarly. He trained her during the days. She had moved up from hand-to-hand to knives, which he did his best to teach her to stab and throw. She had warned him about her lack of coordination, and despite her self-confessed insufficiencies she managed to grasp it well enough. Guns didn't decapitate, strangle, or remove a heart and therefore wouldn't do her much good, so he wanted her to learn to use a small sword. The lesson on slicing off a beast's head became another of those surreal, out-of-body moments for her. In fact, she found it so strange that on a few occasions during this lesson, she began to giggle. Nias did not find it quite as funny as she did, and looked at her with a piercing, arched brow combined with a disdainful glare.

At night, Jade felt they had moved into far more dangerous territory than knives and swords and even cracking an evil Daemon's neck. Inexorably, he continued on with his hideous and sinister plan of treating her with respect, kindness, and attention. He spoiled her. It had quickly become clear she couldn't cook at all and somehow, suspiciously, he could. She still wasn't sure how a militia-leading Sovereign Daemon that barely ate learned this skill, or for what reason, but it was delicious. As the week wore on, she found any waning resistance to him wearing down.

And she didn't have the will to stop it.

This week for Nias was different. In his almost four thousand years of life, he had never experienced anything like it.

The girl talked to him like he was some normal guy. Not like a Daemon, not like the leader of the entire race of the Djinn, not like a kidnapper, or an ex-resident of Sheol. She didn't seem to fear him, or have an overwhelming desire to please him, worship him, or need him to fix, control, or be responsible for her. In fact, the only reason he continued to control her was because he found it fun.

On further reflection, she did need, or at least seem to want, two things from him; the first was food. Jade was a hot mess in the kitchen. Luckily he had read a few things about human food during a particularly strong bout of ennui. Thousands of years can drag on.

The second was a good, solid fucking. The way she stared at him sometimes was almost more than he could take. He was doing his best to try and pull off the friend thing; it didn't seem like ripping her clothes off again or coercing her into his bed was a valid way to earn her trust, which was, surprisingly to him, what he found himself wanting. He felt a compelling urge to care for her. He had every intention of "playing" friend to her, but he found it was more than playing. Bloody hell, they were becoming closer.

She had an uncanny ability to both learn weapons and repeatedly fall down during the same lesson. This was always followed with a self-deprecating laugh at her fumbles. It was simply lovely. He felt himself swollen with pride at her abilities and much of the time just plain swollen. Her shiny red curls swung around her as she learned to use knives and forced him to throw her to the ground. Some of the time she hit her targets by sheer clumsy luck. "As coordinated as a giraffe" had not been an extreme exaggeration.

Nias knew this scenario would play out to its inevitable end and an unspeakable horrific outcome, but her energy, laughter, and chatter kept distracting him.

He had finally admitted to himself that what he felt was more than lust, although he had never spent this much time with a pure, unadulterated, and unfulfilled need to lick every inch of a woman's body. He felt as if he could never let her go; she was his, at least for the rest of her human life.

His Kitten currently sat on the top of the counter stealing his vegetables, crunching out loud, with her legs swinging, and chatting away incessantly.

"You know, I've only checked in with my business once since I've been here. I should call and make sure everything is going all right. I usually order all the books and do the accounting and help with customers…" and then he tuned out. She was a clumsy, silly, tough, ass-kicking, sex kitten, who would starve if she had to cook a thing, and he had taken about enough of not touching her. Because, while her delicious pink lips yammered on, her eyes scanned him. She did it like she was trying to hide her nasty little yearning tracks, like she was taunting him. This time, as she rested her eyes on his constantly half-swollen arousal, he decided to call her bluff.

He put down the knife he was using. "Would you like to see more of me, Kitten?" he said, as he stalked over to her, put his hands on either side of her on the counter, and brought his mouth in close enough to feel her sweet breath.

She looked uncomfortable for a second as her breath caught, but then she recovered. "What are you talking about? I was talking about work and waiting for food. And we pretty much spend all day together, so I'm not sure how I could possibly see more of you." *She knows exactly what I mean*, Nias thought to himself. Then, he could swear an almost imperceptible evil and flirty tremor passed through her as she glared fleetingly into his eyes.

"Is that the way we are going to play it here, Kitten? Because I can only be pushed so far," he ground out. He was so close to her mouth he could feel her breath on his lips now. And he cocked his head and she closed her eyes, anticipating his kiss, and he stopped, and pulled away. And then he tauntingly said into her waiting, slightly parted lips, "When you are ready to stop telling me not to touch you and taunting me with little fuck-me glares, and want me to actually follow through, I will be in my room." And then he left her, eyes still closed, waiting for a kiss she wasn't getting.

Joss Hu'dor stood in a five-by-five cage. It consisted of iron bars and a dirt floor and was stiflingly hot. Joss remembered leaving this, literally, God-forsaken place with his family, and what would eventually become the Sentry, and while it had been pure and unadulterated torment to live here, it couldn't even compare to the feelings that came with seeing it again. The memories of their time here were unpleasant. That had to be the understatement of all time.

"Why do you not rest, beauty, we will not harm you." Empusa almost sang when she spoke as she walked around the rim of dirt outside his cage. His birdcage, and the thin perimeter of dirt the she-beast continued to circle, composed the whole of the small island where he had been imprisoned.

"Empusa, continuing to tell me the same lie is not only futile, but it has surpassed ridiculous and grown boring." Joss put his hands to his ears, knowing a high-pitched scream would soon be wailing from her mouth. She would howl in this hideous fashion whenever he insulted her, but he couldn't help himself. Considering he couldn't fall asleep, insulting her was pretty much all he had with which to amuse himself for the past week. He knew if he were to fade out, she would not hesitate to sexually assault him during his unconsciousness.

Empusa was a Succubus, and as such, it was in her nature to arouse men without waking them, drink from them, and then, depending on her mood, either devour their flesh as a meal, or keep them for a prolonged period for the blood and sex. Succubae were tolerated and used here by Iblis … feeding off Verge humans; the pheromones a succubus let off during sex or blood play took over their object human's mind. The humans would forget who they were as desire took them. The surge of pleasure would cause them to fade completely after a handful of encounters. Humans became completely addicted to their assailant, and unable to think of anything else.

Daemons were a whole other story…

"Beauty, I *will* have that delicious drink you supply, I must. The smell of it makes me wild. If I hadn't been instructed not to harm you, I would simply take it from you awake." She held her hands behind her back and looked at the ground as she shuffled her feet, continuously circling. Her hair was a mass of dirty tangles; of he had no idea what color. It was possible that she could have been pretty, maybe even beautiful, if it weren't for her dirt-caked face, and mud- and feces-covered gown. Oh yes, and the fact she desperately wanted to rape and eat him.

"Why don't you bathe? You are a disgusting mess of a creature. You have spent so much time playing to your depravities, you have let yourself be covered in others' excrement and filth. Or maybe you prefer yourself that way," he said, grinning, and quickly covered his ears. "You're a beast," he added.

Not only did it amuse him to piss her off, but her constant screeching jarred him back awake. He was really trying not to let her catch on that he wasn't holding on to the bars to have the best angle with which to throw insults; he was using them to keep himself standing.

He had been back in Sheol for eight long days and seven, even longer, nights. If his siblings didn't hurry the fuck up and come to get him he would eventually fade and darken, or become unconscious and Empusa would have him. Djinn didn't have to sleep daily, but it relaxed and calmed them; it helped them to push away the darkness inside them. His siblings' constant desire to do good deeds all but had them forgetting who they were. They lived like humans, with the humans, protecting the humans, and sleeping like the humans. With all the bone and fresh meat and the constant sleep they were able to hold their darker desires at bay. They had been able to control their Daemon instincts for hundreds of years. But unable to do those all-too-human things, he wasn't sure which would overcome him first, Empusa or the darkness. He had never before been in a position to find out.

"I wonder where your master race is, Beauty. Do you think they have left you to rot because you no longer attach yourself to them?" She had stopped to turn her head to the side without turning her body, as she taunted him. Anything she could do to unnerve him she would try, as he would insult her at any opportunity he got.

"I have no idea, Empusa. But if a desire for their intervention is the reason I am being kept here, then I guess Iblis will have to rethink his strategy. Apparently they aren't coming." He had to believe they would come for him. He simply wished they would move things along. He was getting weaker and weaker; he was hungry and so damn tired.

He missed his ranch and the wide-open land he owned in Wyoming. He was utterly alone there. His siblings knew to let him be when he was there; they knew to let him be in general, but when on the ranch it was mandatory. He was thought of as the irresponsible younger brother, the disengaged; the one who absolutely didn't give two shits about their self-inflicted duty to the humans. At least, that was how they perceived him, and he had no intention of correcting their notion.

And then there was the reason why he had separated himself from the rest of the family. For the last few years, he had felt something growing inside him; a force that seemed to be welling up, harder and harder to clamp down on. More evidence of what Iblis had always told him – he was worthless and weak. He was sure the darkness was starting to break through, even despite his presence in the human world.

He had been ambushed and brought here. When Hamartia had appeared she had caught him completely by surprise. When they had transcended to the entrance of Sheol, they walked him in and had those bird-whores fly him to this patch of land in the depths, surrounded by rank, boiling water. Here he had been caged ever since.

Remembering the episode pissed him off and refocused him. The realization of what had happened to his companion for the night even more so. And he swore to himself if he ever got out of this cage, he would snap Empusa's neck before going after Hamartia to do the same.

Chapter 13

As Nias stalked from the kitchen, he dwelled on what had transpired between him and Jade. He continued to become close to her despite all of his rationalizations to the contrary. He now realized how out of control the situation had gotten. He wanted her so badly. He wanted to sink his hands into her beautiful hair and pull it tightly back away from her exquisite face, and then lick the smoothness of her skin again. He remembered the feel of it, the smell of sweet plum and sunlight that somehow emanated from her body. It was the smell of summer, he realized – a sensation a Djinn rarely experienced during a lifetime of Shaitan-hunting and slaughter. The image of owning her in every way had him walking around in a state of absurd arousal reserved for schoolboys.

But it was more than lust. Somehow, at some point, in spending time with her, he had let his defenses down enough to allow himself to see her as more than a possession. Something more was what she could never be, because being with him would get her killed. Humans who became attached to him emotionally died; it was a fact, simply borne out by history; by his history. She was … she had to be … a toy. He could keep a toy.

"Keep her at a distance, Nias!" He growled out loud at himself, as he stalked down the hall. He had to get a hold of this situation.

Once in his room, he slammed the door behind him and shot

a look at the fireplace so fierce that the flame erupted. In a blaze as intense as his raging emotions, it exploded up past the mantle, scorching the paint, melting the picture, and blackening the ceiling above. He had to psychically calm the flames before they started on the rest of the room. If this were his own home, he might have let it burn and bought a new one.

Not knowing what to do with himself, he was actually relieved when his sister, Ella, knocked at the door and then immediately barged her way in.

"So, I can tell you're in quite a mood from the damage and smell in here," she threw at him, crinkling her nose and looking toward the fireplace.

Ella normally didn't joke around. She didn't poke fun at people as the rest of them did. She was a serious person. The air around her was not to be trifled with. She was indefatigably trying to prove she was an equal to her brothers and the entire Sentry. She ran her Sentry Unit into the ground, and they had no choice but to follow her demands to the letter or find a new unit. She gained their loyalty because she was the kind of leader who performed every task she demanded of her troops and then tried to best them at it. If she asked you to go into a Shaitan nest and single-handedly end three Shaitan, you could be damn sure she could end five. Weapons expert, ruthless executioner, and overall menace to their race, the Shaitan never wanted to see her coming.

She was also, much to her own vexation, amazingly beautiful. Five foot six, with shiny, dark hair to her waist, which she *always* kept pulled back too tightly in a low ponytail. She tried to look as plain as she could, but unfortunately for her, she was born with a ridiculously perfect porn-star body, and it irritated her to no end. She tried to hide it with bulky black, masculine clothing, a lack of make-up, and steel-toed combat boots. She had even gone as far as flattening down her chest with surgical tape. But it was no use, she still looked hot, and that was from the viewpoint of a protective sibling.

"One thing I am not is in the mood to discuss it," Nias replied, waving her toward the door.

"I don't really care what kind of mood you are in, Nias. In fact I'm sick to death of your moods; we are all *inundated* with your moods. First irritated you had to obtain the human at all, and then you come here and began what I can only describe as courting her. The two of you have practically taken over the house with training and cooking, and giggling. Yes, did I actually hear you *giggle*? Are you *cooking* for her Nias? Because that is beyond outrageous, as well as bizarre, considering you don't even consume cooked human food. And then what you do at night, I can only imagine, although, knowing you, it is screw like monkeys."

If only, thought Nias.

"Knock it off!" she continued, shouting at him. "It is time for you to go; your time here is up. It has been a week. Joss is likely beginning to fade, and we have no idea how long it will take the two of you to get to him and get him out – or if you can do it at all. Honestly, you are the last person in all the worlds I ever thought would be lovesick." She continued to stand in his doorway as she berated him with her arms folded.

He swiftly strode toward her and, using only his mental energy, threw her to the floor. Then, standing over her, all of his pent-up emotion flooded out of him.

"You will never speak to me in that manner! You may see yourself as a powerful warrior, but, as you know, I can crush you as easily as I stand here, Ella. I'll go to Sheol soon, not because of your demands, but because I feel it is time! Jade is almost ready. And I am not, nor will I ever become, lovesick." As she stood, he moved her out the door without touching her. "The ways in which I choose to gain the trust of the human are my decision, and rest assured, I will retrieve Joss and I will bring him home. Now go away from me!" He waved her away.

"Fine, I cannot wait to leave." She squinted her eyes at him. "But I also came to let you know, Hamartia was spotted in this immediate area with a full pack. We took out many of them. But she got away from us."

"If Hamartia was spotted in the area, you are needed to protect the humans. Do your job, unless *you* would like to escort Jade to find Joss and visit Father?" He saw Ella shiver at the thought.

The last look she gave him before she turned to go unequivocally said, *If I were capable, I would beat your ass.* After she had left him, he couldn't help the smirk that formed on his lips, because he knew she was fully capable of taking care of herself and that was immensely important, considering she meant the world to him.

But as she retreated down the hall, he thought about the half-truths he had given her. Although he knew he was not "lovesick" – a silly human term – he could not pin down how he actually felt for the human. He knew he wanted to keep Jade, but he couldn't, he could not refuse his overwhelming need to protect her, and there was a growing desire to satisfy her. It may have even gone beyond him strapping her in a collar and providing her with a short leash attached to his bed – *unfortunate.*

But the fact was, he shouldn't, and wouldn't, fall in love with her. He rationalized it again – he liked her, he could keep her as a possession, keep that possession safe and happy, but in order to ensure she was not harmed, he did need to keep her at a distance from his heart. Nias sighed, allowing himself a fleeting sadness and then abolished the thought. Ultimately, Ella was right; it was time to move forward, the week was up. It was time to go get his brother.

Chapter 14

As Jade got ready to shower and go to bed, she felt something was missing, her common sense maybe? After all, here she was training with a Daemon to make her way into what can only be described as Hell, to save someone she didn't even know. But, no, it wasn't that, instead it was the lack of any fulfillment from the overwhelming sexual energy Nias poured over her, *all damn day long*. She stretched out on what she was now referring to as *her* bed, slid her legs to the ground, grabbed the sweats Nias had given her, and went to *her* gorgeous bathroom to take a shower.

When she went to look at herself in the mirror she saw herself, but there was another image rattling around in her head. What she thought of in her mind's eye was the old little wood carving of the oblivious monkeys – hear no evil, see no evil, and speak no evil. And that was the way she wanted it; she was on the verge of a breakdown and her escapist fantasy was gearing up to take over. She had lost all grounding on anything even approaching normalcy. As long as she was completely ignoring everything that was happening, she would focus on her dreamy, attentive, harmless, beautiful and exceptionally well-endowed boyfriend. Oh, yes, as long as she was living in a state of pure denial she was taking it to the extreme, she had such a lovely smitten boyfriend here in "Jadeworld". Sure, they had had a tiny little argument, but couples often do.

After showering and putting on her sweats, she began staring at her image in the mirror again and combing out her auburn hair, when that very same infatuated, infuriating "boyfriend" knocked on the door. She shook her hair out. If he was here to talk about their conversation in the kitchen, she wanted to look confident and maybe a little bit pretty, even if she had on ugly sweats.

But when she opened the door she noticed he looked different than he had for the past five days. Completely pissed off and more than a bit anxious would describe it; he ran his hand through his hair. She stood to the side and let him in. He walked in, but didn't sit down; instead he paced for a moment, then turned and began speaking to her.

"My sister encountered a full Nest of the Shaitan very close to the compound. Hamartia was with them."

She recognized the name from the first day she was here, when she eavesdropped on Nias's siblings. Jade knew this was not good news. Doing her best not to be jolted back to dangerous reality, she gave him a confused look.

Nias continued, "Hamartia was at the warehouse when they took you, she is high-caste Shaitan and most likely in charge of the above ground attack on us. She is in charge of much of the … discipline in Sheol. She has rarely ever left The Unseen before; in fact none of us can remember it ever happening. So with the abduction of our brother and her above ground so close to our compound, I believe it is necessary for us to begin our journey."

"Now?" The reality of literally going to Hell, or at least some version of it, began trying to creep into her consciousness. She had flashes of fire and chains and red creatures with horns and wings and pointed tails. Her knees began to falter underneath her. This shock of reality came far too quickly, and she thought for sure she would pass right out. Although she managed to avoid a complete blackout, her legs did buckle and she began to fall. Nias reached out and grabbed her waist before she hit the floor and pulled her up and into him.

"Jade, don't lose it on me already, we haven't even gotten close." He held her easily with one arm and put a finger under her chin to angle her face toward him, and his voice softened a bit. "Hey, look at me," and she did and she felt even more overwhelmed. After trying so hard to check out and then being punched in the metaphysical gut with the images of Hell, she had gone straight to overload. And she could feel the tears welling up in her eyes. So much for being strong no matter what, she couldn't even get her own legs to work.

"Kitten, please don't cry; I'm not good with crying." He moved his arm around to her back and picked her legs up with the other. He walked her over to the bed and set her down. She felt the tears still escaping her clenched eyes. And she wanted to be anywhere else, anywhere this wasn't happening, but she felt his hand on her and then she still wanted to be anywhere else, but not without him. He remained standing, but smoothed her wet hair away from her face.

"Hey come back, you need to look at me, we won't leave right now. We can rest first and we will head out in the morning. Jade, I won't let anything happen to you." As the words tumbled out of his mouth, he still wondered if they could be true, and cursed himself for making that promise.

"Nias, how can you even say that? You are the reason I am in this position. You *are* what's happening to me. You are going to drag me to Hell, or whatever you call it," she sobbed, and she couldn't think, because no matter how upset she was, she could feel that energy wafting off of him and right now it made her feel like punching him.

And so she did.

She opened her tear-drenched eyes and with every bit of frustration she had welled up inside her, over all of it, she used the skills he had given her, turned and sat up on her knees, made a fist and punched him as hard as she could square in his gorgeous face.

Smack! His head flew to the side, and his fucking shiny, silky hair went with it! As he grabbed his jaw, she screamed as loud as she could. "Damn you!" Then she put both her hands over her face and began to sob, sagging with an overwhelming release.

"Do not be nice to me anymore, do not train me or read to me or cook me food. I want to go to your stupid Unseen world right now and meet the Devil himself. I only hope I will have the opportunity to spit in his face before he kills me and sends me … wherever a person would go when they are murdered by the Devil." Both fists clenched and ready to wallop him, she got up and stomped forward. But he caught her wrists. And she felt his strength and saw his arms in the black t-shirt he always wore and his muscles were like hard steel under flesh. And, damn, her conflicted body just wanted to be held by him again.

"I hate you, I hate that you have the power to make me want to rip all your hair out and fold myself in it at the same time. You caused my misery and I want to curl up in your body so you can make it all go away. What is wrong with me?" she sobbed. "Can't you stop that sexual fucking energy that constantly follows you everywhere and makes me want to tear your clothes off when you're around? I just want a fair chance at hating you!"

He stood above her, holding his jaw, stunned. She was right. He knew she was right, and it was killing him that he was hurting her. He knew he should let her go, somehow put her back into her life before he completely destroyed it. But he couldn't, and even if he could let her go, he knew she was no longer safe. He couldn't abandon her to the Shaitan, no matter how upset she was, or how much she hated him – he was keeping her. She belonged to him … or was it belonged *with* him?

"Jade, I'm going to sit down. Do your best not to punch me again." He smiled at her, and she looked up with her swollen and angry eyes and the slightest quirk formed on her magnificent face. And in that moment he knew, with every fiber in his being, they would be all right; whatever crazy bond they had formed was still intact.

He sat down, then he laid them both down; he took her in his arms and she curled in to that space he offered like it was made only for her. He considered briefly whether it had been.

She fit so perfectly against him, he felt like it was the most comfortable he had ever felt with a woman. *Except for the fact my jaw aches from where she struck me.* And for a moment, his heart swelled with pride.

"You come off so tough, don't you my Kitten? All sardonic wit and bluster! This front you put up for the world to see, it sometimes makes me forget how innocent you really are. I often truly just want to throw you down wherever we are and take you in the rough fashion my body's ache demands." He could feel her shiver beneath him now, feeling her fear, and it reminded him of her innocence and made him react more gently toward her. He released his firm grip on her, pushed her head back and began to kiss her, starting to fall into the one place he swore he wouldn't go.

She turned her puffy eyes to his full, pink lips, his erotic, sparkling golden eyes stared back and she wanted more. She wanted it all. Her body was taking over again, like it had that first night, and this time her mind and heart were hurtling right alongside it.

Part of her wanted him because he could take her out of this fear she felt threatening to consume her. Another part of her screamed from within at that weakness. Still another wanted him like an animal would, carnally and without remorse.

When he pulled back from ministering to her wanting lips, she sighed, looking up at the mischievous twinkle in his eyes. He looked as if he had just thought of something on the edge of getting them in trouble.

"Let's just stop with all the tears and play a little game, an educational game. Can you do that, Kitten?"

She looked up at him, wondering what he was up to; by the

gleam in his eye it was something devious …and perfect. Now she was paying full attention to him and not to the pounding of her own heart. He was a sly one, and yes, she wanted to play, and she looked up at him a little more sharply.

"Okay," she managed, knowing by the look he gave her when he said it, and the physical shift he made afterward, she had given him some kind of permission. She didn't care.

"My sweet Kitten," Nias ran the backs of his fingertips across her cheek, "I am just as content to lie with you; really, I believe I have successfully distracted you. I won't tease anymore."

The only thought that entered her mind was *I'm done being teased.*

He grinned at her and moved her hand to his stomach, then he had to readjust his erection in his jeans. As he made a move to pull her into his arms, he kissed her softly. He was surprised by his own satisfaction with the situation. She smelled good, and felt good pressed against him. *What has gotten into me?*

"I do not think so, I was offered education," she sassed. "And I want to learn." She pushed her face into his neck and gave a purr that gave him shivers.

"Okay, but you have to do exactly as I am telling you. Do you understand?" He quirked an eyebrow to emphasize his point.

"Yes," she said with a quiver in her voice.

"I know in some ways you are untouched, but let's look into what else you've experienced? Have you ever held a man's hardness in your hand?" He gave his signature smirk.

She considered this question and knew if she answered it, all bets were off.

So she slipped back to the comfort of her theme song *Lalalalala.* It was good to be back. She would take a tip from Scarlett O'Hara and face the consequences tomorrow, and, besides, every time she went to object or tell him what to do he kissed her witless again anyway. And this was another one of those times. Gasping, then sighing and relaxing into the playground that was his mouth on hers, any protests fled quickly.

He finally released her mouth, allowing her to answer breathlessly.

"Yes, I have had boyfriends before, not for long, but long enough for that," She said with a tiny panic.

"Really?" He pulled his shirt off and she got a good long look at his body. He was sculpted muscle under soft, warm, bronzed skin. Everything about him sleek and velvety. He took her hand, which was curled into her body, and placed it on his groin, forcing her to rise up to one elbow.

"Like this." He put his fingers over the top of hers and moved her hand up and around over his jeans, showing her the way. He began to thicken beneath her hand, and then continue to grow even larger.

"Oh!"

"Is that a no?" No it wasn't a no, but it was an, 'Oh my God. How many of them do you have?' Because it was entirely too big, so much bigger than any other she had felt, bigger than she thought they got; she inwardly giggled.

"Because our game is just beginning. Can you handle this right now?"

"Yes, Nias, I need this right now."

He gently placed her hand above the buttons on his jeans, and she proceeded to unfasten them. With a quick rip, he released his enlarged thickness, and wrapped her hand around the warm thickness; she tried to stifle a low purr as she felt her first touch of it, but somehow it escaped her mouth, leaving her lips parted enough for him to sneak his tongue inside. His tongue slid in, twisting and rolling; it was intense, more than a kiss, more like a possession. He had one hand behind her neck, pressing her mouth to his, and the other was guiding her to stroke him, but she no longer needed his hand to guide her.

"It might be just a little bigger than what I've felt before." She smiled and confessed, wrapping her fingers more tightly around him, firmly pulling and retreating slowly, and he started to rock his hips with the movement of her hand. His eyes only half-open, a smile crossing his lips

"So I hear," he answered absently, pulling her back in to entangle her in sweet kisses. She had to stifle a moan as the scene began to encapsulate her. It felt surreal, euphoric somehow. His tongue caressed and danced inside of her, while she stroked his arousal. He pulled back slightly again. "And how do you feel, Kitten?"

"Wet, my legs are clenched together, I feel… needy." The honest words tumbled out of her mouth without pause; as she couldn't help wiggling and bringing her legs tighter together, another purr escaped her.

"Where, where are you wet and needy?" His eyes closed and he pushed his head back into the pillows a little, his hips kept time with her movement, the ripples in his stomach curving and releasing in time.

"Between my legs, Nias, you know it's between my legs. I can't stand it! Touch me like you did before, please." The memory of that night flooded her mind.

"Not yet," he taunted her, using the erotic tone that was his voice always whispering promises.

"Why, why won't you touch me?" she begged.

"Because you haven't earned it." And he laughed, but it was almost sweet, like she was in on it with him; the laugh wasn't cruel, but not touching her was. She began rubbing the top of his erection, loving the feel of it; even if he wouldn't pleasure her, she wasn't letting go. She saw him notice her looking down at her hand while she manipulated his tip. And he turned a sharp gaze on her …

"Would you like to taste it?"

"No," she said too quickly.

"I think you would."

"You think you can talk me into anything, don't you?"

"I am pretty sure, yes," he said with a nefarious laugh. "Lick me. I'll give you instruction." His words alone were making pleasure rise in the cleft of her thighs. If she touched him with her mouth she thought for sure the sound of him, the slow bucking of his hips, and the friction of her own legs would make her come. But she moved her mouth between his legs anyway; it was like velvet over metal, soft and completely hard all at once. His instruction was precise.

"Lick slowly from the base, underneath, up the shaft. Cup me here," he placed her hand, "now run your tongue around the tip… again. Yeesss." And she did. A giant moan escaped his sensual mouth as she continued.

"Now take it full in." He ran his fingertips across the sides of her face scraping his nails on her scalp and finally fisting her hair on both sides guiding her slowly at first and then faster up and down his engorged shaft until he groaned her name and his pleasure released inside her mouth, at which point he rasped out the words, "Now swallow." And she did that too.

As she lifted her mouth slowly off of him her beautiful blue eyes were at half-mast, full of languor and a yearning desire. Her pouty lips were swollen and the look she gave him had him beginning to thicken again before his body even gave its last shudder. But he wouldn't be giving in so easily.

He kissed her half-heartedly and got up to leave.

But Nias had a huge grin on his face she couldn't see when his feet hit the floor and he stood up. He was teasing her senselessly now, he knew she was aching for his touch, but he couldn't help it; she was way too much fun to tease. His sweet innocent was a vixen at heart; at least he was doing his best to make her that way.

As he reached full upright he heard it, the sound he'd been waiting for.

"NO!" And she grabbed him by the slacked waist of his

unbuttoned jeans and yanked him back down on the bed with her. He found it impossible not to let her in on the full-blown amusement her protest created.

"You did that on purpose, you tease. You are wicked!"

"I am a Daemon, Kitten, what did you expect?" And he kissed her ferociously, driving her to a senseless abandon as she pitched and roamed his body with her hands, exploring every accessible inch. And then suddenly, improbably, she pulled back herself and made a demand.

"Pull this damn sweatshirt off, the bra too, and the bottoms, both of them, all of it." He gladly removed her sweats and panties, balled them up and threw them at the wall, then dove back into her with reckless abandon. She was on fire, her hot skin felt so much better out of the binding clothes. He took her breast immediately into his mouth, pulling at it with his teeth, and flicked at her tight nipple with his tongue, pinching and rolling the other between his finger and thumb. She grasped his hand and moved it between her legs and he smiled around her nipple, biting her as punishment for her impatience. Then pressing his hand inside her warm folds, he slid straight to her overly sensitive bud, and traced it with his fingertips. She trembled at his touch, lifting his fingers up and then sliding them back down. He tortured her toward a crescendo, short bursts of breath followed by numerous loud moans followed. She was so exquisitely vulnerable, flush and open to him. He continued a tiny, circular motion focused right at that space, which made her sighed purr the loudest. She called his name into the air and when she arched her back and let out a long, soft cry. It told him he had brought her to peak. The beauty of this ritual made him shudder slightly with pride and pleasure. He let the smile dying to escape spread across his face and warm his heart, just a little.

He moved immediately to curl her up into him. He would have never admitted it out loud, but lying anywhere with her pressed up against him safe and possessed by his body was possibly the closest he would ever get to Heaven. They lay together on the bed, exchanging soft, lazy kisses until time seemed to fall away.

She loved it here in this bed, in these blankets, in his arms, and whatever happened after this she wasn't going to feel regret. It wasn't inside her anymore. She knew her own feelings and she was feeling more than lust. She liked him and regardless of what he believed his feelings to be she was almost sure, mostly by how he treated her, he felt more than lust and a desire for her assistance. It was stronger than that. She couldn't read his thoughts, but she knew they were falling for each other. It was crazy and how it would ever work out she had no idea. Could they date? If they survived Hell together could they cook and read and watch movies together? She burst out laughing, because it was hilarious, but it sounded so great!

"You are supposed to be getting some rest, not amusing yourself." His deep voice cut through the dark.

"I'm sorry, I was just thinking how much I like this, right here, right now. I feel kind of like I'm floating. Your crazy energy wraps around me and I feel like I'm being lifted, like I'm not actually lying in this bed, but just an inch above it."

"Anytime, my Kitten; now sleep." 'Anytime,' he had said, and she drifted to sleep thinking just that, 'anytime.'

Nias agreed with Jade's final assessment; he was lying there thinking how much he liked curling up with her too. He thought about her belonging to him. How she belonged in the little alcove in his soul she had created for herself. He may have brought her to this house, and eventually staked his silent ownership, but she was the one who had truly snuck into his life, with her absurdity and her impudent backtalk, with her inability to cook or stand on her own legs when he kissed her. Those were only some of his favorites; damn, she made life better. And then there was the fact that he had already thought of a hundred ways he would fuck her senseless. *Oh, there's another one. That makes a hundred and one.*

Right now, his thought was there was absolutely no way he was taking her anywhere near Iblis, or Hamartia, or close to Sheol. No one would harm this girl, his girl. The thought of causing her harm completely overwhelmed him, and all the feelings he had been drowning for the last year came crushing back. Humans were too fragile; *she* was too fragile. He had not wanted to let this relationship progress past ownership, but still she was breaking him down. He had worked too hard at building up resistance to this, dare he refer to it as love, for a human? He could feel the bastion he had built for himself failing him as pieces of the wall were falling away in tiny bits. Slowly the fear of not being able to protect Jade became the reality of not being able to protect ALL the humans he had spent so long defending. Especially *her*... He had not only failed to protect *her*; the truth he was desperately trying to keep at bay was he had caused her demise.

His memories of the barren sand, the biting cold of the wind, came rushing back to him; *her* death, all on his hands. And then days later he still remained watching, contemplating over and over what he could have done differently – *she* was being taken away.

Inside his stomach lurched and the nausea returned. He knew he had no right to the happiness Jade brought him. He moved her gently out of his arms. "Fuck this," he said out loud to himself, and stretched himself back out in defiance. He folded the duvet back and stood straight, pushing his hulking shoulders back. He would protect Jade at least from a trip to The Unseen.

She would want to come with him, to help; he knew Jade wouldn't want him to risk going to Sheol without her. Her heart would overcome her fear and make her act recklessly. It was easy to see in her eyes where her heart was. Even if he had to lock her inside, he had no problem with that. *He would hide her from danger and chain her to protect her from herself until he got back with Joss.* He would go against the plans of the Goddesses and take on all of Sheol alone before he would risk her there.

If he had to take the Sentry to Sheol with him, that was a chance he was more than willing to take. Things had changed; he would *dare* anyone to challenge him.

Nias still planned to leave the next day. All he needed to do was arrange things and then head out. Phaeton would have to be informed and a few Sentry acquired to help him move into Sheol and traverse the layers. She would have greatly increased his chances for success at the likely expense of her own life, but there was no way he would let that happen anymore. He discovered he had made the decision days ago that he would not be letting her go with him. Faced head on with leaving, there was no choice to be made. He would tell the family, come back to say goodbye and lock her away, for her own safety.

He refastened the buttons on his jeans and found his t-shirt. As he reached for it, he noticed her clothes bunched against the wall, and he had a mental picture of her swollen lips rising off of him and then of her closed eyes and tangled fiery hair as he pleasured her. The vision made him want to forget it all, wake her up and stay in bed for the next week. But the thought of Joss fading and surrounded in darkness launched him back to the tasks at hand. His brother needed him and, with or without the help of the girl, he had a difficult road ahead of him. Still he had to force a newly formed thickness uncomfortably into his faded jeans, and he walked out of the room, leaving his sacrifice behind.

Chapter 15

His brethren didn't pluck souls from the bodies of Homo sapiens, but they did play rough with the lucky willing. This fact was nowhere more apparent than in Club Djinn on one of Phaeton's party nights. Unsuspecting humans mingled with Djinn Daemon in a party the pagans would have been proud of. Nias transcended outside the club and stood in the doorway for a moment, chuckling to himself, as he always did, at the way his people hid here in plain sight, and at the attempts of the newcomers to properly pronounce the name of the club. They often wanted to put an extra syllable in, saying "duh-jin". *How appropriate that the extra syllable is – "duh".*

As Nias walked in to the main room, the lights in the club were low and the atmosphere strong with extravagance and sex. The main floor had several sets of plush red-velvet couches, which faced each other, and sleek modern coffee tables held the space between. The bar was lit with a recessed lighting, which came from underneath. An immense gilded mirror gave off a warm glow. Bottles of the finest alcohol sat on glass shelving to either side of the mirror and were underlit, enticing passers-by to each libation. Scantily clad go-go dancers ground out their seductive movements on the circular platforms placed throughout the large, dimly lit room.

Wrain, one of the Sentry, was standing across the room with a human girl pressed against the wall, his hand on her ass, tongue in her mouth. This, as far as Nias could see, was the most innocent thing happening in the room. Half-dressed, or fully undressed Daemon and humans were going about the typical party routine, at least for this place. The room smelled like a pungent mixture of smoke, sex, alcohol, and who knew what else. The slow, rhythmic grind of *Dazed and Confused* swayed in the background and the girls moved their bodies in time with the beat.

A topless blonde eyed Nias from head to foot and began to make her way through the crowd straight for him. Staring straight into her eyes as she moved he shook his head slowly from side to side, silently telling her he wasn't interested. He had no desire to engage in the revelry this evening. Nias had never been one for a public display and as he stood there now he only wished he could be back in bed with Jade, whom he was definitely *not* falling in love with, he reminded himself for about the hundredth time since leaving her side.

Nias felt truly conflicted and a little confused by his decision. He loved his family and his brother deserved to have every asset at his disposal to assure his safety, but he couldn't bring himself to risk Jade's safety. The very thought of it made him start to shake and sweat, a physical manifestation of the intense feelings he was trying so hard to deny. He would have to tell the family his decision and then follow through.

Phaeton's booming voice was easily heard coming from the furthest corner, where he was holding court with several highly amused women, an underwhelmed Ella and some of his Sentry. Nias approached him and after a few minutes of cajoling, they reconvened in the back room. Nias leaned up against an overly lit vanity counter the girls used to apply stage make-up; Ella stood with her arms crossed, most likely annoyed he hadn't left yet, and Locke and Phaeton took seats.

Nias sighed and got right to the point. "I will leave in the morning, but I will not take Jade." He stood with all his height and dominance, daring any of them to challenge him.

Ella nodded and spoke up first. "Good, I was against it from the beginning; she couldn't possibly be ready in a week. It was foolish to begin with. She would have gotten you killed." Although Nias was glad for her support, he found himself wanting to defend Jade's abilities, but he wasn't about to give voice to his feelings in that regard.

Phaeton looked at both Nias and Ella as if they each had two heads, and then turned to his brother, his face flashing his frustration. "Nias, have you lost your mind? The Goddesses gave us this girl for this specific reason, to be of assistance to us."

"I will take the men who have been at my side for hundreds of battles. We have defended one another many times and will do it again. I got us all out of Sheol and I can get myself back in and our brother out safely."

"I demand you take the girl with you, she is trained well enough; Locke has informed us of her progress. She may be injured, but she is not our concern – Joss is." Phaeton stiffened as the two of them squared off; it was obvious where the main conflict was going to occur.

His mind screamed that Phaeton was right. Her abilities were desired, hell even needed, on this mission. But he could not overcome the growing feelings in his heart. He knew the probability would be that the mission would be a failure, or at least cost many lives, and he didn't care. Hers had become more important to him. His vision clouded and tunneled to where he could see only Phaeton. "Jade will not be harmed, brother! I won't have it. Even if it means my death, I will get Joss out and I will not risk her to do it."

The room was silent at Nias's outburst, and Locke looked back and forth between the two he had sworn to follow. But there was only one he truly called friend. He cleared his throat. "I am with Nias on this. I see why she should stay. If he and a few Sentry can get to Joss, feed him, and get to a place for Joss to rest, Joss and Nias are sure to be able to find their way out." Locke turned and gave a knowing look to Nias, as if he were truly glad for him that he had come to this decision and was following through with it.

"Thank you for your support, Locke," he growled, but gave his friend as much of a smile as he could muster.

Phaeton looked at all three of them in turn, then turned to face the wall in barely contained rage. Finally he gritted his teeth and spoke. "As Sovereign, I will give you my permission on this because fighting you when you are being stubborn is futile, but I assure you, I will not lose two brothers in this struggle of wills with the Dark One. I will give you three more days and if you are not back, I will come in for you both and only blood and corpses will be left behind me, and the all-out war we have fought so hard to avoid will begin in earnest. Go, but know, as much trouble as you cause me, I will not lose you to him, or any of the Shaitan. I will be getting you back, damn the consequences." Phaeton did not speak loudly; there wasn't any need for it. Nias knew it was a certainty that if he were not home, war would commence at Phaeton's hand.

"Brother, I believe you've just admitted you love me, but don't worry, I won't hold this weakness against you the next time we fight," Nias teased him. Having won this small battle against his family for Jade's safety he felt as if a giant weight had been removed from his chest.

When Jade woke it was dark out and she was still sated. She stretched her arms and body in the soft silk of her sheets, expecting to find Nias there with her. She even thought he might be watching her sleep, like he had last time they slept together. As she reached over and felt the cold mattress next to her, she realized that, unfortunately, her fake boyfriend, the one who practically gave her orgasms ordering her around and kissing her, had gotten up and left the room.

She was starving and planned to find him and force him to feed her – food this time. She giggled to herself. It felt so good to be in this bed; the sheets were soft, the duvets were thick, and life was like a dream here.

As she looked around the plush room for the clothes that had been removed a little while ago and discarded, she couldn't help but remember the process which separated them from her body. But instead of her clothes from the day before, she found someone had placed new things on one of the dressers sitting next to the headboard, on either side of the bed. She had been supplied with broken-in looking, although new, low-rise denim shorts, a black tank, black hiking boots and a backpack full of things.

She reached down and grabbed the pack, placing it on the bed, and unzipped it. Inside she found wrist sheaths, each holding an extremely sharp blade, and the short sword she had trained with, along with a back holster and leather strap which Nias had shown her how to put on and then quickly remove the sword during training. He had made her remove the sword over and over again, swinging it in just the right way as to point the blade toward an enemy and sever its head. There was water, protein bars, and a small, quilted, blue blanket. She also found another knife, which she knew was to go into her boot.

She moved the bag to the floor and sat down on the silk sheets. Absentmindedly she smoothed her hand over the luxury of them, staring at the floor, then the bag, and then the clothes, which she now realized were meant to be worn in a rugged and sweltering environment. Damn, today she was going to Hell. The reality of it suddenly weighed heavily on her shoulders. Nias had most likely gone to make further arrangements. What those could be she had no clue and didn't want to guess.

She suddenly wished she had paid a little more attention to the weapons and a little less to his tall, amazing, muscular physique as he had moved around the training room. He should have worn looser clothing, damn him.

As she dressed and then tied her new boots on, her fear started to increase. Panic crept up and tried to take her, but she imagined herself as a monster-slayer. *Ella can do it*, she thought. She pictured herself as Ella: stern, angry, and mean. Her imagination would once again come in handy. *Goodbye incompetence, hello ass kicker. Yeah, right.*

She searched through the house for Nias for around thirty minutes, and couldn't find him, and with his abilities he could actually be anywhere in the world.

She went to the kitchen to find food. While she was picking through the refrigerator, the Sentry she had met when Nias was trying to make sure she still had use of her powers walked through and she asked if he had seen Nias. He had brown hair that came down close to his shoulders and brown eyes, which sparkled a bit when he spoke to her. He was a big muscular man, and he looked like he would as soon hug you as he would kill you if you moved wrong; but all the Djinn Sentry looked that way. The Sentry all dressed similarly as well; button-down shirts in muted dark colors, knife holstered to the left side by the arm, black washed camouflage pants, and black steel-toed boots. Either they thought anything dark was the best color for them or, more likely, it was better for sneaking and thrashing and slicing up the Shaitan in the dark. He stopped his gait through the kitchen and turned to face her.

His brows rose and he looked at her like he was surprised she didn't know. "Phaeton's party at Club Djinn is tonight. The Hu'dor family is usually in attendance, unless other matters are pressing."

"Oh, well, I was sleeping and I guess he didn't want to wake me." She was a little incredulous.

"I could take you if you like, but we would transcend. The club is in another part of the city."

"Um, okay?" She wasn't sure if she should go or not, but she was a little curious. It hadn't been what they said that made her wonder, but it was the way they talked about it. The way Locke had teased Nias made her want to see it for herself. There was a distinct pull inside her telling her not to go, that she should simply eat and go back to the room, take off her boots, and finish the night sleeping. When he got back he would wake her. There was no reason to learn anymore about any of them than she already knew. *Yeah, right, I am so going.* "I'm Jade, by the way."

She could have sworn he was smirking. "Yes, I know. My name is Hector."

She took his arm and the house around them winked out. When the world came back, she sucked in a breath with a tremor. She could see they had arrived about a block from the club – there was no mistaking the bright-colored signage around the building. But that wasn't what made her shake.

It was the realization they were not alone, and then she heard a voice similar to those that she half-remembered from her ordeal in the warehouse. It came out in a breathy whine.

"Hello, my sweetling …"

Chapter 16

The world hissed and popped around Joss.

The black lava walls of the immense cavern he had been held in for the past week leaked a constant bubbling and spitting lava from its bumpy creases. The rough water surrounding the small dirt platform on which his cage was perched was fetid and rank and the smell was permeating not only his nostrils but it had now coated his exposed skin and clothing with a thick layer of its putrid odor. His clothing, such as it was, remained the same t-shirt and lounge pants he had on when they captured him.

Empusa stopped the constant circle she walked around him and screeched, her upturned eyes betraying the jealousy of no longer having him to herself.

Wings could be heard flapping in the distance and then, directly above, as a giant flying beast brought Hamartia down to one of the nearest platforms. Mid-level caste airborne creatures, the Ifrit were ridden by wingless high-caste Shaitan from the entrance caves to their desired locations. The Bird-man was the color of a dark festering wound; a deep, dull, grey-hued purple, with blotches of fringed feathers a dirty brownish green. A feathered bird's head sat on the shoulders and its body had the general shape and size of a ten-foot-tall man. Its feathered wings spanned more than fifteen feet across, starting at its shoulders and folding into its back when it stood erect.

It was a long journey to where Joss was being held. It would have taken Hamartia hours, maybe days, to get to him on foot. Joss thought about how many levels would have to be passed to free him, and how those same levels would need to be traversed to get out. He let out a regrettable angry sigh as he sagged against his cage.

He turned in his dirt-bottomed cell to face Hamartia, each hand grasping a bar, using all the strength he had to show her he would not be easily defeated. Strong, although reluctant, a warrior in his own right, he was proud and would not let any of them see him fade. If it happened, it would have to be at the point he fell to the ground, because until that point, he would continue to stand and look physically powerful. And if the darkness captured him first, well then, that would no longer be his problem.

The enormous man-animal settled down onto a dirt patch, which held no cage. Hamartia gripped the large chain reins, forming a stranglehold around the beast's neck. The Ifrit was an angry and malcontent prisoner of its position as simple transportation. Conquered in battle by the Ghouls, Hamartia's race, in a massive slaughter, the few which remained in Sheol were all male and forced to be subservient or suffer the fate of their brethren, who were killed a thousand years past.

The loud brush of its wings blew gusts of dirt and air in his direction and with them a different, but equally as vulgar, odor wafted toward him.

"Ugh!" he groaned. Facing his head to the ground he placed one of his hands over his nose and face, but it didn't help. "I had forgotten how nothing ever cleaned itself down here," he said loud enough for all to hear.

Once the Ifrit landed, it went down on its hands and knees like a dog, head bent to the ground, allowing its passenger to dismount. Hamartia flung a leg over the midsection of the birdlike Daemon, placing one foot to the ground and then the other.

"How are you faring, Joss; I hope you are enjoying your time in the Valley of the Angel of Death. I missed it here and am anxious to get back to work. Like you, I am *so* hungry." She twisted her mouth in a macabre fashion and looked to the cavern's ceiling as if fondly remembering the last time she fed. "I see Nias has not come for you yet. I find it curious. Although I told them you were being watched by the Empusa, I didn't think he would push you this far. He has to know you are beginning to lose your strength. I can't imagine they believe I'm feeding you." She chuckled a little at the thought.

"Why do you say Nias as if you are sure he is the one coming for me? What is happening?" Joss was a little worried at her conviction. Maybe something had happened to Phaeton and Ella.

"Nothing, nothing has happened, no one has been harmed … yet … although would you really expect truths from me?" Again, it looked as though she were amused. "But please, love, who *else* do you think would come? Nias would never stay above ground with you in danger here. He is the consummate hero. A hero like Nias can never truly change." She took a deep, shaky breath.

Did she just lustfully sigh? he thought to himself.

"We may have won a few tiny battles against him, I know he pouts. But he knows he is the best candidate for the mission, he knows the Unseen like no one else. Phaeton will continue his futile mission of saving the human animals and my Nias will come," she smiled.

"Your Nias? What are you talking about, Hamartia? Do you actually believe he will give you praise? Cater to a Ghoul?" He made a special point of looking into her eyes when he laughed at her, and continued. "Nias is surrounded by beautiful women who desire him. You are disgusting. Iblis couldn't even tolerate you!"

He saw her cringe at his words; he had hurt her.

"The Shaitan have amassed more souls than Iblis ever dreamed of with our creative ways. He has let us grow strong, while he is content with the truly damned and his fetishes. I will make a far better leader!" She paused for a moment and then stupidly, Joss thought, continued her angry dialogue. It must have been her anger making her divulge so much information. "Nias could never have been taken above ground; he is always on guard, he is too quick, and my legions fear him. We took you instead, a solitary target. He is without so many of his powers here; I will have him, and soon after, the rest of your siblings."

"You will have him? What does that mean?"

She evaded his question. "Who is the girl, Joss? The girl being protected at the compound; he came for this human when I decided to question her."

"I have no idea; Nias knows a lot of girls." And he took the opportunity to smirk back at her; it brought him almost as much joy as torturing the Empusa, but not quite.

"He looked at her like he cared!" She was shouting over the water. Even Empusa stopped to stare.

"I don't know," he stated blankly. His arms were feeling the strain of holding himself in place. He was done conversing with her and turned to face the opposite direction, an impotent move but the only one he had.

She stared at his back, dissatisfied with his answer. Pausing for a few seconds, she turned to Empusa. "Empusa, I am returning to the surface. When he fades, bleed him and you may have him. But do not end him until Nias arrives. His feelings for his brother are the only way we will ever get Nias caged. And I need him caged." She returned to her place upon the Ifrit and it took flight as Empusa smiled and turned towards Joss, staring at his fine, toned back.

It won't be long now, Beauty.

Chapter 17

Nias left his siblings and went to Fforde, Wallach, Kohle, and Wrain, the strongest of the warriors he had always had beside him, until he had decided to never battle again. They had been confused at the time and tried to talk him out of his decision, but only Locke knew the truth. The rest of them he had never involved, and after the events that made him abandon his position, he could see no reason to involve anyone else.

While speaking with Wrain about what was needed and what would be involved in the rescue, one of Nias's previously regular intimate partners, Diana, a Djinn, sauntered up to say hello to him. Although they were frequent bed partners and she admittedly thought he was beautiful, she was only interested in the sexual bond they had formed. He had accepted her as a partner for this reason. He had never promised her more and she had not wanted more. Nias had found this to be a perfect arrangement, since he had no desire to attach himself in a relationship. She eased into Nias's space, almost wrapping herself around his body, with one hand on his lower back and the other on the front ridge of his jeans. She completely ignored Wrain and the conversation they were having, expecting Nias to wrap an arm around her while he finished speaking and then provide her with his full attention.

"Hello, Nias, I would love to have *words* with you when you finish talking to Wrain," she whispered into his ear, putting a heavy emphasis on the use of "words" into the statement; they both knew what she meant.

Nias found he not only felt uncomfortable with her proximity, but he actually wanted to shake her off. It was a strange and unexpected reaction. His heart and body betrayed him … and he recognized then how extreme his attachment to Jade had become. He hadn't been "exclusive" with a woman in so long, it had not even occurred to him that his loyalties had been given solely to her. This was bigger than him, and he now realized all other female relations had been over as soon as that beautiful girl had first purred into his ear. Giving her pleasure, receiving it from her, holding her, or listening to her laugh or ramble on brought him to a place beyond his expectations.

He was about to shrug away from her when he sensed something dark and foul in the vicinity. He wasn't the only one. Diana released him and backed away as tension filled the room from the Djinn in attendance.

He transcended without thinking of the consequences, straight to the source of the darkness. His sense of smell detected the recent presence of the Shaitan. There was a groan from his right and he hurried over to the crumpled form lying there. A quick examination revealed it was Hector, a younger Sentry from Phaeton's compound. His chest wounds were mortal.

Hector reached up to grab Nias's sleeve. "They took her." That was all Hector could manage before he expired, his arm falling limp at his side.

Rage welled up in Nias. He immediately knew who the "her" was that Hector referred to.

Furious, he transcended with the body of Hector back into the club and a storm followed in his wake. A burning wind swirled around him, picking up bits of dirt and trash from the floors, napkins and coasters, and ashes from cigarette trays; anything not bolted down flew into the air and struck anyone and anything in its fury. Chairs crashed to the floor and bottles of alcohol smashed against the wall. His rage was uncontained and spinning around him in a physical manifestation.

He threw fire at the DJ booth to stop the music. The party froze in place when he settled, but he had no intention of being subtle. His voice was a commanding boom through the abrupt silence.

"Warriors escort all civilians to the door and come back immediately!" The humans, although completely safe, were unaware in whose presence they were, and he had no intention of explaining it to them right then. He needed to find out if anyone knew of the local nests; and if not he would initiate a search party using everyone who could be reached to find her. *Why are they still not moving?*

"NOW!!!!" Although he wasn't the current Sovereign, the Sentry still responded to his commands as if he were. Every Djinn, male and female, knew if he were in this state they needed to act, immediately. The Sentry began ushering the humans toward the front door as quickly as they could. Clothes were being straightened and thrown back on. After the room was cleared the Sentry began to reappear settling before him. Nias stood now, with his back straight, his feet spread apart, and his hands fisted behind himself.

"What nests are in the area? The girl, Jade, who was to go with me to Sheol has been taken." He looked to Locke, who was always in charge of the home operations and kept the maps with current nests, the successful Shaitan conversions, and any Verge humans they knew of.

"There is one in the bay area, but it has no recent movement we know of." Locke was standing several feet from Nias, with a look of concern in his eyes for his friend. But Nias had no time to even think about taking any friendly advice at the moment. There was only one thing on his mind, and that was finding Jade. All other concerns had fallen away.

"Who was with Ella when she destroyed the nest near the compound? Were any traces of a move left behind?"

"They were all destroyed, Sir, with the exception of Hamartia. The last scent we had of her was by the Sentry on site in the desert ad-Dahna. She was coming out of Sheol after just a short time spent inside. As ordered, she was left untouched and transcended out immediately, with a new pack of six bottom-caste and two Palis." The Palis were nothing more than foot-licking, club-carrying blood-drinkers, but they could provide some added muscle when needed.

"The girl must be found immediately! South Corps spread throughout San Francisco in case she stays close. Wrain, find Ella and bring her here to lead them. Phaeton and the North go to the Compound and comb the streets there. Serv and I will go to the desert and check with the guard there. If we find nothing we go to Qum. Go now!"

Phaeton looked at his brother and simply nodded, and that nod showed his love for his brother was far stronger than any egotistical need to be in charge.

Nias and Serv transcended into the heat of the endless red mounds of the Arabian Desert. The winds were strong, whipping around him and red sand blew into his face and eyes. He froze for a moment, letting the sand thrash against his skin. He needed to center himself if he was going to be any help to Jade at all.

When he opened his eyes he found the Sentry on duty slain. Heads bashed in with a wooden club, the weapon frequently used by Hamartia's pack of soul-sucking killers.

His face hardened … this is where she would be. He only hoped he could reach Jade before it was too late.

Chapter 18

Jade had been wearing the backpack provided for her, but she didn't have any of the weapons out or fastened to her body. Right now she was too angry to care. The oppressive heat of her new location struck her at the same time a burst of adrenaline did, similar to what she had felt in the warehouse, but far, far stronger. She was not going to be used as a pawn in anyone's games right now, and she damn sure wasn't going to be taken prisoner again. Two kidnappings in a week were more than enough.

As she was in a state of shock and anger herself, she couldn't use her abilities to make the tall female beast grasping her arm any less angry. So she used every bit of the torrent of conflicted emotions bouncing around in her head and mentally bludgeoned it with them. She assaulted the thing with the weapon she did have access to, her mind. There was a virtual mental *smack* and it fell backward. Jade swung the backpack off her shoulders and ripped the zipper open as quickly as she could, grabbing the first thing she felt; the short sword sticking out slightly through the top.

Nias had told her they were stronger and the only chance she had of defeating a Shaitan was to surprise it and attack first.

"No fear, Jade, be angry and slice its fucking head off!" she growled aloud, and leapt toward it with the sword at the best angle to cut it down. She swung the sword with every bit of force her anger supplied, but unfortunately she didn't chop through the neck where she had aimed; the beastly woman towered over her and the blade struck it in its chest instead. Jade left a deep and gaping wound from which blood immediately poured down its torso. It was injured, but it hadn't been stopped; it only seemed more irate. The beast woman swung its immense arms and grabbed for her, a horrifying snarl coming from deep within it. She jumped backwards and although she got out of grabbing reach it caught her face with its claw and ripped a four-fingered gash vertically from her mouth down her neck through the front of her shirt before she could fall back and out of the way.

The next scream she heard surprised her when it came shrieking out of her own bleeding mouth. She had fallen to the ground on her bottom and when she cried out she simultaneously launched her feet forward at the thing's knees. She caught them hard, and after a satisfying crack, it fell to the ground, apparently out of commission, at least for the moment.

She got back to her feet, threw the pack over her shoulder, and gripped the sword in her hand, knowing her life depended on holding onto it. Then she ran her ass off. She went as fast as combat boots in soft, constantly shifting, sand and blazing desert sun would take her.

Then she heard Nias behind her yelling, and as she turned to face him, she fell right though the earth.

Jade was shrouded in a blackness, which was so dense it seemed impossible. She fell and fell, and hit the ground sideways, legs first, and could tell by the sharp cracking sound and the sudden shooting pains she had broken at least one of them.

Nias had transcended past Hamartia while she shouted at her minions to find their transportation, leaving Serv to deal with them. He had almost caught Jade as she fell through the quicksand hole, but just missed her, watching her fall into the entrance.

He slid through the opening himself and began to descend down into the Unseen. He called softly to Jade, not wanting anything that might be waiting to hear him. He found her in the darkness, huddled on a small black lava ledge within an alcove, covered in blood and obviously in pain but with her weapon drawn before her, ready for another battle.

"Jade, it's Nias, I'm going to walk toward you, put your weapon down. You're okay right now. Can I come to you?" He could see pretty well in the darkness. She was definitely in shock and he wasn't sure if she was able to process what was coming toward her. He could see her face and neck had severe cuts and by the placement of her leg he imagined it had broken on impact from the fall. He let his energy reach her first, wrapping around her. He couldn't make the pain stop, but even though she had to be unaware of what he was doing, he heard her release a small sigh.

"Okay, I swear I won't slice you to ribbons. Of course, you can come over here," she teased, even though he knew of the agony she must be feeling. Her strength of character never failed to amaze him.

"How is it you manage to tease in a situation like this?" He knelt beside her, lightly placing his hand to her arm, trying to avoid her injuries but wanting her to know he was there. He heard her begin to weep, but then stop herself. She straightened her shoulders a bit, like she didn't want to appear weak.

"Is she right behind you? Did she come through as well? She scares the crap out of me!"

"No," he said trying to assess the extent of her damage. "She will most likely wait for transportation. We have some time."

"Did you see me cut that thing? I did good, right? I couldn't quite reach her head, Nias, but I tried. I was so damn scared I actually staggered her with the power in my head. I've never done anything like it. A force came out of me and pushed her back. It gave me the time to get out the weapon." She was rambling too much. He could tell she wanted to be strong for him.

"I did, I saw you; the force must have come from the extreme fear. Your abilities seem to have some room to grow. You may have been scared, but you appeared fearless. No trained warrior could have been more courageous or fought as well." He looked over her injured body, remembering how she fought, and swelled with pride. All he wanted to do was to hold her tight to make her feel better. But there was no time for that now. Hamartia would be following soon.

"But, Nias, I think I'm broken. I think you said some of your tricks don't work here, right? Can you fix me at all?"

He chuckled softly, "Yes I can fix you. I am so sorry you are, as you say, broken. You have a very strange way of making a situation lighter, don't you? There are not many people so amusing when they've been sliced and crippled."

"I told you I can't help it. When I'm stressed I either check out completely, or I make jokes. I have to laugh or I will completely lose it. Then you would have a real mess to clean up." He could see in her eyes that she verged on a breakdown, and was fighting to hold a tight smile on her lovely, but frightened, face.

"Any energy or magic that flows through my body will still function. I have no ability to manipulate any force outside myself here. No fire, no transcending. The strength I have inside myself is fully functional; the healing blood is still within me. I can see you in the dark." He chuckled. "You are a beautiful disaster, Kitten."

She laughed painfully, "Not so sure about the beautiful, but I'm definitely a disaster. And I freaking hurt." He placed the back of his hand to her uninjured cheek, and stroked it lightly.

His rational mind still knew he had to separate himself from her. He cared for her too deeply. He didn't want to see her injured even worse or killed because of her proximity to him. He was a huge liability to her. He couldn't fool himself any more with thinking of her as a toy or possession, it was absurd to deny it any further.

Yes, she needed to be kept safe. But not by keeping her. He would kill everything that wanted to harm her, and then release her back into her life. They could never be together.

But right now, she needed repair, and he was going to have to take an irreversible step to help her.

He took a deep breath. "Jade, if your leg is truly broken it is an interior wound. With the cuts outside your body, my blood can fix them from the outside, but with an internal injury … Do you understand what I'm saying to you?"

"Huh? I really hope I'm not understanding what you're saying. Because what I think is you're saying you need to put your blood inside me in order to fix me." He could see her wince.

"That's exactly what I'm saying."

"Are you saying I have to put your blood inside my body, by like drinking it, like a vampire?"

"Yes." His body had a physical reaction thinking about her mouth strapped to one of his veins and drawing from it. His groin began to ache.

"No."

"Woman, you are way too fond of that word." He gave her a flat, dry, ominous stare he knew she couldn't see, but couldn't help. "If you won't take my blood, I would have to leave you here, acquire medical supplies and come back. Then set your leg and you will need to sit, for days, possibly weeks, before you could climb out."

"No, smearing blood on me is one thing." One thing she had enjoyed thoroughly, if he remembered correctly, and he was damn sure he had too. "But drinking blood is just so gross."

"Okay. Wait here. I will climb out, transcend to a hospital, get supplies, and climb back down to you. Remember Hamartia is still above ground, and when the other Shaitan come for her she will pass this way. Hopefully she won't see you. Huddle closely to the walls."

"Oh. Fuck you, Nias. I get it. Enough with your sarcastic drama." He smirked at her, knowing he had won that battle of wills. "Give me the blood." She cringed with a slight shiver. "But I swear to God, if I grow fangs or turn into a bat, my first act as a vampire will be to drain you dry."

Chapter 19

Hamartia stood in the desert with anger seething out of her, the lower-caste Shaitan staring at her after the Sentry had distracted them long enough for Nias to get past. Unfortunately for him, he was only one, but he still had managed to dispatch a small number of her forces before he himself was felled.

"If you will not cease with your ogling, I will end every last one of you. I cannot believe he has gone after that girl!" She paced in the sand, ranting, and the minion took a step back from her. "She should have been killed long ago."

Hamartia was trying to not let the jealousy she felt at the girl's presence show. She was failing miserably. The girl was obviously more than a meaningless tool for him. Nias never would have jumped in after her unarmed and without Sentry to back him up. It was an emotional response, completely uncharacteristic of him, and it made her want to tear someone apart and consume their dismantled flesh. Her entire body turned red.

She stalked through the sand toward a four-foot-tall grotesque hunchbacked Shaitan, her new first in charge, and spoke to him. "Nias is finally in Sheol. I have at least achieved my goal of getting Joss imprisoned and Nias one step closer."

Her lieutenant cow-towed to her, "Yes, my mistress has done excellent work. We are already leaking word to the other siblings of Nias's descent. They will come for him. With the absence of all four siblings we can begin our fight to control the entire Djinn Sentry, and then move toward the Dark Father himself." The Shaitan's tone was one of subservience and praise; brownnosing.

Hamartia, being more than angry at this moment, became annoyed at its ridiculous speech and childish laughter. She picked it up by its neck and grabbed the skin outside its chest, scratching and tearing away the flesh. Then she wrapped her hand around one of its ribs, snapping the bones out and backward. The creature screamed in pain, but she ignored it, baring and gnashing her teeth. She slammed its back to the hot sand, still holding the neck with one claw, and wrapped the other around its heart, tearing it out, still pumping, and throwing it to the side. When it landed, the fine sandy dirt clung to its sticky surface and it lay there like any piece of discarded trash. The group of Shaitan visibly cringed, giving her even more pleasure.

Hamartia sighed, feeling a bit of relief at the release of her dark emotion. Almost smiling, she turned to address the remaining creatures and offered no explanation or apology.

"We go to Sheol. The first to find Nias and the girl will contact me. Stay back, Nias can kill you as easily as he stands breathing." She stood taller, he was so handsome and strong; she took pride in him, in his ability to kill. "And the girl has some kind of power I do not know. When we have secured him, you can kill the girl as reward. But she will be mine alone to consume." She couldn't help but bare her teeth again and then pointed toward the hole.

"Move in!"

If that she-Daemon was coming down here, Jade wanted to do this quickly. She turned to Nias, trying to look all matter-of-fact now.

"Bite into my wrist, tear it like I did before and begin to drink." Despite the disgusting situation, the thought of getting to suck any part of him made her throb and moisten; good God, even her breasts began to tighten and pulse.

Her face was slashed, her leg turned in a way a human leg should never go, and tears were silently escaping out of her eyes and rolling into her cuts. And still she was aroused by him. She was a mess of conflicting physical and mental states, and she definitely didn't feel strong enough to argue about this anymore.

His hand came from behind her head and ran through her hair, scraping his nails past her ear like he had done earlier. She blushed just thinking about it.

She allowed him to pet her until she felt almost calm, and it was working, as it always had. She moved closer to him, keeping her one knee bent, careful not to cut her exposed legs further on the sharp ground, or fall from the cliff where they were perched. Nias put his hands beneath her bottom to help her, easily picking her up and placing her in his lap. Then he put his wrist in her hand, trusting she would raise it to her mouth when she was ready.

She melted into his warmth, her head falling snugly against his chest, his hand in hers. She had no faith he cared for her the way she was beginning to care for him. She was heartbroken about how she had created an imaginary bond which didn't seem to exist between them emotionally, but there was no way to deny when he was this close to her, when she inhaled his musky base-level masculine scent and felt his firm, powerfully built chest, the sound of his heart pounding beneath her, she was enveloped in a euphoric feeling of physical safety.

Raising his wrist to her lips, she ran her tongue over the salty, firm skin to find the vein and used her incisors to pierce his tender flesh and tear it out of her way. He let out a loud hiss and she felt his cock buck and grow under her, and then his soft moans began as she sucked.

All at once his blood tasted metallic, salty, and sweet; the fluid was thick and flowed plentifully and rapidly into her mouth. His blood was the opposite of repulsive; it was heaven. She felt greedy and sated and lazy simultaneously as she drew on his vein. Nias continued to groan softly and thicken and there was nothing,

nothing she could do to stop herself from squirming.

That was all the encouragement he needed. He wrapped her waist with his free arm, pulling her tightly into his body and pushed her down on his rock-hard erection, while she continued to drink from his wrist.

When he moved his hand to trail up her thigh, past her way-too-short shorts that were riding into her and slid two fingers into her slickness, she felt an intense euphoric flush of ecstasy roll from right between her legs, where his fingers worked, up through her stomach to her chest, making her breasts cry to be touched by him and her body want to be filled completely. But instead, she pulled his warm fingers away. She couldn't do this again. Her body wanted one thing, but her heart wanted another. He had left the clothes and the bag by the bed. He was only using her. She felt like an idiot. All she wanted was a normal life and here she was, in Hell with a Daemon she was falling in love with. It had to stop. She felt like she was spinning out of control.

It was the curse destroying her life, AGAIN. Her gift, HA! She wanted it gone.

As she pushed further away from him, she knew he had let her do so. He was too strong for her to have done it on her own. There was no way she could have moved him without his consent, but the irked look in his eyes both complimented and contrasted with the ache she was feeling.

"Kitten, come back to me," he rasped, and he sounded like lust should: smooth, raspy, and darkly melodic. Apparently she was standing, her leg miraculously healed, because he rose and tried to pull her back into him.

"Nias, I can't do this." She leaned against the cave walls to steady her legs, which were so full of unsatisfied desire they threatened to fold. "It doesn't work for me anymore, no more touching, really this time!" She simply couldn't get any more attached to this Daemon, this beautiful man who, in the end, would be leaving her. She wanted to have a life, a real life. And she knew this man was the key.

Not listening to a word she said, he wrapped his hands around the back of her neck, pulling into her as if to kiss her, but instead licked the blood from her mouth. His tongue ran slowly over her inflamed lips as he cleaned her face of the sticky fluid, and she purred. His body was so long and sleek and forcefully built, and although she couldn't see him, she imagined his golden eyes looking deep into her own. And it just made her mad.

Sharply, she pushed him and held him away with a stiff arm, hand on his chest. They were separated as much as was possible on the ledge.

"Stop it!" She lowered her head to look at the ground and catch her breath. He was not making this easy.

"I need all of this to stop, Nias, all of it. When we first met you said you didn't have anything to do with me acquiring his power, but it sounded like you knew where it came from. I am coming with you to find your brother. In return you will do everything you can to relieve me of this curse."

"I do not want you to join me." He looked in shock at her words.

She hated the fact he made her feel like this. Vacillating between anger with him and desire for him was driving her crazy. So she jabbed him in his broad, muscular chest just to make her point. "Well, I am."

He tried to take her hand, but she didn't let him. She was firmly planted against the wall. Standing her ground.

"Kitten, listen to me, your powers are a gift. You shouldn't want them gone. You should learn to control them a little, but any power bestowed by the Goddesses is greater than you believe them to be. They can most likely be cultivated. You are beautiful and perfect the way you are."

Did he just say she was perfect? *Sigh*…Ugh, stand your ground, Jade! She silently chided herself.

"I find that, somewhat against my wishes, my body only wants one thing, one person in its bed, and it is you. I think it would be best if you didn't come."

Somewhat against his wishes! His body … and his bed! If she had had enough room, she might have kicked him in the groin, vomited, or started bawling. As it was she really wanted to do all three. There it was, undeniable proof; it was lust for him; it was about his body, his bed and even that was against his wishes.

"Thank you for fixing me, again. I'm sorry I started something I have no intention of finishing here. It seems your blood makes me a little confused." *Yeah, confused, what an understatement that is.* "We will find your brother and stop these things from coming after me and you will rid me of this curse. That is final."

"I care for you, Jade, but I actually agree with you it should be this way. I need it to be this way too. It seems a fair deal. Although I still prefer you not accompany me," he said softly. Jade arched a brow in his direction that undeniably said, do not make me punch you again.

"This is the part where I pull myself up by the boot straps and move forward," she said softly to the ground.

"What does that mean?"

It means heartache has always been a close companion. We shall just continue on our way together. She thought it, but she didn't say it aloud. Jade tried to lighten her own mood, but the situation was painful, not funny at all. "It means I'm ready to go find your brother and get out of here. You said we could survive this together and that's what we'll do."

He felt like he was floating, lounging on a plush mattress, leaning back as a pair of hands roamed over his bare chest. The caress aroused him, making his groin ache to take his lover completely. He felt her hot breath in his ear, and she whispered to him how much she wanted him.

He thought he heard something else then. A voice sounding like it was from miles away. "Joss … wake up!" but it was so faint … and who was Joss? He struggled for a moment to think, but then the message became more urgent and he forgot the voice. Endorphins and hormones flooded his mind. The hands moved down towards his waist.

As they slid under his waistband, there was one last urgent shout in his head. "JOSS!!!" In that instant, he felt the metal bars against his back, and his eyes snapped open.

He saw the bars on the opposite side of the cage, and latched onto that reality, tearing himself away from the arms gripping him from behind through the bars, and stumbled his way to the far side. He grabbed onto the bars and pulled himself up, breathing hard. *My name is Joss!* He held on mentally as tightly as he could, as Empusa screeched her displeasure behind him.

He had to clear his head. He looked over his shoulder and saw that the shirt he had been wearing had been pulled off and tossed aside, well outside the cage. He must have dozed off and Empusa tried to take him, and the pheromones she had given off had started to permeate his being, already doing their addictive work.

Another few minutes and he would have been completely lost to her. Luckily, she was not advancing on him now, or his already compromised system might betray him, even though he was awake.

She resumed her pacing outside the cage as Joss contemplated his situation. He was exhausted; Hamartia had clearly given him to the Empusa. If he thought about it, he loved sex, and blood-letting. The situation might not be as hopeless as he thought. As he worked it out, recovering his faculties, it might be possible for him to turn the situation around. But could he do *this*?

She wasn't shaped like a monster; she only acted like one. He thought there was a chance she was pretty underneath the filth. Was it true?

He couldn't believe he was considering this. His mind was swimming, fighting against the exhaustion, the brain toxins invading his senses and the darkness within him. The truth was, he would soon collapse and she would have him anyway.

"Hag, let me see your face." She screamed the high-pitched wail at him, but as she did, he could clearly see a young woman under there. Man, the scream had to go, but this idea seemed better than the Fade or darkness, at least a little better.

And then he saw it in her eyes. She desired someone to give themselves to her willingly, without having to wait for the time he could no longer do anything about it. Maybe, just maybe, he could do this and maintain control of himself. He shook his head and finally the fog cleared.

He struggled, leaning against the cage, but still found himself getting the words out. "Empusa, would you consider a deal?"

Chapter 20

After the extremely brief and one-sided "discussion" with Nias regarding whether she would come with him, Jade sank to her knees and sought out the edge of the cliff and felt around until she found a ladder-type apparatus. The ladder felt like the branches of a tree, rough and possibly petrified. She had no idea how it was attached to the wall. She went down on her hands and knees, turned herself around, and placed a foot a few rungs down. She still couldn't see at all, as the blackness was stifling; a sharp stench of foul air blew up from the gigantic hole. She hadn't smelled or felt it while sitting on the ledge. Her hair blew up behind her as she went down. Despite their argument, Nias moved to grab her arm and stop her from what she was doing, but she was determined. He reached and got a firm grip on her wrist.

"I have a tenuous grasp on this ledge, and one foot on a rickety ladder. I suggest if you want me alive, you let go slowly. If have to force myself out of your grip, chances are I am headed for a fall no blood will help me recover from."

"Do not do this, Jade; I don't want you to go. Climb up, I will help you, I will transcend you to Phaeton's and come in later with back-up."

"No. You just told me you couldn't transcend down here. You would lose too much time climbing out and then back down."

148

"You use that word with me way too often; if you want to act like a child, I should like to spank you like one." She laughed in response; this not touching each other was a terrible plan.

"*Somewhat against my wishes*, as a very stubborn man once said; I very much look forward to it." And she continued her descent. Unable to stop her from climbing down without risking the fall she had described, he followed; *thank God*, she thought to herself; she so did not want to go alone.

The updraft increased and a smell of rotten egg came with it; this she knew was the smell of sulfur. She could see an orangey glow, which ironically resembled a beautiful sunset coming out of the darkness. The heat continued to increase.

"Okay, so far I smell sulfur, and it's amazingly hot, and I'm pretty sure that glow is fire. Is the whole place one big stereotype? Did we have it exactly right up top?"

"There is far more down where we are headed than humans could ever imagine, Jade. Some of it is amazing."

"Amazing, umm, right, only a Daemon would use an adjective like 'amazing' to describe Hell. The fact you keep calling me by my real name is freaking me out more than anything."

"As we climb down into Sheol, my calling you by your name should be the least of your worries. If you insist on continuing on your current path, I suggest you at least listen to me. When we arrive, I am in command; you will never, never leave my side. If you do either the Shaitan or the heat will kill you. Do you understand?"

"Yes."

"I will wrap you in energy, the same that you keep pulling out of me. It can protect you from the fire and heat."

This was beyond a nightmare. When Nias hadn't cared if she lived or died it was completely different. Now that she had become so important to him, ever since seeing her fall though the sand, he wanted only to get her out. It was his worst nightmare come true;

another human, another woman was going to die and it would be all his doing. He was a murderer, no better than the Shaitan below.

Infuriating, stubborn, cocksure woman; beautiful, strong, courageous, sexy woman. If she would just stop sucking on me, possibly I could make better decisions. If I could just stop putting parts of my body in her mouth maybe she would stop sucking on them!

"What do you mean by the same energy I keep pulling from you? You have been blasting me, enveloping me in it; it's like I'm in a constant state of nymphomania around you!" She continued climbing down the rungs, but looked up at him to see him in a faint glowing yellow light bathed in shadows. He stopped climbing and began to laugh, and turned to his side to look down at her, half his face in the shadow of his hair, half illuminated male perfection.

"Ahh, my Kitten," he said with his favorite cocky smirk, "my aura is only what you take from it. You decide what you want to pull from me; many see me and just pull fear. It is so delicious to know what you take, exactly how you need me. However, now it will be almost unbearable not to touch you."

"So if I take what I want from you, which I feel quite embarrassed about right now, you don't affect other women like this?"

"Certainly I radiate a somewhat sexual energy, like I said, all my siblings do, but it isn't enough to coerce you into giving yourself to me. I would never stoop to that level. I have never needed to; women can't wait to get their hands in my pants. No, you want me that badly. Don't you?" That had not been a question but an accusation. This entire banter was nothing more than a defense mechanism for him, preparing him, and her, for the time when they would have to part. The part he didn't mention was she was the only woman he had ever wanted as badly as she wanted him. His desire for her was not a decision he made, it was a compulsion his body and soul insisted on.

"I choose not to answer that question, Nias; first of all, because you would enjoy it so much, and second because I refuse to incriminate myself any further."

"I believe that was the most precise answer I could have gotten. If we weren't separated by a ladder with one thousand feet of burning air below us, I would have absolutely no self-control and would feel quite justified in at least a small innocent kiss."

"Could you please never use the word innocent and your kisses in a sentence together ever again? If there was ever a more severe oxymoron, I sure don't know what it could be." She paused as a wave of hot wind passed over her. "The heat is sweltering. I just felt a wave of it and it seemed like it came from nowhere. I think my proximity to you is simultaneously a blessing and a curse. I think I feel safer than I should. Might be time to override my pull, or whatever it is, and start pushing out some different signals, Nias. Cause I think I just lost some hair to that fire."

Nias had felt the heat come up in a sheet and pass through their bodies as well, so he swept an enveloping energy down on to her. The time for flirtation was over, for more than one reason now. He not only wished to keep her from getting more emotionally attached, but his lack of focus on the conditions would get her killed.

He hadn't entered his old home in over five hundred years. Five hundred years above ground, trying to do good things, trying to protect those he could, trying to be an advocate because he had failed to be one for thousands of years before, when he was a part of this fiery world. This world where screams, malevolence, pain, and torture were considered a necessary amusement. The Shaitan fed off of it; it was their energy, their source of power, their one true enjoyment.

Jade and Nias climbed down for hours. He could sense Jade becoming tired. He wished he were able to help more. He knew by the heat, the heat she could no longer feel, they were approaching the end of the ladder. And then the real danger would be upon them.

Chapter 21

Jade began to see the light beneath them fade, like the light from a distant city that appears to wane as one gets closer. So now she found herself descending into what appeared to be darkness. She continued to unwrap a hand from each wooden bar and grasp the one below it, moving her feet in time with her hands. Over and over she performed this motion, for what seemed like forever; the end had to be near, or the monotony would drive her mad.

"It's getting dark again?" she asked Nias.

"We are coming to the bottom of the ladder, when your eyes adjust you should be able to see enough to move forward. You have about five more steps on the ladder and then a small platform. When you get to the bottom wait for me. Do you understand, Jade? Do not move on without me!" His voice deepened a touch, a renewed forcefulness to it.

"We may have our differences," *like you bringing me into Hell,* "but down here I am sticking to you like glue."

She reached the end in exactly five steps, as he had said, and she couldn't see anything at all. She was terrified; she felt no heat, she was blind, and for a few brief moments she stood completely alone. So when Nias came off the set of steps a few seconds after her, she grabbed him by the waist and buried her face in his chest.

"I will not be scared, I will not be scared, I can do this, I will do this…" She mumbled over and over into him. Even though she couldn't feel the heat around her, she could feel the warmth from his skin. Her hands had slipped underneath his t-shirt when she grabbed him and her long nails were digging into his back.

"Hardly the time for this, my Kitten," he chuckled slightly. She opened her eyes and realized what she was doing, and pulled back a step.

"I didn't mean to do that. I am trying to pull it together … pulling it together, I am pulling it together," Jade said more to herself than to Nias.

He didn't want her to let go. He didn't want her to be frightened. But he also knew what made her feel better, and this was hardly the time or place. Although his body's instinct was to take her in his arms, encircle her, and have her right there, he instead took her hand as she smartly pulled away.

Nias raised her hand to his mouth and lightly kissed the tops of her curled fingers. "Do precisely what I tell you and we're going to make it back from where we came, above ground." He tried to comfort her by using his other hand to push her hair behind her ears, one side at a time. He took her chin in his hand and pulled her face toward his. Staring into her eyes, "Kitten, you are here with me, right? Stay present."

"Yes, I'm with you, I can even see a little bit better, I can see your eyes."

"Good, that's perfect. Now take off your pack and get out your knife."

Having perfect night vision, Nias watched her swing the backpack off and place it on the ground. Squatting, she unzipped the back and retrieved the leather knife cover, which held a Gerber Mark II that Nias had selected for her to train with.

"Strap that to your ankle with the snap, like I showed you," Nias instructed.

"Got it, should I get the other weapons out too?" She found

several items in the pack and stood with them. He took a silent inventory of the goods he had asked to be placed in her room several days ago. She had all the weapons he had trained her on and her mind controls. Hopefully it would be enough.

As he assessed her situation, he also assessed his own; as he hadn't prepared for the descent he had none of his weapons. The ball and mace he treasured was left behind. They had done a lot of damage together and he yearned for the comfort of it in his hand now. He picked up the pack and retrieved the extra Gerber, which he pushed into the space between his belt and jeans. *This is better than nothing*, he thought.

"Put the sword holster over your shoulders; it will go under the backpack. Put the wrist knives on as well." When the leather straps of the sword carrier were attached to her back, he grabbed the length of her wild flame-colored hair, twisting it tight; then he wrapped it around itself into a knot, securing it in place. Leaving a hand there, he slid the small sword into the leather sword holster for her. He had to force himself not to linger with his hands in her hair, as he wanted to drag her to him again. He loved to tighten his grip in her hair and he knew how it made her feel from experience. Again a frustrated growl unwittingly escaped from between his lips; he took her hand again, and wondered where his years of easy, emotionless existence had fled to.

"Let's walk," Nias said, forcing his strict tone to return. "When we see a Shaitan, follow my instructions. Some of them should be easy for you to manipulate with your mind. Others we will conquer together. I need information about where my brother is being kept, and so we will not end them all immediately. You should know, some of the Shaitan could pass for human; they look almost identical to Djinn. Very few are as pretty, but some." He gave a sardonic grin.

"Don't worry about me. Let's just find your brother and get the fuck out of here, as soon as possible."

"We're going to be fine," he prevaricated, determined to make it the truth, but anything could happen. He wondered about his father. Remembering the thousands of years the Djinn, his Djinn, had lived in the depths of this world.

His father, Iblis, would he ever let him leave again? Nias had taken an entire race with him when he left, and The Beast was livid. Iblis wasn't able to go above ground, thankfully, because of his personal limitations. His father would do anything for retribution and to get his Djinn back. They could only hope to avoid him. It would be like avoiding lust at one of Phaeton's parties; it could happen, but the chances were less than slim.

It is amazing how warm and fluid his hands feel in my hair, Jade thought idly, momentarily escaping the reality of their situation. When he pushed the long curls back from her face and tucked them behind her ear, she felt so taken care of, and a long slither of goose flesh ran from her head, down the tender skin at the sides of her waist, and culminated wetly between her thighs. He didn't have to tell her he would take care of her, she knew he just would. Jade closed her eyes and felt as though she was actually melting with contentment. And then, he took her hand. She felt like stomping her feet like a four-year-old because when she looked up at him expecting, well, expecting she didn't know what, his face was stern again. His beautiful, exotic, sexually charged eyes were blankly staring ahead, plotting their course.

This would have been a great time for her stupid gift to actually work on him; she would have loved to be able to know what the hell he was feeling. Of course, her annoying brain wouldn't work on this man. Her empathy rarely showed her something that would actually please her, and she'd love to know if it would have this time.

Jade stepped off the platform under the seemingly endless ladder and turned around to find a wide set of stairs before her. Made of sharp, black lava rock, they descended even further downward. A heavy, dark vine intertwined about thirty feet above, creating a complete rounded ceiling with a denseness that allowed nothing through. Ten feet down, it became an almost pitch-blackness. She tried not to anticipate anything beyond her next step. Just like when she had been in Phaeton's house, trying not to think about whom Nias was, she wasn't going to think about what Sheol would bring. It would do no good, *Lalalalala.* Contemplating and speculating was a waste of energy.

Damn, if these stairs didn't seem to go on forever too.

It took a full day and well into what would have been the night, had they been anywhere near the sun to see it rise and fall.

When they finally reached the bottom of the stairs, the vines ceased and the sky opened up, streaks of yellow and orange and red lit up the sky and colored an otherwise ominous world. Somehow the sky was lit with the colors of pure fire and yet it remained full night. The ground consisted of powdery black dirt interspersed with chunks of the glassy, black lava rock. It was fascinating; she was staring into Hell. *How many people have gotten to do this while alive?* The black ground bled into an aura and physical reality of darkness. Shadows of wicked mountainous formations were evident only by their own shadow in contrast to the burning sky above them.

And then she heard the noises. Like being sucked in through a magic mirror or a vortex in some bad sci-fi movie, her vision had come first and then it seemed the rest of her senses finally caught up.

She was suddenly assaulted by a cacophony of smells and an increase in heat, which must have meant it would have killed her quickly if it wasn't for the presence of Nias. The smells came in grotesque waves of heavy sulfur-laden sweat, rot, mold and mildew, urine and feces. And then there was the sound. The sounds around her weren't screams or crying like she would have imagined. What she heard were moans, almost quiet, deep sorrow-filled moans of hundreds, no thousands, of souls. Some were higher-pitched, which were no doubt female. She didn't know whether to cover her ears or block her nose first; it was amazingly sudden and overwhelming.

Nias gripped her hand harder and pulled her closer to him. Squeezing her hand, he kept his elbow straight and his arm at an inward diagonal behind him so that her body was within inches of his, and she fell into step with him, their legs moving together simultaneously, left foot, right, left, then right. She wasn't losing him, and he had such a firm grip on her she knew he wasn't planning on losing her either; she felt he wouldn't let anything take her. His eyes never stopped scanning the scene in front of them, apparently looking for anything that might attack. To think he was looking for unusual activity caused her to smile; it almost made her laugh, because it was all unusual to her, bizarre, but the situation wasn't amusing in the least. She could see where he had gotten the skills he had used to train her, surviving in this place. It was surreal and blistering hot.

"Nias I am really warm, I'm close enough to you, right?"

"It's hotter than you could ever tolerate here; I have you surrounded. If you fall to the ground gasping for water and feel your skin singe and begin to peel away, you'll know you're too far away. No matter what happens, stay within fifteen feet of me. Unfortunately that means if I have to attack something you are going to have to move with me."

"Yeah, me walking away from you down here ain't gonna happen. So what is the moaning and the smell? I don't want to ask but, I think knowing what to expect might help me get through things here."

"This is the Verge. A place for human souls not designated for the worst and most extreme pain as given to those who have been taken for eternity. They committed lesser crimes, such as killing in self-defense when there may have been alternatives; crimes which are seen as verging sins against all gods not deserving of a lower level of damnation."

"So this must be purgatory; humans call this purgatory. Can

they earn their way out?"

"Some." It didn't seem like he wanted to expand on his answer, so she let it go. Honestly, she didn't feel like she could take in any extra information right then. Staying in the moment was hard enough.

As the wailing got louder and the smell became unbearable, the lost souls became visible to Jade. She froze for a moment at the sight of them and then continued her stride.

"We need to move quickly, we are not alone with the Verge. The Watcher Shaitan protect them, and use their pain as energy. They would love nothing more than to bleed you dry; your living soul and body would bring even more strength and pleasure to them and could sustain them for months."

Jade closed her eyes and took in the negative aura of her new surroundings. "I can feel the desperate ache and exhaustion. I can feel the Daemon as well. They are full of excited angst, and yearn for more."

A deep, dark, brownish grey sludge covered the ground all around where the human souls walked. In some places it was so deep, the people were in to their shoulders. Others were floating en masse, as if in a lake with far too many swimmers. They were all moving, endlessly moving, trudging forward on fatigued legs or crawling through muck, constantly pulling themselves through the muddy quicksand. Not one was stationary. The sky was even darker than before and seemed too low, pushing them toward the ground and forcing a slouch. It was an illusion; the sky was higher than it seemed, but too oppressive in its tone and shape. It pushed them like a bully, onward through their fatigue.

"They're forced to always move. If they fall they will be punished. And they will fall, the Shaitan wait for it, like a game," he said, turning his head to the side and down toward her face. She was pretty sure he was looking to see if she was okay and not losing it, but there was more than a little sadness in his eyes, like a haunting memory was assaulting him.

Jade walked through the scene in a state of suspended shock. She felt somewhat disconnected, as if she were ill, in a kind of separation fog. Not being able to help herself, she walked into the mire, her boots sinking to the ankle. She felt somehow compelled to ease their suffering. Maybe if she told them to repent, or asked around to see what the rules were, maybe she could help some of them get out of there, as insane as that sounded. Surrounded by their soft, pained moaning, her presence was completely ignored.

"Jade, don't walk away from me! They can't communicate with you. We can't help them." Nias jumped into the slush and grabbed her waist again. Then he walked her out, back to the dirt road, where they had been traveling.

Jade felt the excitement streaming from the Shaitan a second before she saw Nias draw the knife from his belt and stab a creature running toward them. He easily slit the creature's throat, throwing it to the ground. He grabbed her, pulling her toward him and removed the sword from her back holster; it came down on the neck of another advancing monster, severing its head completely.

"More are coming, stay within fifteen feet of me, use any control over their feelings you can and remember your training. Got it?" He was standing in an attack position, completely alert and scanning the area around them, only turning for a moment to look her straight in the eyes and make sure she had heard him. *He does that a lot,* she thought to herself quickly.

"Yes, break the neck, sever the head, remove the heart and stay close." The fog of the unfamiliar lifted as adrenaline charged her body. He handed the large and now-bloodied sword back to her without turning his gaze. Jade slipped her hand onto the hilt and swung it in a circular motion through the air, getting a handle once again on the weight of it. Nias had the seventeen-inch knife poised and readied for another attack; in his massive hand it seemed closer to the size of a butter knife. He used it like an extension of his own arm.

Nias watched her swing the sword's blade out of the corner of his eye, and she did her best to reassure him with a nod.

"I'm good; don't leave me and I'm good," she said as she stood ready with the short sword held out in front of her body.

"There is no way I would ever leave you here, Jade." His black hair swayed with his movements, and she found herself having to actively remove her glance from the profile of his beautiful face and reengage her focus after hearing the sincerity in his voice.

"I feel a group of them coming, their creepy excitement is moving toward us, but I can dull it, I think." She grabbed Nias's t-shirt to make sure he would still be there when she closed her eyes. She thought about the feeling she would want them to have, instead of the crazed excitement they felt when they saw her; calm, calm was good. She was pushing the excitement out of them and replacing it with calm. She opened her eyes to see how it was working. "I think I just slowed them down." She smiled quickly.

There were a couple of ugly hunchbacked creatures with long, curling horns coming from the tops of their heads, holding wooden clubs, coming through a pocket of humans crawling on hands and knees. There were three more coming from around a small mountainous rock formation next to a pool of sludge.

"They are definitely slower, Jade, but they still coming toward us. I need you to move toward them with me; just like I told you in training they won't expect you to attack first. Keep your back to me and if I turn, you turn, if I jump, you jump."

"Got it, holy cow, I got it! I'm scared, not stupid, Nias." He laughed at her, and moved forward quickly toward the pair who were closest.

With the sword in hand Jade said, "Turn, I got this." Nias had no choice but to do as she said and turn, as he had no intention of losing her. She raised her sword and started to run toward the Daemon. The beasts stayed calm, like her mind told them to, although they continued to saunter forward slowly. "Good little Daemons, come to Jade so I can kill you," she said in a low, evil tone that surprised even her. Gritting her teeth she slashed at the bigger of the two; with a clean blow she decapitated the thing straight through its neck. She actually hissed "Yesss," at which point Nias frowned at her. He pushed the other one over and stood on its chest, moving one boot to its chin, turning slightly and cracking its neck.

"Niccce," she hissed again, and raised her brows at him.

"What has come over you woman? Have you gone from scared witless to super-Daemon killer in mere seconds?" He looked at her, completely disbelieving.

"I can feel them; I know they aren't even alarmed when we come near them. We should move toward the other ones quickly." Jade ignored his question and turned to move toward the other three, and Nias walked behind her, obviously a little shocked.

"Come on, I will still die from the heat if you can't keep up, you know." She snickered.

Jade headed for the rocks and the three other Shaitan, but one of them seemed to be moving more quickly than the others, its version of calm at a different level. Nias was completely uncon-cerned; he looked at it as if he were going to swat a fly. When it drew near enough, he used the beast's own momentum to dig his knife into its throat, and it gasped on its own blood and fell to the ground. He withdrew his weapon and hacked at its neck twice; the execution was bloodier than the others, but equally successful. The head removed, he kicked it to the side and went for the other two slower-moving Shaitan.

Jade pushed one to the ground, looking at Nias while she did it, for instruction. She leaped onto its chest, moved her foot slightly to its head and pushed. Nothing happened except it began to struggle, trying to get up, and scrape its claws on her legs. But Nias placed his feet on its wrists, holding the arms down, so she could end it.

"No, more angle, Buffy the Daemon-slayer, twist your foot out a little," he said dryly.

"Oh," she said, twisting, and achieving the desired effect, causing the crack she wanted. "I did it," she said excitedly.

Nias scowled at her again and in a continued flat tone said, "Well done, much better."

He removed the head of the third and last Daemon using his knife again. And after Jade did a few understated silent cheers to herself, for which Nias was having little patience, they trudged through the mud back onto the path and continued deeper into Sheol.

"I did awesome, right?" She couldn't help it; her adrenaline had not had a chance to quiet down yet.

"Cocky will get you killed down here, Jade. Move closer to me. The larger, more powerful beasts will not be so easy to take down. Besides that you went a little dark on me," he said dryly, with no amusement to his voice, as they continued the walk. But when she caught up to him, she held his arm, with two hands pulling slightly, using a bit of left-over adrenaline. And Nias wrapped his arm around her and kissed her on the top of her head, lingering longer than necessary.

"You were pretty awesome," he grinned proudly.

She had been amazing, but he was starting to get used to her extremes. When she was scared she cried; when she was aroused she purred and drove him to the point of insanity. Now, he saw when she was aggressive she was a crazed killer. He would like to take some of the credit for her new, heightened personality; he knew she was unfolding into a new woman. And if the old one had been amazing, well, this one was indescribably intoxicating. He continued to hold her hand, because he wanted her by his side. But the more he cared for her, the more he knew he would have to leave her in her quiet, safe human life at any cost when all this was over.

The endless night continued, the colors in and around them like a fire burning in the night. Nias took her by the hand and they walked together. He stayed in a heightened state of awareness and protection; his body language threatening and alert.

They passed through a long, cavernous tunnel and were met with a sharp drop, a cliff. Jade moved away from him to see what lay in the ravine, her curiosity getting the better of her as they moved further from the fight and The Verge.

Having warned her multiple times not to leave his side, he realized it seemed she couldn't obey him right now; this world was too strange for her. Unfortunately it was way too familiar for him. He followed her quickly, staying right on her heels. He would try to hold on to her hand, but if the woman continued to pull away from him he would have to find some chain and use it to confine her. He already knew that over the cliff Jade had run to was a river of fire and putrid water with spouts and geysers rising. A small wooden bridge connected the two cliffs on either side. If there were any way he could avoid taking her on that bridge he would use it. They would be opening themselves up for way too much risk on that death trap. Unfortunately they might not have much of a choice. Nias wasn't about to tell Jade, Hamartia couldn't be far behind them now.

Chapter 22

As Jade moved swiftly toward the edge, Nias saw the Ifrit move in behind her. He knew the Ifrit. They were forced to work for upper-caste Shaitan, and they had never been content with their position. Nias quickly moved in front of the giant Daemon, grabbing the belt loop on Jade's shorts to make sure she didn't run and fall off the cliff when she saw it. Additionally he blocked the monster from a direct path to her. The bird, having recognized him as Djinn, moved forward on its human-shaped legs, trying to intimidate with its ten-foot height, and chicken-like quick jerks of its head, expanding its wings slightly, but Nias stood his ground.

Then it spoke to him.

"Well, Nias, all hail the mighty Djinn, welcome home." Its tone was bitter, sarcastic, and envious. This one Shaitan was no threat to Nias. He removed the large knife from his waist. Its height prevented the birdman from noticing the action Nias was taking. Jade jumped and released a short yelp when she saw it. He tugged at her waistband, letting her know not to move and preventing her from falling.

"Ifrit, we seek transportation to the prison of my brother. Take us to him," Nias demanded. He had every intention of using his previous status to his advantage in Sheol.

The bird gave an evil grimace and a deep chirp, almost like a cough; what it meant to do was laugh. "I do not work for you, Nias. It has been too long; you cannot order me to service just by demanding it."

"If that is your choice, bird, than I shall oblige you by putting you in your place first, and then demanding you obey me; in fact it will be my pleasure." He raised his weapon with his free hand to strike at the animal and it screamed and squawked at him. It knew alone it didn't stand a chance.

"Kitten, would you please make the creature happy to provide us with a ride. I would like to move quickly from this area and, although it would be fun, if I hurt the beast it will only slow us down." Nias used a flat tone, but he was thinking, *and give Hamartia time to catch up to us.*

"Um, okay." She closed her eyes and did her best to smile. It came out more like a grimace, but her mental ability must have worked because the birdman's demeanor changed.

"I'm sorry, Nias. I forgot my place!" It threw an immense wing in front of its bird head, and then it bowed to them going down on its knee during the pronounced gesture. "I know where Hamartia keeps Joss. I can take you to him."

When the Ifrit continued to move toward the ground, eventually going to a position on its hands and knees, Jade turned to Nias and said with a slight panic, "Wait a minute, what is it doing? Do you expect me to ride that thing, like up in the air?"

Nias turned to her and glared.

"Because that is going to be super-fun!" she said with an exaggerated sarcasm and a fake grin.

He sighed at her. And shook his head as if thinking *Woman, what am I going to do with you?*

She and Nias walked over to the beast. When she got to it, she realized she would need a step ladder to get on the thing. But she was doing this. *Get this over with,* she thought, *do this, get brother, go home curse-free, do this, get brother, go home curse- free...* it would be her new mantra. Kind of like *follow the yellow brick road*; everyone needs a mantra on an adventure.

"Do this, get brother, go home curse-free," she repeated out loud.

Nias heard her and turned to look at Jade as the Ifrit patiently waited. He was torn now; he needed to get his brother, but he had an even deeper need to see Jade through this and get her out. She was doing her best to hide her fear, but he had come to know her well enough, he knew … inside she was scared to death. A now-familiar wave of emotion went through him, and he couldn't stand to put her through this anymore.

"Listen, Jade, if you can't get on this bird and continue, I understand. Hamartia is sure to be right behind us. But it doesn't matter… Fuck." He looked at the ground and then back to her eyes. "It doesn't matter. If you can't do this… and *trust me* I can see you are talking yourself into being strong here. If you don't want to do this, I will hide us in The Verge humans, and take you back as Hamartia passes. I don't ever want to see you hurt. I want you out of here; I want you away from me and all this, forever. Say the words, and we leave."

"And then those things will come after me, and I continue to live with the curse. No, I prefer to make sure you live to speak to the Goddesses, whoever they are, on my behalf; and I am here to watch the monster chick die."

Although Joss seriously doubted his own plan, it seemed the best solution. Joss knew why the Sentry hadn't come for him yet; he should have had days before the fade. But his siblings were completely unaware of the enormity of the darkness within him. He had never wanted them to know about his differences from them. He didn't have the ability to resist sleep like they did; he was becoming so tired. He knew in another twenty-four hours it would be over. He would fade, and as sleep pulled him under, the Empusa would suck him dry of all his blood and his memories, and keep him as her thrall for any Succubus who wanted him to rape and feed from him, forever.

Or, far worse, the darkness would completely take over and swallow all of the humanity within him. He could feel it already, the darkness looming over him, slowly consuming him from the inside out. Although he was managing with sheer force of will, with his stubborn nature, to keep the beast at bay, it had managed to begin its infestation within him.

His siblings thought he kept himself isolated by choice, because it was his nature. But the truth was, he lived far away to keep them safe, because if the darkness were given free rein of his will, he had no idea what he might be capable of. He was different. He had known that since he was a child. And Iblis knew it too.

"Empusa," he said, as she stopped screeching and looked up at him. "I do like to tease you about being hideous." She began to start a wail, but he cut her off. "But I believe you are quite beautiful under all that filth, aren't you?"

She looked to him with desperation, "I am beautiful! And I shall have you, it will be sweet, Joss, you will enjoy me. I know you will," She leered at him, freakishly. No, he wouldn't enjoy her, but he would endure her.

"Well, I was actually considering as I stood here, I would like to make you a deal."

She looked at him again, this time a fascination on her grimy face, and she stopped her constant pacing and put her hands to the metal bars. He would have loved to touch her hands softly then, as a way of convincing her of his intentions. But she was too gross.

"Go on," she said hungrily.

"What if you didn't have to wait for my sleep? You will find my willing participation in the acts you wish to perform with me would be worth so much to you...maybe even enough for you to give me freedom?"

"Never, Iblis would kill me; he would kill us both, gladly, for disobeying him." But he could see her considering the offer. "It would be so satisfying." She released a sigh of pleasure thinking about him. He could smell her desire mounting. *That is good*, he thought.

"You could leave with me, the Djinn could protect you." He was so absolutely lying. He would use her to get out of here, as a way to gain his freedom.

"You would do this, Joss? You would take me out of here?" No, he wouldn't. But she sounded so desperate. He almost pitied her – almost.

"There is a huge condition. This is completely non-negotiable. You would have to bathe. I will give you my blood, you will have me, but you cannot look or smell like you do." She let out a hint of her former screech and looked him in the eyes. Then, he saw her utter hopelessness. And knew he was getting out.

"Let me out, I will help you." She stared at him for a while longer, considering the proposition.

"No, I will find a place to bathe and return." He could hear excitement as well as fear in her voice. He definitely did not want to give her a chance to change her mind. He was going to go with her. Even if it required touching her while she was dirty. He was leaving with her.

"Let me help you bathe, you won't regret it, I promise." And he touched her soiled fingers. She actually felt like a woman. Like a filthy woman, but he had expected her to be scaly or rough.

"Beauty, I can't resist you. I'm not sure there is a woman of any breed who could. Although there is a very good chance we will both die regretting it, I will take you." She began to laugh, with a depraved cackle.

Then she grabbed the key from her waist pocket and unlocked the gate.

The birdman Empusa used as transportation stood on the platform closest to them. When she demanded it to come to her it flew over and they mounted.

And flew to what Joss believed was her home.

A shack by his standards, the crumbling structure stood in a tropical forested area; it smelled of salted water and sand and the area was dense with tall, swaying, gray palm trees. The sky was a deep red with hints of yellow scattered throughout. They were outside of the dark zones in the Unseen. It looked like a sunset above ground in the middle of summer, when the days are hot and the expectation is that tomorrow will be as well.

Joss was still shirtless, and he had no choice but to wrap his arms around Empusa's waist as they flew. His mind was confused, vacillating between his plans to escape and then wondering what she would look like when she was cleaned up. At this point it didn't matter … he was at least out of the cage, and that was more freedom than he had had in over a week.

They dismounted the Ifrit, and Joss pulled the dirty female by the hand toward the slightly ajar, peeling, white wooden front door. Joss pushed through the door and looked around. He didn't care at all how she lived. He wanted her clean and happy and then he wanted transportation the fuck out of there.

He considered uncommitted sex with this dirty woman a tiny price to pay for his freedom. Otherworld creatures, Daemon, Rulers of the Light, and many others, male and female alike, didn't place a moral value on sex. They invested in monogamous relations only when they didn't desire anyone else. Sex, for them, was a pleasure, not a sin. But when they chose a partner it was forever. They allowed themselves perfect sexual freedom and when they were finished and found their true mate, that was it. Unfortunately many never did.

Joss knew he would be one of this type. Too much had happened. Although a true bond had always been his goal. His young life, a painful memory, had included nothing close to love. The word itself was a torment. He had dreamed of finding this evasive thing with a true mate. But now it was plain it wasn't to be.

Never one to wallow in pity, he had accepted this and committed himself to the pleasures he could still enjoy, sex being one of his favorites. Okay, his absolute favorite.

A human had come up with the theory sex was a sin, and the rest of the humans had believed it. The Light and Dark alike considered it amusing that it was thought of this way. One of the only things they did agree upon, actually. The Daemon had tried to dispel the lie, even the Djinn had tried above ground. But it was so ingrained the humans had chosen to believe anyway. Things people were sent to Hell for were horrific and gruesome, not fun. The whole notion was ridiculous.

They made their way through the door. Empusa's home was simple but clean. It looked like she hadn't been there in a while.

"How is it this place is so clean while you keep yourself so filthy?" he said, as he headed for the back of her sparse front room.

"I am rarely allowed to come here." He could hear the sad undertone in her voice.

"Do you even know where the shower is?" he said, as he looked back at her. Her hair was still matted and stringy and her dress was a brownish mess. She smelled faintly of sex, old blood, and other things he didn't want to decipher. When she noticed him looking at her in the brighter light of the red sky, she seemed to become nervous and ashamed. She didn't seem to be used to people evaluating her aesthetically.

She pointed a soiled finger at a door in the back of the home and he rushed her into the room behind it. An old, slightly rusted, claw-foot tub stood at the wall toward the back of the, at one time, white room. The back wall had been torn out, or maybe it had decayed. Regardless, the room stood open to the trees with scraps of palapa and thin wood exposed to the forested land.

He turned the water on, running his fingers underneath and waited for it to warm only slightly. The air was so hot that keeping the water cool would be far more comfortable.

"Soap?" He was going to get down to business; this would not be a production. He would make sure she got in and would give her a thorough wash.

"I think I would prefer a few minutes of privacy, actually," she mumbled to the floor, and then surprised him even further by saying, "You could end me now, Joss." She looked at him as he stood waiting for the water. He looked at her like she was nuts. Then he remembered, indeed she might be. Even so, the sincerity and vulnerability in her last two statements were not lost on him. "You are far stronger than I am. Nothing is in your way. We are alone. I wonder why you don't." Her voice was so ordinary when she wanted it to be, when she was calm.

"You don't care, do you?" He sat on the edge of the metal tub looking at her.

"I do," she said with a deflated lilt. "But you would have done it by now." She raised her eyes to his. "I am just pointing out the obvious to you, that you have chosen not to. You are an interesting man, full of contradictions." The corner of her mouth raised in what looked to him almost like a smile before she looked away again. Odd, he was suddenly thinking the same thing about her.

He tilted his head as he perused the woman, and realized that was what he was starting to think of her as, odd, not evil. "Look at me." She raised her head. "I have no intention of hurting you anymore. I will stick to my deal, if you will." Except he wouldn't take a killer above ground. He would not lead a Succubus, even an emotionally wounded one, to a trough of defenseless blood victims. She would have to stay in Sheol.

"I don't kill, Joss. I never have. I have ended no one. I can almost see you thinking I am a killer. You said it out loud earlier. My job isn't as a torturer or a Protector, I am a just a Watcher. I consume blood like you do, for food; I have sex like you do, because I enjoy it."

"Even if I believed that, you prey on the unwilling. Nonconsensual sex and bloodletting is something I would never wish upon anyone, Empusa. You are a Watcher and a literal nightmare. Please do not tell me you have never done this. You are a notorious taker from

The Verge."

"Beauty, the only things I leave behind are wet dreams, full of sex and pleasure. A few holes and an iron deficiency are my worst crimes. The sex I give should be considered a gift. It is the most pleasure anyone in The Verge will ever feel again. I wait for them to fall and take them. They wake happy." She took her dress off, exposing nothing underneath but dirty, incredibly feminine curves and sunk her body into the warm water. "I know you know what my kind are capable of. I never take a Verge human more than once. They survive after being with me. My many sisters and brothers are not so magnanimous."

"I am not going to win. Discussing sex with a succubus is like discussing blood with a mosquito." He tilted his head and looked at her. The dirt was beginning to lift off of her body revealing … quite a bit. He turned and left the room, shaking his head and laughing a bit at her comments – "a few holes and an iron deficiency?"

Her screams were the next thing he heard. Then a cringe-inducing rip of metal, water hitting the floor, and the excruciating screeching he had heard her make as he insulted her from the imprisoning cage. But it was broken. It was being stopped in between thrashing blows. As she was being beaten her voice was being knocked out of her. Joss ran to the kitchen in the front of the house and found a large, jagged knife. He felt an uncontrolled fury. Whatever was hurting her would be ended.

Running barefoot across old wooden boards he placed his hand on the loose door knob and crashed into the room. Her body was thrown against the door and something moved to kneel before her as he began to push through.

The being stood, a black giant, visible through the crack Joss was creating by force. It dragged the female's body from the door and tossed it easily to the side, slamming her against the overturned tub and sending more water onto the floor.

When Joss was able to open the door completely to view the small, devastated room, he saw the Daemon and couldn't help but freeze, shocked by what, and who, it was.

The enormous male stood at more than seven feet tall. Red sky cast it in shadow and it appeared, a dark blue-black angel of death, with black-feathered wings and a naked chest of muscle, sculpted like metal. Hard-cut power pulsed from it. It wore a pair of black-leather pants fashioned from a raw, uncured animal hide. Curled horns came from its head and its disturbing chiseled face smirked.

"Welcome home, son," Iblis said in deeply amused and heavily accented speech. Joss fell back against the wall behind him, the shock of it and its sheer malevolent power knocking him off his feet.

The dark angel walked toward him and took him by the throat with long, sharp fingernails. It took an immense amount of pleasure in piercing them into Joss's neck. Iblis leaned in close. Joss felt his hot breath waft into his nostrils. His father flicked his tongue at Joss's cheek and kissed him sweetly.

"Hello, baby boy." And then he proceeded to tear Joss's flesh to ribbons.

Chapter 23

Jade looked at Nias incredulously, and then pushed him roughly aside. "Really, I am fine to do this," she said, as she walked right up to their bizarre mode of transportation, grabbed a hold of its back, and strained to pull herself up, throwing her leg up and over it, as if on a horse. "Ha! I did it!" she said, as she sat up and gave a glowing smile.

"So I guess we are moving forward." He shook his head and smiled at her with apprehension and more than a bit of concern before he also mounted the bird. He put his huge muscled arms around her waist and pulled her against him. Even separated by the backpack, being right between his legs, a place she could fondly remember licking not forty-eight hours ago, made her turn around to stare at him. Big, sparkling, erotic golden eyes looked back. His lips were two inches from hers and it felt like he stared straight into her soul for a second. Then a deep growl came from within him. Somewhere no human growl could come from, and he deliberately moved backward and yelled at the Ifrit, "Yaa!" He took the thick chain around its neck and placed it in her hands, with his to the outside.

"Ifrit, take us to Joss. Jade, hold on to these reins like your life depends on it, because it does."

The half-man half-bird stood on his legs, ran, and jumped off the cliff, taking flight. Its massive wings pumped beneath them.

They were abruptly weightless, soaring through a heat wave in a swirling fire-colored sky. The air which pulled at her hair loosened it from the knot Nias had placed there. She felt his hand scoop it into a solid mass and hold it in place, pulling enough to run a shock of dark pleasure through her body. He left one of his hands on the reins, and she felt like she had become bound by the other.

The Ifrit dove down toward the water and barely left enough room for their legs to hang as it passed over spitting patches of molten lava coming up through the surface. As the bird cleared the grotto the gigantic ledges pulled away and the sky opened up. They were surrounded by an evil beauty so profound it took her breath away. She closed her eyes for a moment to feel the hot air stretching across her face and knew the euphoria could only be completed by his touch. As he didn't seem to be offering, she moved backward. Her back and weapons still separated them, but her bottom was against his denim-covered sex and his legs pressed against hers, holding the two of them together. She closed those few inches that had seemed like miles. He must not have minded as he intensified the grasp on her hair, pulling her in even more and silently curling his arm, which held the reins, around her. She shuddered and exhaled.

And then the pain-filled horror of the damned came shooting through her brain. The sheer nightmare of the agony would have struck anyone with terror, but as she was empathic, she could actually feel the horror and pain they felt. She couldn't feel the actual infliction, only the misery accompanying it, but that was more than enough.

Nias could feel Jade's body jolt violently when it hit her and he knew she was feeling intense pain. She grabbed her head in her hands and moaned.

"Ahhh, my head. It hurts, Nias," she screamed. "It feels like my brains are going to explode right out of my skull!"

"What can I do to help?" Nias said helplessly in a flat, calm tone. He placed his hands over hers and squeezed slightly, trying to help using a little pressure, then began rubbing two of his fingers at her temple while she bent over and continued to moan softly.

The wind was still shooting past them as the Ifrit continued moving through the air. But there was a sudden shift and the bird started heading in a different direction; it was going down toward the screaming – and fast. Nias shifted Jade and tilted her face up toward him to see her, feeling powerless over her pain. He knew the mental influence she had over the Ifrit had faltered when the pain had become too intense for her.

The sky seemed to melt away, changing from the beauty of fiery oranges into a mean flurry of blues. Intricately laced bright blue, mixed with navy and royal, darkening to shadows.

Nias pulled back on the chain around the birdman's neck, and it made a choking sound, but continued to dive toward the ground.

"Dammit, Ifrit do not put us down here!" Nias boomed, realizing it was the malevolence below Jade she was being assaulted by. They were coming in toward a landing on the ground; there was nothing he could do about it. "Kitten, can you hear me? We are going down." It seemed as though she could hear him, but he could tell there was no way she was going to be able to function when the bird landed and pushed them off.

They were about twenty feet from the ground when Jade could clearly see the fires and realized they were headed for a crash landing in the middle of a death zone. The Ifrit landed roughly and immediately stood shaking them to the ground.

Before Jade even saw him move, Nias had the knife in his hand and the bird's feathery throat slashed, just below the metal chain they had used to hold on with. It put its feathered claws over the gushing wound and its eyes looked around panicking, like it was looking for help and knew it wasn't going to find any.

Nias put his boot on the thing's chest and pushed it to the

ground violently. "I warned you! I am only sad I cannot draw out your pain before you end. Causing Jade to hurt as you did was the worst affront you could have made to me." Nias pushed it to the side with the toe of his boot in anger, but by the time his words of hatred had finished the thing was already gone; whatever life force that had been inside it no longer remained.

Jade was shocked by the violence Nias had exhibited in assaulting the creature. But as it had stranded them in a barren land full of fire and screaming, she was glad he had killed it.

They stood behind a rock formation similar to the ones she had seen in The Verge. She could see the light of the fires coming up over the rock and the screams were piercing. But her mind strayed away from the terrain as she thought, *Did he just say causing me pain was the worst thing it could have done to him?* She felt her heart swell, and found instead of being disgusted by the violence of the act, it was his words she was focusing on and they caused her to feel hope. *I am so not right,* she thought to herself.

Her eyes began to focus and she looked around at the landscape; and if it were possible, it was even more bleak than that of The Verge. The rocks were all the same sickly shade of beige, depressing and morose, but punctuated by flames that shot up like terrible geysers. They licked at their periphery like they were living things, desiring to reach in and consume them both. She was sure Nias being here was the only thing stopping the seemingly living tongues of fire from engulfing her in their deadly embrace.

Unfortunately, to add to the negative atmosphere, the pain in her head was coming back. Although her immediate impulse was to clutch it and smash it with her hands, she knew they needed to move forward. Banging her head against a rock, no matter what imagined release it might bring, did not seem to be the best course of action. And standing here staring at Nias didn't hold any promise of alleviating things, either, as delightful as that would be. He was right next to her, and she reached out to grab his arm, hoping it might somehow help. She squinted, trying to block out some of the now-piercing light.

"Jade, I need you to come with me while I look around these rocks and see what we are going to face here. How are you feeling?"

She was sure he would be able to see the pain was back, so she made an extra effort to smile and say, "I am great now, thank you so much for your help." She couldn't keep the sarcasm out of her voice or the stupid grin off of her face. "I'm sorry, can you just wait one minute?" Her voice softened as she pulled the backpack off and placed it on the ground, unzipped the large middle section and found the water she had inside. After taking several huge sips she offered it to Nias, while she took one of the power bars from inside the pack and tore it open. She almost puked when the sweet smell mixed with her headache, but took a bite anyway. She took two more as Nias drank the water and she watched him put the cap back on and place it back in the bag.

She knew he didn't need food like she did. After drinking from his wrist and realizing how it had affected her, and his response, she wanted to know what it would be like to reciprocate. She actually pushed her hair over her shoulder to expose her neck. She pulled at the skin a little while she imagined it happening.

But Nias never saw her actions because he spun around like he had eyes in the back of his head and sent a quick Chuck Norris-like side kick into the bare stomach of a testosterone-laden male Shaitan wearing a strange wrap around his hips, with curled horns protruding though his wavy black hair.

The Shaitan flew back, but never hit the ground because there were several more that looked almost exactly like him to catch him before he landed. These males were coming straight for her.

Jade didn't have time to think about which weapon to use. As the closest "man" reached for her, she grabbed his hands and pulled them in sharply, like Nias had showed her. She ducked underneath him and he flipped over her, landing flat on his back. She turned to finish him, but before she knew what was happening Nias put his boot on its neck, twisted, and cracked it. As she stood there, stunned, Nias shouted, "Jade, look behind you!" But she had no time to react and something smacked her down to the red earth below them. It startled her and started to swing a clawed hand down on her neck when the fear inside her manifested and smacked it, and it flew backward, seemingly on its own. Once again she had used a power she had no idea she possessed, but this was not exactly the moment to sit and ponder it. Quickly she got to her feet and hid behind Nias's back, because she saw several more coming toward them and she was having a small moment of terror.

Then she heard Nias confidently say in a sarcastic tone, "This is a great time for you to use your skills, Jade." She closed her eyes and pressed up against his back like a thief hiding behind a corner would press himself against a wall, and focused her mind. The pain tried to prevent her from pushing anything out. She tried desperately to stop her own fear from taking over completely and finally found some clarity. She thought about the opposite of aggression and got peace, calm, serenity. She centered herself, concentrating on those feelings and pushed the message out of her mind and into the minds of the Daemons, while Nias prevented any of the group from taking them down.

Jade felt the shift as the effects of her power altered their mood, and they slowed their movements.

"Jade, take my hand," she heard Nias say, and when she opened her eyes she saw his open hand next to her. She latched onto it. "We are going to walk away right now!" He spoke again with a calm authority she knew meant, "Move now!" He turned around to move them toward the side of the rock formation and around to who knows where. But as he did, she caught a view of the Daemon they had been fighting and there had to be twenty of them now. She began to run, keeping a firm grip on the mental control that was the only thing slowing down the Shaitan.

Nias continued to hold on to Jade's hand as they ran around the side of the huge boulder. They came to a wooden bridge similar to the one that crossed the chasm between the two cliffs in the Verge. This time, though, Nias wanted to put as much space between Jade and the vicious Shaitan as he could, so throwing caution to the wind, he ran across the dusty, barren, red earth and continued to move as quickly as he could across the rickety bridge. Jade held on to his hand and he never had to look back to know she was no longer frozen in panic but moving forward with a strength that continued to amaze him. Having her hand in his and finding a safe place for them was the only thing he could think of.

When they safely exited the overpass he used his knife to cut the eight ropes which held it to both sides of the precipice.

"Hey, what are you doing? Are you sure there is another way out of here?"

"I am completely sure if they end me and kill you, our time together will end abruptly. And so an alternative route will have to be found. It is possible to keep going through the bottom and get out of here. But that will be used as our last alternative, I can assure you." He spoke quickly and urgently as he severed the last rope.

"Don't even tell me. I don't want to know why," she stated bluntly.

"Keep walking, I would prefer if they had no idea which way we are headed. If Hamartia should come by with some Ifrits, they could join her and come after us."

"They are really strong; they are fighters or guards of some sort, aren't they?"

Nias said nothing; he thought silence was the best course of action. He did not want to explain how much of a miracle it was they had both left with their lives. The Shaitan they had faced were the same caste of Protectors Iblis himself used for his personal guards. And when you are that evil and do as much harm as the Dark Father did you needed an amazingly relentless, vicious group to serve as protection. They would not only desecrate her body and mind; they would greatly enjoy every minute of it. As a gift for good behavior, Iblis gave a Protector a new murderer to play with for a few hundred years. Sometimes one of these Shaitan would become so powerful from the pleasure derived from the torture, Iblis would have to end its existence. Many Protector Shaitan considered the torment they inflicted during the time spent with the damned human well worth dying for. They were sick fucks he never wanted to see near Jade again.

Nias continued to walk Jade through a winding maze of caverns for about an hour until he was absolutely sure he had lost the Protectors, and anything else that could have been following them. When he got them to a large sand-filled cave, he took the opportunity to give Jade a rest inside. He knew here she was safe; it was even cool enough for her deep inside the caves. These caverns were an old stomping ground of the Djinn. Phaeton, Ella, Locke, and himself had come here to hide out when they couldn't stand to be around their homes any longer. Sometimes they had spent days together up here, in these black rocks.

He stared down at her as she sat in the sand and leaned up against the rock wall. Nias had tried desperately to not let Jade into his heart. He knew he felt strongly for her, and he had realized it would be next to impossible to let her go. She was the solitary thing in his endless lifetime that had made him happy. Truly happy, for no reason except for the fact he now realized he loved her and it was tearing his heart out. There was a pain inside Nias stronger than any he had ever felt. Being with Jade in the pack of deadly Shaitan had shown him it wasn't only that he cared for her; it wasn't just that he didn't want to let her go. She was no one's possession. She was the woman he loved.

Before he met her Nias could have never even said he knew what the hell that meant. But it ripped him apart because he knew they could never, under any circumstances, be together. His Father would kill her. Like he had killed Rachel, he would kill Jade. Nias could never see her hurt, and Iblis could never see him happy.

Chapter 24

The moment they entered the cavern she could see he wasn't right. Something was going on in that impenetrable head.

"What's happening? Are you okay? Do we need to leave?"

"No, we should rest for a while. It is safe here. If you need to sleep this is a perfect place to do it. When we leave here we will be going through a place where you will need all your strength. I will have to find someone who has seen Joss and can tell us where they have him. We need your mind strong."

"Are you worried about him? You look shaken. I've never seen you like this. You are the strongest man I have ever met. I'm sorry I haven't even considered what you must be going through worrying about Joss." She reached out to lightly touch his hand.

"No, he should be fine, unless he has done something stupid. He is being watched by Empusa. She is a succubus; she won't harm him until he sleeps. Djinn can easily go two weeks or longer without falling asleep. Iblis is obviously planning something which doesn't require hurting him immediately."

"You slept with me. I mean, you fell asleep with me twice in less than two weeks."

He sat heavily in the sand next to her and leaned against the wall. His proximity enveloped her like it always did. And she felt a tremor of need run through her. *God, can I not want to jump him just for a minute?*

"I wanted to, I wanted to be next to you, whether you believe me or not." He paused, as if trying to keep something from coming out. But then it tumbled from his mouth. "It has never been solely a sexual attraction between us, not for me, anyway." He turned his dirt-streaked face toward her, but didn't move the rest of his body. The sparkle in his eyes was a little fragile. He was looking at her to see what her reaction to the fraction of feeling he had exposed would be. He licked his lips and squinted a bit, as if bracing himself. She thought he looked like her reaction to his comment was truly important to him.

She exhaled and unconsciously ran her fingers through the sand. Looking down now toward her own hand she replied, "I have never in my life been as immoral a woman as I've acted with you. I have been filled with a desire for you, so strong it ached, since the moment you carried me out of that warehouse and away from those beasts. But spending this week with you has only added to that passion and you have become more to me than I even know how to explain to myself. I don't believe you lie to me. I believe you trust me and for the first time in my life I feel like I trust another person, which is honestly more than I ever thought I would find." Jade leaned over and placed her lips to his amazing cheekbone and lightly kissed him. Nias looked frozen in place for a moment, but his body showed physically how he felt about her. The stimulation made him swell so quickly in his jeans he had to slide his legs flat in the sand or be crushed in the bent position.

"Don't get me wrong, Jade." He looked toward her, the grin she loved returned to his gorgeous face. "I want you every second we aren't about to die." They both laughed. "But you should know, it has always been more than just sex with you."

Damn, she was going to kiss him. He smelled amazing, like musk and dirt and of a faint salty sweat, a smell unique to Nias. She noticed now his hair wasn't perfect any more, either. It was messy. He leaned back against the wall, his chest and stomach's lean muscle pressing though the black cotton t-shirt. His massive toned bicep flexed simply because his arm was bent placing his hand on his leg. His jeans were a deep, worn-in blue with a coat of powdery dirt on them; his combat boots were covered with mud and those dirt stripes on the tanned skin of his face were begging to be cleaned off, with her tongue. He was the picture of masculine perfection, of strength and dark, broody sex. He could have been in one of those overly sexual male fragrance campaigns right then, one you see while flipping through the pages of a magazine and have to stop and glare, and say, damn. If only men actually looked like that, like they couldn't wait for you to put them in a tub of warm, soapy water and scrub them clean. Combined with the fullness of those slightly pink lips and his enormous erection, he was way more than a girl could stand to be separated from. It wasn't her fault she simply had to have at least a small piece of him attached to her body.

Before she had a chance to make a decision, her body made one for her. She got to her knees and slid one of her legs to the opposite side of his lap, straddling him. Suddenly she was just there. His back was against the wall and he bent his knees back up, holding her between muscled thighs and rock-hard abs, and rock-hard erection, and she wiggled her way right into the middle. As soon as her sex landed on his, it was over. She leaned in next to his ear and purred.

"I have missed that sound, Kitten," he said, putting his hands on her waist. He was still somewhat docile, maybe a little stunned, by the conversation.

"I miss having a reason to make it," she rasped. "I want to have all of you." She *really* did. He felt so good, her body ached to have him fill her completely.

"Elucidate," he teased.

Nias cocked an interested brow and looked like the incarnation of lust itself, with a sharp, wicked, golden stare so hungry it would have scared her if she weren't so turned on by it.

"You know exactly what I mean." She matched his glare. "You just want me to say nasty things to you because it pleases you to turn my innocence into a dirty plaything."

A sinister growl came from him. "Yes, it does. So go on, I'm listening." His fingers tightened on her waist and then began to wander down to her ass, which, in this position, hung out of her shorts, giving his hands plenty of access to skin.

"You are going to make me spell it out for you, aren't you?"

"I would love it, Kitten. It is so much more fun that way." His words were so arrogant, but the look on his face was anything but. His face belied his true feelings, feelings matched by her. Feelings of need, want, desire, and ultimately, love. That was the only word she could put to it. How could she have missed it before? He looked at her like he loved her. And she loved him right back.

"I want you to make love to me. I want you to be my first. We have never promised each other anything permanent. I'm not asking for it now. I just want you inside me. I need you inside me. I don't want to wait anymore."

"My sweet Kitten, you are killing me." He growled even louder than before. "I just don't know if you're thinking clearly right now. There is too much happening. The situation around us is frightening. I love that you come to me for comfort. Your body, your touch, brings me to rapture. But this is a decision human women consider precious; it should be special for you. I have a rough edge, I can be demanding, I am sarcastic and, much of the time, an ass." He smirked as if almost proud of these flaws. "But I have formed a desire to keep you safe and make you happy, which, much to my regret at this moment, includes protecting you, even from me." He kissed her fiercely and pulled her body into his by moving his hand from her rear. Rubbing his hand up and down her back, his kisses came to her as sweet pecks.

Jade sighed. "You are so much sweeter than you allow people to know. You need to be careful, because I am about to mistake you for someone worthy of my heart," she teased, not wanting him to know she already felt that way. "Now, if you can stop being mushy, I would very much appreciate it. I assure you, I am a grown woman, and am in no way unsure about my decision, to have you screw my brains out."

"I will be as gentle as I can, which I'm afraid isn't going to be very gentle at all."

"I expected nothing less."

A growl came now from deep within him. And his erection bucked underneath her. His hands fisted her hair on both sides and pulled her in and slowly those unbelievable soft lips connected and conquered her. On every level of her being she burned for him. His tongue was passion; it was thirst. He was savoring her mouth and her tongue like a man who had been in the desert and was getting not a drink, but a swim in an entire pool. He consumed her.

Nias wanted Jade so badly right then, his need became overwhelming. Hearing her tell him how she felt so much more for him than he suspected had him burning for her. He wanted to fill her completely. He needed to taste her again and have every part of them connected. Her tongue coiled with his and he could feel the burning heat from between her legs. He could smell her need for him, her wetness. He pulled back because he knew it would make her cry out for him to return to kissing her. Except he bit her bottom lip and pulled on his way back, and when she pressed her lips together to grimace at him he licked right through the tight center of those pouting lips with the tip of his tongue, a forewarning of what he wanted to do to her.

He put his hands at the bottom of her tank top, the one he had picked out for her with the panther on it. He smiled at his decision now, thinking about how, when he had transcended to purchase it, he had dreamed of ripping it off of her perfect breasts. But seeing as she didn't have anything else to wear he pulled it up over her head, leaving it intact. When he did, it caught the long mass of auburn curls and they slid through, flopping down to her back when he reached the end. He pulled her hair into a tight ponytail, twisting it around his fingers and used it as a rein to steer her neck toward his mouth. He ran his tongue up her neck and over the large vein, which he could feel throbbing beneath her smooth skin. He could almost taste the blood running through her, and had to smash the urge to cut a tiny hole in her neck with his incisors and taste her.

"Kitten, stand for me. I want to put the blanket down so I can properly take advantage of you." She laughed, and slowly moved off of his lap. Nias reached for the backpack and took out the blanket, carefully unfolding it on the ground so as not to get sand on top of it. But as he finished straightening the corners, he felt her hands come up behind him, undo his button, and take down the zipper of his jeans. He always went commando, so that was all she needed to release him from the tight fabric and take him into her hand, and start to stroke him. The thick head and shaft didn't feel like it could get any harder until then, when it became almost painfully engorged in her hand. Then she slunk around to the front of him where he dropped her shorts to the ground, along with her pesky, unneeded bra and panties and he pulled her mouth back to his. She tasted like heaven and smelled of sunshine and plums, and he reached down to feel the moistness between her amazing thighs.

Jade couldn't take it anymore; she reached her hand around to his perfect butt and pushed him down. And he laughed out loud. His sexual energy was once again absorbing her. She was blissfully drowning in him.

She sank down next to him. His muddy black boots came off next, followed by his jeans. He took her tightened nipple into his teeth and rolled his tongue over the tip, at the same moment, three of his fingers thrust into her. She shuddered at the instantaneous shock of pleasure ripping through her entire body. His fingers plunged deeper and moved within her, carefully circling that perfect spot within her that somehow he knew was the most sensitive and erotic, and she gasped. Arching her back, she spread her legs out a bit, making more room for his hand to sink in and stroke the intense pleasure point.

"I want you inside me, now!" She was so hot, she couldn't bear it anymore.

He pulled up on top of her to look her in the eyes and kiss each one. He was resting with both his forearms on the blanket.

"You are sure about this, right?"

"Why, aren't you?" She was feeling a bit nervous until she heard him moan out the words "Oh no, I'm quite sure." He licked her lips quickly and then opened her mouth with his tongue to kiss her.

Nias's hand slid back down past the skin between her breasts, over her rounded belly, through her coarse curls, and finally traced the moist line between her legs. She was ready for him.

"Take me, sweetheart, take me in your hand and make yourself feel good. I want to see you pleasure yourself with my cock. I can go as slow or as hard as you want me to." He bent his head down to the space of skin which rested between the base of her neck and her shoulder and licked. He kissed and nipped the sensitive flesh up her neck and her ear, then back down. Her body sparkled in a light sheen of sweat, need, and heat.

Gently he guided her hand to his rock-hard arousal. Jade placed its swollen head at her cleft and began to rock as she ran it around her sensitive bud, and she moaned aloud. The feel of the thick, warm mass rubbing over her was making a tight, unbelievable ache pulse from between her legs and low in her belly.

"That's right, Kitten, make it perfect. I want to see and feel you come for me. Look in my eyes."

She did. She looked into his eyes and the blaze of lust he felt was all over his beautiful face. It made the ache stronger and the pleasure pulse harder and it rose as she stroked her own wetness with him.

And just when she thought the look in his eyes alone would push her over that edge, he took his shaft from her hand and pushed his way inside her.

"Ahh!" She wanted to weep, he was stretching her and the sensation was amazing, and he continued to fill her a few inches at a time. Out and then slipping back in a bit further with each stroke, until she could feel him reach her barrier. When he pushed through, he bit down on those tendons at the base of her shoulder and neck and the feeling of the pain spread between the two centers. She screamed and smiled because the pain his teeth caused at her neck was exquisite and the sharpness inside her was immediately replaced by his massive, complete fullness. When she thought she had taken him completely, Nias put his arm underneath her bottom and pulled her hips upwards. The angle allowed him greater ease to push himself the rest of the way in, and he began to rock his hips back and forth, gliding his thick mass in and out of her.

"Oh, my God," she cried, "that is amazing."

He hissed as he nuzzled her neck, his voice muffled. "Are you all right? Should I slow down?"

"No, go faster," she said as he placed her bottom back to the softness of the blanket-covered sand. She put her arms around his neck and her hips fell into the rhythmic thrust with him.

He began to pound inside of her and the feeling rose from that same point his fingers had stroked earlier, but the sensation was so much stronger. And without her approval, her mouth began to release moans, which came from deep inside her chest as the pressure grew.

He yanked her hair back to whisper in her ear, "I have never seen or heard anything as beautiful as you are to me right now." He said it with a sweetness, contrary to the pounding, animalistic movement of his body.

Jade did her best to focus on his eyes, but each time she moaned her eyes wanted to close. His hand ran back between her legs and started to rub her cleft in time with his thrusts and she thought she would come apart at the seams. The tight pressure pulled itself out from inside of her, where his burning arousal touched. And outside, at her tight nub, her body vibrated. She became liquid beneath him.

Her explosion came in endless waves through her core. She looked straight into Nias's eyes as her entire being turned to a melting, liquid heat and the tremors became fierce. He was relentless as he accelerated the pounding of his hips and the circular stroking of his fingers and she came completely undone during her climax.

She started to convulse slightly and come back to earth, and realized her nails were dug deep into his back. Her claw-like nails had torn long scratch marks the length of his back and she was still piercing into his flesh when she felt him release, letting out a roar of pleasure. He crushed his lips to hers and wound his tongue around hers in his last deep thrusts of passion.

Satiated she kissed him, and melted into the soft earth.

Before she realized it, she was stretching and awakening. Looking around as Nias still had her tangled up with him, she asked, "How long?"

He chuckled and stroked her flaming red hair. "A couple of hours. Don't worry, I stayed awake, no one came near while you were out. But unfortunately, we need to get moving again."

She slowly, reluctantly, untangled herself, then forced herself to dress. He was up, dressed, and ready to go by the time she shook off the haze of her intense, lingering pleasure. He hugged her close and kissed her passionately. Then he took her shaking hand and intertwined it into his rough, warm, dirty fingers. He looked into her eyes and kissed the top of her hand, smiling.

"I wish my hands always smelled of your sex," he teased.

"Um, ew!"

"Humans have the strangest hang-ups," Nias said. Jade turned her head toward him and squinted her eyes, smiling, then she

switched his hands, holding the other instead. He rolled his eyes
at her and laughed.

Chapter 25

When they reached the bottom of the rocks, he stopped. "We are going to have to move fast when we reach the roads. We will be out in the open; the Shaitan and Iblis himself will be looking for us. There is no doubt they informed him of our last position and Hamartia may have joined him by now. Remember to stay close. Use your capabilities whenever possible." Then he sighed deeply, having one more request of her. "There is one more thing. I need nourishment."

"What does that mean? You need blood?"

"I'm sorry, but yes."

"I had actually been thinking you might. I'm ready."

Nias reached for her wrist, but Jade pulled it away. Pulling her hair to the side, she offered her neck.

"That might hurt," he said, but it made him hard to think about it. Her neck was pale and the vein smelled so good.

"It'll be faster and I'll feel better with you closer; you know it won't hurt me," she said, the second part of the sentence in a mumble, staring at the ground. He knew he would enjoy it too much, even in this situation. His body felt as if it were on fire, and he licked his lips in anticipation. He didn't know if he could bear to be bonded even more with her and then leave her, but he had no choice.

"The bond between us will be complete when I take your blood. We will be connected." Jade shook her head and continued to offer, stepping closer. He could feel the heat of her body at her approach, could smell her sweet scent; and as he needed the strength to face Iblis, and didn't have any resistance left, he dove in to take the sweet nectar he craved.

Jade felt his teeth punch a hole in her throat and his arm wrap around her waist, and she felt ecstasy. He drew from her and she shook; it was amazing. After several long sucks of her vein, the now-familiar feeling of orgasm began to rise from a new wetness.

"Kitten, I'm going to have to fuck you again if you react this way," he said as he pulled back only enough for her to see his moist, red lips and raised brows.

He went back to her neck. His finger went under her shorts and between her thighs, stroking through the line of her nether lips.

It was right when she moaned that she opened her eyes and saw the dark shadows move beyond the rocks and fire.

Hamartia came toward them with fury in her eyes.

"I see you have found each other." She was stalking toward them with the rancid and worn fabric of her dress flowing around her. Her matted dreads did nothing to make her look any less untamed. Ten Marid Protectors were with her, and Nias cursed under his breath. He could see Jade begin to reach for the sword she had replaced on her back.

Nias moved his hand to the one she had raised toward the weapon, gently taking hold of her wrist and bringing it back down close to her hip.

"Easy," he smiled at her, with a hint of pride curving the corners of his lips. Nias thought it best to find an angle to deal with this situation. Ten Marid Protectors could not be easily defeated by a human and a Djinn directly. He would need some advantage, which, at the moment, wasn't before them.

Nias leaned in to Jade and whispered to her, "Do not use your power against them yet. If they take us we will finally be with Joss and the three of us will have a better chance of defeating them and finding our way above ground and safety. We need to find out where Joss is." She nodded her head in acquiescence to his plans; which, considering how she liked to do exactly what she wanted, whenever she wanted to, relieved him greatly.

"Nias!" Hamartia screamed at him. "Stop whispering to the human. You said you would discard her. Instead you followed her into Sheol without the Sentry to back you. And I can smell her sex all over you." She looked ferocious, and he had a pretty good idea why.

"Jealous, are we dear?" he said sardonically, not caring if he made her even madder.

"Do you find me funny, Nias? Human, do you think he finds me funny?" She continued to yell her words at them and fisted the sides of her dress. She motioned to the Protectors to move toward her with a sideways wave of her hand, and then proceeded even closer to the two of them. Nias clutched Jade's hand and saw Hamartia watch the movement and twitch noticeably. As she came closer the smell of decaying flesh came with her.

Nias responded with another volley of words. "I believe you have some crusted blood on your chin, darling. If you hope to entice me, you might want to wipe your mouth of the damned." He talked to her nonchalantly, but his defenses were keenly aware of the placement of every Protector and exactly which way he would move his hand to retrieve his knife from the back of his jeans, where he had it tucked. One hand in Jade's and one upturned behind him, he was ready to kill quickly if they came at him.

"Human," Hamartia said to Jade, but then swung a look of triumph quickly over to Nias. "Let me tell you a story that is truly funny. Have you heard of Rachel, human?" A low growl began to escape from Nias's throat before he even recognized he was angry at her remark.

"Not laughing now, Nias? Trust me; we have been keeping her busy for you." Hamartia's mouth went crooked and slightly upturned on one side and then she sputtered what seemed a sad, crackled version of a giggle; as if she so rarely attempted such a thing, it actually hurt. "Humans are just too fragile. You should never get attached. I thought you learned that last year. But apparently you forgot, because here we are again, human at your side and your obvious affection oozing out of you."

He took a step towards her. "She is baiting you. Stay still," Jade said, holding her hand out to stop Nias from moving. He was surprised she felt confident enough to speak, and it helped to keep him focused. It was their only chance to get out of this alive.

"She tells you what to do!" Hamartia yelled. "Stupid, overconfident human."

Nias softly placed his hand over the one Jade was using to attempt to constrain him, and recovered his sarcastic manner. "Contain yourself, Hamartia, don't get your panties all bunched up and start laughing all in the same moment, you might hurt yourself over there. If I could call that a laugh; really it was just creepy."

Jade spoke up. "Whoever she was, Hamartia, she has nothing to do with me. It was a long time ago, none of my business. Do what you intend to do, or go away." Nias squeezed her hand. He could feel Jade push at Hamartia's emotion with her mind. But there was no noticeable change. She wasn't strong enough to fight Hamartia mentally and he wouldn't allow her to do it physically.

"Rachel was the last human to be close to Nias, and coldbloodedly, he let her die and left her for Sheol. He has never come for her, not that it would have done any good." She cackled.

Nias wanted to slice her heart out for even speaking Rachel's name, but the emotion of what she was saying crashed into him. All the pain of it seared him. He had killed her, it was true, and he could no longer protect the rest. He was a danger to anyone around him and an impotent ruler. He would stand up to her, but the emotion connected to her truthful words made him hang his head toward the ground and catch his breath.

Hamartia pressed her advantage as she paced around them. "Nias found Rachel and fed her to the Shaitan. He brought her to die. Didn't you, Nias? And now, human, do you think you will be different?" She gritted her pointed, moldy teeth and growled. "You think I'm stupid. More than anyone, I know you cannot view his perfection, spend time with the strength of his intoxicating energy and not love him. It can't be done. You have strength, more than Rachel ever had, but you have kissed him, lain with his notorious appetites and his flawless body. You still reek of desire for him." Again she gnashed her teeth at Jade and saliva came from her bloody mouth. "You love him, and even if you knew the whole truth, you would stay with him. I am an ugly female but do not be fooled, I am female. I know how you feel, human."

Jade turned to track Hamartia and kept her in her sights. "You have no idea what I feel, monster. You and I are nothing alike. You do not feel like I do. You could never love like I do." Jade wanted to yell back at the ghoul that Nias felt as strongly about her as she did about him, but she knew it wasn't the case. And yelling back at the beast "someday he will love me with all his soul, as soon as I can convince him to" probably wasn't a persuasive argument in her favor. What she did know was, Nias was a good man, an unruly pain in the backside, but the most caring person she had ever met. She couldn't believe Hamartia was telling the truth; there was more to the story, she could feel it. Not that the beast was lying outright, but that it was a lie of omission. Her intuitions or powers seemed to be increasing. She had never before been able to tell if something was a half-truth. And she had never before been able to assault anyone physically by using a mental control. In all the time she had had these powers they had remained constant, never increased, and now, suddenly, she was capable of more. She could feel energy welling up inside of her.

Jade gripped Nias's hand because she could feel he needed her. She would be his advocate even if he couldn't be his own right then. She was done being the follower. It was time for her to take the lead.

She closed her eyes, conjured up a giant nasty ball of power and threw it at Hamartia. The invisible force hit her in the side of her head. It smacked Hamartia's skull like a jagged rock and left a bleeding open gash to show for itself. Jade was so pleased she closed her eyes and hurled another, and another. One was slamming her in the stomach, knocking out all her air, and the next slapping a force to her cheek that resounded with a crack and broke the bone at its center, right under her eye.

As the Protectors rushed them, Nias drew his knife and Jade pulled out her sword. They stood back to back, ready to take on the entire faction one by one until one of the groups was extinguished and the other victorious.

Chapter 26

Jade saw a shadow and looked up to witness the gargantuan black-and-blue angel of death fly down from the angry cobalt skies like a living nightmare. A macabre energy reeked from its bloody skin; the thud, swish, thud, swish of enormous feathery black wings slowing and lowering its giant body to the ground in front of them. Deep belligerent cursing emanated from its mouth and a seething, vicious anger came from its piercing glare.

The malevolent glower moved from Jade and Nias to Hamartia and the Protectors, where it remained.

"Hamartia, you will not touch them," the deep male voice boomed. "And give me space," he said as he continued to flap the black wings hovering above them. Hamartia and her faction cowered and jumped back to create room for their leader.

He landed extremely close to Hamartia and she winced and put her head down and to the side, as if bracing herself for his wrath. "I put you in charge of collecting a small group of my Djinn progeny and you have made a ridiculous mess of the entire endeavor. Nias stands before you ready to kill you all. You think you can take him on and win?" The creature didn't laugh; he moved his bloodied hand and lengthy claws back and struck her in her already-bleeding head wound. The force of the blow sent her flying a dozen feet through the air and he didn't seem like he had even strained to create the impact. Stalking his giant frame and half-collapsed wings up to her feet, he glared down upon her, his aura that of a treacherous storm.

"He would kill half of these men without losing breath, and with the help of the girl it seems they would have taken the lot of you with ease. Your job was to cage him, collect all the siblings, and report to me. I heard you lecturing him like a jealous child. You are my servant, my disgusting soiled used toy, not worthy of his waste." He kicked her as an afterthought, but it seemed to break something inside her because she curled into a fetal position and shrunk away at the impact.

"I am sorry, Iblis, I can fix everything. I will fix it," she begged, with her face in the ground.

"After all I have gone through, all I have plotted, to get Nias back to Sheol, you think you can now simply confront him? You stupid … If he were so easy to defeat do you not think I would have just sent Shaitan to bring him to me? I had to have you bring his worthless brother as bait to bring him here!" The giant dark angel pushed at her again with his toe and she rolled to her side. Cowering, she put her hands to her face. Jade was scared of the woman; this woman had ripped Jade from her life twice, had her tortured, and then brought her to the entrance to Sheol. But it was less than nothing compared to the fear Iblis instilled in her. Jade pressed her back firmly against Nias. She needed to know he was there.

"I think I might like to see him kill you. I used to very much like to see you fight in the ring, Nias. Make sport of her, be my guest," Iblis went on, waving a hand to show Nias she was all his. Nias had free rein to end her. But before Jade felt Nias make a decision either way, Hamartia began to beg. Nias remained stoic, as if simply taking in everything transpiring here.

"Iblis, please!"

"Please what? Your lust has made you even stupider. I told you once how ugly and disgusting you are to me. And you want my beautiful son, my most perfect creation for a…for what…for a mate? Get away from me; go back to your pit. You are not even worth laughing at."

Hamartia pulled herself to a seated position. Something near a whimper escaped her lips. Then she called to the group of Protectors she had brought with her.

"You, come get me, we shall go." Jade could hear the hurt and anger in Hamartia's voice, but she had been humbled. Jade couldn't believe herself, but her next thought was to attack her while she was down, end her now. Nias must have felt her flinch; maybe he knew her so well now, her body's slight reaction told him she might want to lash out. So he reached his hand backward and intertwined his fingers with hers, a slight squeeze of his hand let her know he wanted her to stay still, hold their ground. Once again, he had known what she was thinking and what she needed before she even knew herself.

Several Protectors stalked forward and placed clawed hands beneath Hamartia's arms and pulled her to her feet. The Marid could definitely pass for human, Jade thought. If their massive, masculine bodies had been clothed and they had a baseball cap to cover the horns and shade the odd coloring of their skin, maybe a nail trim, it would be easy. It was frightening. Jade thought about how many of them were above ground right now passing for humans and causing the shifts in thought or decision that would turn a human into a killer, a suicide, or something else equally as horrifying.

Hamartia brushed at her dress, as if this gesture would somehow bring her back to esteem. But, as always, it was torn, bloodstained, and filthy. She kept her eyes to the ground and left, to where Jade could see that the Ifrits were waiting to lift her back to her home.

Jade felt Nias tense in her grip. Nias appeared to be done with the show his father was putting on.

"What have you done with Joss? I demand you release him to me. I am taking him home."

Iblis laughed at this. "Nias, so nice to have you back. I have always found your spirit intoxicating. But you are never leaving. This is your home again." He stated this as if he were saying, "We are having tea with lunch." It was a fact to him. Walking away from Hamartia's receding form and over to tower over the man who towered over Jade, he became even more frightening. Jade and Nias held their positions, weapons up, until Nias released her hand and curled his entire arm back behind him and around Jade's waist. He pulled her into his chest, where he wrapped her in tight, absorbing her into his hard, tense chest and abdominal muscles. She clutched his ropey forearm, gaining strength from the contact.

"You care for this human, care whether I kill her, don't you?"

"That is none of your concern." Nias gripped Jade so tight it pushed the air from her chest.

Laughing, Iblis stepped even closer and leaned in toward Jade's ear. Nias tried to back up, but the creature stopped him by grasping Nias's bicep. She thought she would puke when it sniffed her and whispered in her ear. "I can smell that you fucked him. I can see he cares if you die and therefore I will have your sweetness for my amusement whilst he watches and then kill you slowly."

Nias was living his worst nightmare. How could he let this happen? Why had he fallen in love with her when he knew it was a death sentence? "She is mine, you will not touch her. Do you understand me, you evil fuck? Do not get near her," Nias growled from deep within his chest. He was like a wild animal, ready to strike. He went into a slight crouch, crushing her within him.

"My prodigal son returns to be the hero and save the day. It is quite amusing. You killed this human the minute you let her near you. She is all but dead and you know it to be true."

Nias hated his Dark Father from the core of his being. He had stolen everything Nias had ever cared about. The Cause, Rachel, he had even been forced away from his beloved friends and siblings. Now Iblis had revealed to Jade what he was and Nias would kill him or die trying.

Jade gasped, as if she couldn't believe what she had just heard. "Did he just call you 'son'?"

Iblis threw his head back and laughed. The deep boom echoed around them and made the flames jump, as if they were excited by his pleasure.

"She doesn't know? You didn't tell her, and you brought her into Sheol? Did you tell her of Rachel, how she came to be with me? Nias, you are stupid with these frail humans. You thought to care for her and then walk her in and out of my home. You are as arrogant as ever." He continued to chuckle at Nias.

Shaking Iblis's grip from his arm, Nias held Jade firmly before she could pull away.

"Kitten, do not move. I will protect you, I promise. I will get you out of here." He felt desperate. More than anything, he wanted this woman. He loved her. He knew it would never be, but the thought of her hating him, along with everything else, was too much.

"Come with me, princess; let us go see how he intends to protect you." Iblis extended his hand out to Jade, and when she failed to move he jerked her out of Nias's grasp, readying for flight. Nias latched on to the thin fabric of Jade's tank, pulling himself with her. He had no intention of losing her. Iblis did not take flight but transcended the trio into a darkness all too familiar to Nias.

Jade was thrown into the creepiest place she had ever been and, given the past few days, that was saying a lot. The hot wind was the only thing that had remained a constant in her surroundings from the time she had begun the labyrinth that constituted Sheol.

Settling in to a new area of Sheol, a deep violent darkness pierced Jade through to her bones. The wind tore through the shadowed branches of the leafless trees, looming death winding through like a phantom in the shadows.

Iblis had transcended her, and thankfully Nias too, into an entirely new landscape. The sky was an odd dark swirl of purples and deep grays, like in a Van Gogh; it had a life of its own, almost more intricate than the grounds. Still it cast a light shadow behind the barren black trees outlining them and the victims of this realm. Hundreds, no thousands, in fact countless numbers of the dead could be seen from where they stood. The dead hung from these skeletal remnants of flora that appeared to have never truly lived. But those who hung and lay dead, it seemed, would not be given this reprieve for long because others who were clearly in the same predicament were being reawakened and afflicted all over again, by their own hand. Jade did the only thing she could and averted her eyes, staring instead at the ground.

Nias clutched Jade's waist to his body. She looked up to his eyes to tell him she would be okay and he let her stand on her own two feet.

The immense dark angel loomed behind them and practically startled her out of her skin when he gestured to signal them to follow. But Nias didn't move.

"She will see Rachel, son. It pleases me to show her my work." Iblis's eyes were lit with mirth. An evil love of the pain he caused obviously gave him joy. "Your lover will see what happens when you try to take things from me. Like an entire legion of my strongest Daemons. I warned you and because of your arrogance I took your Rachel. She was too weak. You should never have gotten so close to her, and never have left her unattended in her depression. It was your arrogance and underestimating me that killed her." He turned, almost curling his upper body toward Nias, and hissed.

There she was. The sick fuck had caused the suicide of a woman Nias loved and then hung her remains in front of him. It was devastating. It was also a message. *Abandon any hope you have, son. This life will only offer you pain. Love is beyond your reach.*

When Nias saw her he let out a moan of pain. Ripping his knife from his belt, Nias moved toward the tree and climbed up to cut her down. When the rope was cut he used it to lower her to the ground, then slowly descended the crisp branches and trunk.

Jade watched as Nias knelt to the ground and took Rachel into his arms, cradling her upper body with one flexing arm and stroking her dirty, bloody hair with the other. Jade wanted to scream. She was looking at a woman freshly cut down from a noose and she wanted to die at all the selfish thoughts going through her head. She wanted to scream at him not to touch Rachel that way. Tell him she loved him and she wanted him to love her, not this other woman. And all of these selfish feelings made Jade want to throw up. She wasn't that kind of person. That was the kind of behavior she had felt coming from others she had turned away from, that made her want to be a recluse. This man was making her crazy.

The woman now in his arms was younger than Jade. If she had to guess, Jade would say Rachel was around eighteen or nineteen. She had dirty blonde hair and skin so pale it looked translucent. Her brown knee-length skirt and what used to be white top were in tatters. Rachel wore black Mary Jane shoes with a tiny silver buckle on her muddy feet. She also had a rope burn on her neck so raw it bled, with torn, exposed blisters surrounding it.

Nias, her Nias, almost wept for this barely conscious young girl as she started to stir. At first, the girl only mumbled, but after a few moments she opened her eyes and saw him holding her. Rachel tucked her head of ruined hair into him with obvious shame and she began to whimper softly. Nias held her tight and began to rock her, the look in his eyes at once fury and utter pain. And then he left her, leaping at his father with a fury Jade had never before witnessed.

Jade's instincts took over as she went to the young woman, cradling her, as Nias and Iblis engaged in a titanic battle. All she could do was stare at the terrible fight and gently reassure the girl that everything would be all right.

Even though she had a foreboding feeling that nothing would be all right ever again.

Nias's vision went red as he leapt at his sadistic father, wanting nothing more than to tear him apart with his bare hands. He rained a few blows into Iblis's midsection before the Dark Angel growled and picked him up by the shoulders, throwing him into an outcropping away from the two women. "Come now, Nias, is that any way to treat your elders?"

Jade started to feel her flesh heat up. Nias, Iblis, even Rachel, were supposed to be here, but Jade definitely was not suited to this climate and as Nias was forced away from her, his protections started to falter. "Nias!" she shouted, and launched a wall of mental energy at Iblis that seemed to catch him by surprise, making him stumble back a couple of steps.

Iblis turned to her, sneering. "So, you do have a few tricks up your sleeve? Even better. I can't wait to kill you myself." He took a few steps towards her as Nias leapt onto his back, tearing at one of his wings. Iblis roared and reached back, flipping Nias over his body in the direction of the girls. The good news was this got him closer to them, so his protection could envelop Jade once again. The bad news was he heard and felt a sickening crunch in his wrist as he tried to catch himself.

Struggling to his feet, he noticed Rachel begin to stir and her eyes go wide at the sight of him. "Nias," she whispered, but there was no time to respond as Iblis backhanded him to the ground. And Nias realized he would have a chance in this fight, possibly, if he were free to move around. But the truth was, he couldn't with Jade here, and he couldn't go blow-for-blow with Iblis.

If he fought the only way he could win, then Jade would die from the heat. If he didn't, and lost, then Iblis would certainly kill Jade, or at least keep her here forever to torture her. There was no way out.

He held up his hand to stay his father's wrath. "Wait! Wait." Iblis paused as he could feel the eyes of both Jade and Rachel burn into him from behind. "What is it you want, old man? What will it take for you to let them and my brother go free?" He turned and went to Jade and Rachel, stroking Rachel's hair, without waiting for his father's response.

Nias was beyond grief for this girl. Rachel had become a part of his family. She was like a sibling or a child to him. He had practically adopted her when she was fifteen and only had her with him for three years. The pain in her eyes had seemed ancient.

"It is okay, sweetheart, you'll be okay. I am taking you with us now." He was tired of making promises that didn't come to pass. But now that he had finally held Rachel, he couldn't leave her. She was coming with them. He would do anything to save Jade, Rachel, and Joss.

Nias looked to the Black Angel, his father, and knew it was time to make a deal with the Devil.

A sharp gust of cold wind surrounded the entire group, and then Nias found himself in his father's throne room without Jade and Rachel.

"You cannot leave Jade to die! I will do whatever you want," Nias said, panicking.

"I have given them a cooler atmosphere. Climate change is in my power in Sheol, you know that. I wish to speak with you alone. Would you truly do anything to save your brother and the women?"

"How about I rip your scaly head off your decomposing heartless excuse for flesh."

Iblis laughed and began running two of his knifelike-nailed fingers up and down his torso, petting, admiring his own flesh. "How about you listen, you insolent child." Iblis sauntered closer, daring Nias to attack again. "I will, in exchange, let you freely walk out of Sheol with the valueless suicidal rubbish you seem to be attached to, your loathsome brother, and the human woman; although her I would like to keep, she has something, doesn't she? I mean, beyond your absurd devotion. I felt her power firsthand."

Nias raised his voice in an angry, threatening manner. "I will give you what you want, but all of this needs to stop."

"After you are out, you will return to Sheol permanently. And for this I will let your brother and the two females leave Sheol safely and remain that way."

The giant angel circled him. Nias knew Iblis was using his stature, his height, and the demented tone in his booming voice to try and intimidate Nias, but it wouldn't work. Iblis could stalk and threaten all he wanted. Nias would make his decisions based on the wellbeing of the ones he loved, never on threats or intimidation.

"I want you back. I want you to pay slowly and endlessly for taking my children. For protecting the worthless humans."

"I won't do it. You know I won't. I'm leaving. I'm taking Joss, Rachel, and I am taking Jade."

"And then what? Everything goes back the way it was, except you live happily ever after with the human?" Unrestrained evil wafted from his skin; it nearly pushed Nias from his feet. He stepped backward, righting himself. "You have little chance of making it out of Sheol. Even with the help of the girl and your brother. I will send every available Shaitan to come for you. You won't get out. Even if you do reach above ground, how long can you protect them? Eventually I will pick them off one by one. Then I will begin on the Sentry and give the Shaitan full leave to kill humans. I will not even consider their souls, although surely some of them will come to me."

Chapter 27

"Let us finalize our deal, son. You wish the release of your brother, your lover, and this suicide victim. In exchange I will have your willing and permanent return into the Unseen."

Nias thought about Rachel and then his brother, and finally his love, Jade.

"I have no decision to make. It would mean far more to me for my loved ones to find safety from you, and your Shaitan, than my continued existence above ground. I come willingly." Nias had removed any emotion now from his face and body. He would find numbness again.

"I have more demands, son." The seven-foot-tall Daemon squinted and arrogantly moved toward Nias with a gait that reeked of his barely controlled madness. "You will not only remain in the Unseen, but you will remain at my side. You will be my right hand once again. And to ensure your siblings and Sentry do not come for you, you will not tell them. You can tell no one. You know I have Watchers everywhere."

Nias knew the meaning behind Iblis's words. He never said anything not to be taken literally ... Iblis intended he not even tell Jade. "So this entire scheme was to get me to come back and work for you again? This doesn't even make sense. You have already taken my life. I cannot be with my family. Rachel, although you would release her, now has been tortured to the point of possibly no mental return. You have left me with no choice with my love; I would never again risk keeping a human close to me. Especially Jade, never Jade. So why would you want me?"

Iblis scowled and started a tirade. "I want them back, the Djinn are mine. They work for me. You work for me. Unfortunately, somewhere along this long path they began to listen to you. So after you are back for a time; when you do go to them, and you tell them why the best course of action for them is to return to Sheol, I believe they will. I don't care how you convince them, but I know you can. You convinced them over five hundred years ago to leave, to abandon their homes, bloodletting, the Verge, and me. You convinced them to help humans, which is preposterous! You must come back to me, stand by my side, and then bring them all back home."

"Yes, fine," Nias lied. Fine, he accepted he would find his End here. He would never ask the Djinn to come back. Nias would find his End. Jade and Rachel would no longer be factors if he were gone. And he knew if his family stayed together, stayed alert, they would remain safe as well. "I will escort Jade, Rachel, and Joss back above ground and transcend them home. I need to be absolutely sure they are returned safely to their lives. I also require proof they are content and unharmed. That means completely left alone by you or any other Shaitan interaction. I will return to the entrance in three days, where you will supply me with transportation, at which point I will remain with you as long as you wish," *or until I cease to exist.*

The burning wind kicked up in the dim stone-walled expanse of the throne room. It sounded hollow, empty, blank, and reminded Nias of what he had committed himself to.

"I accept these terms ... Enough!" Iblis replied with a dismissive wave of his hand. "So, you shall go see your brother. Or what's left of him," Iblis said, with dull amusement. Clearly Iblis didn't care if there were anything left of Joss or not. "And then we will put on a show for your companions."

Jade felt the force of Iblis's disturbing, powerful magic as the transcending began. She had to physically shake the gross filmy after-effects of it from her skin, hair, and clothing when she settled. *Yuck*, she thought. Unfortunately the essence of his magic lingered and it even seemed to have seeped inside her.

She had been in the realm of the suicides, or whatever they called it, alone with Rachel. She had gone to Rachel when they were alone and held the girl. Rachel had been so damaged she didn't speak, so Jade sat next to her in the dirt, under the tree the girl had swung from, and held her tightly. Strangely, when Nias left, so did Jade's jealousy, and instead it was replaced with genuine concern and pity for what Rachel had obviously gone through. She had searched Rachel's emotions and come to the realization the love Nias and Rachel held for each other was completely different than anything she might want him to feel for Jade. Nias was like a big brother to Rachel, a protector, not a lover.

Now she found herself standing with Rachel in a dank cave with black, jagged walls. A woman, her skin torn to pieces, lay at Jade's feet. This woman lay like forgotten garbage in a heap on a muddy dirt floor. Because the light was so dim, it took Jade a few moments to realize the mud had formed as a result of the woman's blood loss. Only a sparse amount of red light ran through the chamber emanating from small torch-like spots of fire in the ground. She couldn't even bring herself to approach the body.

Nias suddenly appeared by her side. Jade practically threw herself at him; she hadn't wanted to think about it, but she hadn't been sure she would ever see him again. Nias pulled back from her to look into her eyes. There was a flash of overwhelming sadness on his beautiful face. He recovered quickly, but she could swear she'd seen it.

"Hello, my Kitten." Typical of Nias, he stroked at her hair and ran the backs of two fingers down the side of her face. The light came back on in his eyes as he grinned at her. It felt like only the two of them stood there. He pushed her hair behind her shoulders and then grabbed her by the top of her shorts waist, pulled her to him and swept a kiss across her lips. "I want you to always be safe," he said, kissing her more forcefully this time.

"I know that, Nias. I have known that for a long while now," she said, as their eyes were glued together, and she was smiling back at him.

"That is really sweet, Nias, what the fuck? I am chained to the wall over here!" Although weak, the deep and distinctly male voice still dripped with sarcasm.

Jade remembered Nias had no problem with seeing in the dark. When his eyes locked on a man attached to the rough stone wall he took Jade's hand and led her to him as her eyes started to adjust. Jade quickly grabbed Rachel's hand and guided the girl over with them.

Thick metal chains were fastened to the curve of the cave wall. The man was bound by a metal collar, wrist and ankle cuffs were secured by padlocks, and all of these were secured to the wall by those chains. His legs barely held the weight of his body, which was being kept vertical almost exclusively by the neck closure. It seemed to be choking the air from his throat. Red welted stripes crisscrossed over black bruising on his bare torso. The man was as tall as Nias with the sinewy yet intensely cut muscular build of warrior, who was obviously built to protect and defend in a ruthlessly brutal world. His hair hung to the side and nearly reached his waist. She couldn't tell the color in the faint light, only that it was dark. The pants he wore were shredded, and his feet were bare as well.

When Joss looked up at his brother, Jade sucked in her breath. Yes, he was hurt, but, by God, he was striking. He had the resemblance a brother would have, but this man was far more angular, his eyes even more exotic. Nias was beautiful, catlike, a sleek, sensual gorgeousness. Joss looked like a Daemon. Something far more mischievous lurked inside of this one. She took a step back from him. Nias's eyes sparkled, invited you in, said "come on, I've been waiting all my life to fuck you", or at least to her they did. But Joss's eyes glinted and slanted up a touch. Eyebrows slashed instead of arched. He looked dangerous.

When Jade and Nias got to this man's side, a thing Jade recognized as a Marid Protector approached with a leather whip. The Protector came at them like he was going to attack. But Nias used his elbow to bludgeon the creature's face and knock it down. As he went to step on its chest and break its neck, Iblis appeared and called out to his other minions in the area to join in and fight.

Now Iblis and Nias were working together to make a show of Nias's group escaping. Iblis couldn't simply let them walk out and expect the Djinn not to find it suspicious. Nias broke more necks. The fighting went on. Iblis allowed several more of his Protectors and a few Palin Watchers to die, but never called for anyone to go for back-up. Nias saw Jade mentally push calm toward all the Shaitan and, as before, in varying degrees, they slowed.

With another of his evil chuckles, a swirl of dust came up into their eyes and as they covered their faces, Iblis and all his minions disappeared.

"What just happened? Nias, where are they? They're gone?" Nias felt Jade's power rush back inside her. They were definitely gone.

"Yes, I think they have gone for now. I'm sure they will return, though."

"Weird," Nias overheard Jade say to herself, "too weird."

Chapter 28

Nias moved closer to Joss and checked to see how bad his situation was. When Nias touched his brother's face, Joss startled and pulled away from Nias's hand.

"We need to find the keys." Nias looked about the cavern for a moment.

The Shaitan had not kept them far. A weak-looking Rachel had them in hand before he had even thought to look. Nias could see why Joss hadn't simply ripped through the chains and left. Djinn had an adverse reaction to steel. They could touch it, but it wasn't pleasant, and it was the one metal that overcame their powers. They were unable to break through it. No doubt this was a weakness Iblis had manufactured in their creation to use in controlling them, one which unfortunately worked. The Shaitan often used weapons forged of the substance when fighting the Sentry above ground.

"My gods, Joss, what the hell did you do? We were told you were being watched by Empusa. We should have had plenty of time left to get to you and get you out before any harm came to you," Nias said, as he stood inches from his brother's tattered body.

Joss lifted his eyes to his brother and coughed. A scowl ran between the man's eyes, drawing his brows together. Pushing up on his feet slightly so he could capture some air, he spit out the words, "Fuck you, man, get me down." And despite the bleak situation, the two brothers gave a slight laugh together.

Nias had Jade undo the shackle at his brother's neck and Joss fell forward into his arms. Jade finished undoing the locks. Nias pulled his brother away from the wall and lay him on the ground.

"Yes, I may have exacerbated the situation a little," Joss said, without looking anyone in the eye. "This is it? You and a girl came for me, making out?"

"You're welcome brother. I see they've only managed to break your body, but your rebellious smart-ass mouth remains fully intact." Nias continued to hold his hand beneath his brother's head, making sure it never rested on the rocky ground. He didn't even realize he was doing it until Joss shook his head free.

"Yeah, unfortunately for you, big brother, I am still fully capable of cussing you out for leaving me down here to rot."

"Actually, I think it is me who's unfortunate. Seems like all your siblings, with maybe the exception of your mean little sister, have the smart-ass mouth you're discussing."

Joss looked over at Jade and Nias watched him raise his brows as Joss noticed what a beautiful girl she was. "I think I just remembered exactly how hungry I am." Joss bared his teeth in the smile Nias knew could melt any woman to his brother's will, or with a slight degree of change, could bring a man to his knees with fear.

"Joss, this is Jade. She and I just came through a nightmare together to get you out of here. There is no way in Sheol or any world you will be touching her. In fact, remove that stupid grin and stop looking at her altogether," Nias grouched.

"So, I see how it is." Joss turned his tired head slowly and painfully back toward Nias. "Are we giving humans another chance, then, brother?"

"No," Nias said much too quickly, and then forced himself to pause. "She has just been through enough; she shouldn't now be used as your food supply. I can carry you partway, and then you can rest a few hours. Then we get the hell out of here." Nias looked at Jade as she visibly steeled herself for what she had to think would be the arduous journey home. "I'll explain our journey more fully later; right now we need to go." He averted his eyes from Jade and turned to Joss, who tried to sit up. Nias reached to help him, even though it was clear Joss wanted no help.

Rachel shook her head, as if waking up from a long sleep. She had seemed to be starting to recover her senses and approached Joss, speaking for the first time. "Hey, rebel, you aren't just getting up and walking out of here, I'll have to help you." Rachel knelt wearily down beside Joss and picked up his hand.

Joss focused on her for the first time. "Rachel, my gods!" Joss pulled her to him and hugged her. "It is so good to see you. Is our hero going to get you out of here as well, little one?"

"Yes." And then she sobbed. Joss hugged her again and held her for a few moments. Nias's love for the two of them bubbled over. His decision was solid; it made perfect sense. Now getting them out of Sheol became his only thought.

Nias knew the journey out would be almost completely unimpeded. In fact, the most difficult thing about it would most likely be convincing Jade and Joss that it was difficult. The two times so far Iblis had sent Shaitan to hinder their passage, the battle had been won easily. Nias had remarked how Joss was a huge aid in their battle to achieve freedom. But Jade had squinted at him, as if to say, *why are you acting so damn weird?*

Joss was able to get Nias aside slightly, although he couldn't get too far away from Jade in order to continue to protect her from the heat. "It is obvious how you feel about the girl, Nias. You're having a hard time keeping your hands off her. She is absolutely beautiful, and it's obvious she feels the same about you," Joss whispered, as they walked through the caverns and out of the dark zones.

"I guess you're feeling better? If you're thinking of my personal affairs I assume the healing is progressing quickly," Nias replied, trying to change the subject before Jade heard any of it. Nias had not spent much time with his brother in the years since they had lived above ground, but he could always count on Joss to say exactly what he was feeling. Words seemed to pop into his brother's head and then fall out his mouth instantaneously.

"I'm happy for you, brother. You deserve love. You gave yourself away for far too long to the Djinn, and then to the humans; you've finally found a mate worthy of you."

"Truly, it isn't what you think." Nias looked to the ground quickly and then made the pretense he was fine.

They had come to the large ravine where Nias had cut the bridge ropes, and there sat two Ifrit. Iblis had left the flying transportation for their exit and Nias was now faced with the task of making it look like they were forcing the Ifrit to fly them to safety instead of what they were really doing, which was sitting there, docile, waiting, the ignorant animals they were.

"Everyone keep to the cave walls so they will not notice us," Nias said, reaching for Jade's and Rachel's arms and pulling them back toward the wall. Rachel, still quiet, listened and moved quickly. Even Joss did what his brother said, which was unbelievable. All it took was a week and a half of torture and the man actually hid from one of the beasts.

"What are you talking about? They aren't even looking over here. They are pecking at something and it looks like…yuck, is that flesh? It is so bloody!" Jade averted her eyes.

"Jade, this would be a good time for you to subdue them and convince them to give us a ride instead of killing us," Nias sighed, as he walked next to her.

"Okay, I got this, don't panic."

He wished at that moment he were a better actor. He did feel a bit panicked. All he cared about in that moment was that he could pull this off, and get them out of Sheol before Iblis changed his mind or they figured out what was going on. "We truly need to get out of Sheol, Jade. Change their feeling and let us be on our way."

Jade turned and glared at Nias. *Something is definitely not right.*

But given their situation, she felt that expediency was needed and pushed the feeling aside.

She reached out with her mind and found the evil within them and began to twist. She found it surprisingly easy to manipulate and convince the Ifrit to walk toward them. They stopped devouring whatever it was and came over. Joss looked impressed when they merely let them board.

Jade squinted her eyes at Nias and wondered if she had missed something.

"You have grown so much stronger, Jade, even from the time we first entered Sheol," Nias said, as he grabbed her hand and lifted her up onto their now-pliant transportation.

But when the Ifrit had taken to the air, finally Jade and Nias had the opportunity to be alone together, and her uneasy feeling faded, with him wrapping his strong arms around her from behind. Jade no longer had use for the weapons and so Nias put the backpack on himself and squeezed her tightly into his torso. Jade leaned back into him and thought, *Now we can finally put this behind us and figure out what we mean to each other.*

Chapter 29

When they transcended in, Jade felt like she was on a different planet. Well, she thought, *I am actually in a different world.* Whether Sheol was connected to this world or whether she had gone through some kind of giant portal, she didn't know. And she didn't care. All she knew was that she was safe, Joss was rescued, Rachel was with them and improving, and most importantly Nias was safe.

"Oh, thank the gods!" Ella was standing in front of Jade when she looked up and a huge grin spread across the girl's perfectly angled features and then Jade could see her rein her emotion back in and the smile faded. Ella walked toward Jade with a command to her saunter that made it clear that she always kept herself in check and in control. Ella cracked another small grin and it even looked for a moment as though she wanted to throw her arms around Jade, swinging them out for an embrace. This was apparent when she restrained herself and clasped her hand around Jade's and shook it. "Welcome back, Jade, I am quite glad to see that you are well and unharmed." Another crack of a smile flashed across the girl's face as she quickly released her grip. Damn, she was strong. Her hair still in a tight, low ponytail, Ella smelled like vanilla-scented shampoo and a picture of lying in a hot bath ran through Jade's mind.

"Um, hi."

"I am so glad you made it. We sent so many different groups in to find you. It seemed to everyone you all just disappeared at the Verge. Nias, we kept sending them in, but nothing." Ella then proceeded to tightly embrace each of her brothers.

Jade stared at the striking girl, who tried so hard not to be feminine. Ella pulled her black t-shirt back in place and then the tiny grin that lingered on her ample lips was sucked backed into her reserve.

Phaeton strode quickly into the room. "Baby brother, I see you survived, although barely. You look like shit," Phaeton said to Joss as he assessed his brother's wounds and the dirty mess that they had all become.

"Really, because I feel like I've been on vacation, you ass," Joss shot back at him.

"A drink, then."

"Much better."

Phaeton then walked to Jade and planted his mouth directly to hers. It was like when a male guest kisses the bride for too long at a wedding and when he finally pulls back the bride looks dazed and wonders if she'll be able to make it the rest of her life with just one man. Jade lingered when he pulled back and took a few extra seconds to open her eyes. And when she did, a breathy "damn" exhaled from her mouth. Of course, Nias took her by the wrist when he caught this taking place and yanked her away. Jade thought to herself, *this is a ping pong match in which I could never mind being the ball; strong rugged and sexy over there, predatory, beautiful and feline over here.* Okay, fine, the beautiful one had run away with her heart, but holy moly, could Phaeton kiss.

Finally Locke, having heard the commotion, came to Jade beaming and hugged her so tightly with his sleek, muscular body that it hurt. Locke glared at Nias and gave a subtle nod. "I was worried and am so grateful to have you home, my friend. Hello, Joss, are you alright? Should I call someone to look at you as well? I've already sent for a doctor for Rachel."

After the initial shock and excitement of being back home and a huge meal for Jade, everyone became aware of how dirty and tired they were and began splitting off to find themselves a place for the night.

"I am taking you to your room before you fall over. You are filthy; I would suggest a steaming cauldron of water and a scrub. Or you could stay here and make out with my brother for a while longer."

"Very funny, jealous man. But Daemons in glass houses should not throw stones." Jade looked up through her lashes at Nias and he smirked at her. He was delicious clean, dirty, or covered in swamp slime; it didn't seem to matter. "Yes, boiling cauldron of water and soap." He was so right. She felt herself lose equilibrium. She definitely needed to lie down.

"I would like to strip you out of those clothes and place you in that steaming water myself." The cocky half-grin she hadn't seen since they had made love in the caves returned.

"I have to say, the return of your little smirk makes me feel like I am actually home."

"Good night all." Nias gave a quick wave into the air, and ushered her down the hallway. When they got the stairs, he picked her up and cradled her into his arms. He had stopped and Jade saw the sadness in his eyes that had been rearing its ugly head sporadically. He began to take the stairs two at a time and she knew if she could read his thoughts, the chaotic indecision she had felt the first day he trained her would be screaming at her. He headed down the hallway toward the bedrooms they had once occupied. When he reached the doors, her room on one side and his on the other, she finally found the courage to ask.

"Can I stay with you?"

She had a flash of all their time together. From the moment he walked into her bookstore, to the time he saved her from the beasts in the warehouse, and the time they spent together at Phaeton's compound, she had never felt so high, so safe, and as dreamy as when he cooked for her, read to her, and touched her. She looked at him and it was her this time that released a low, almost undetectable, growl. She had fallen for him hard. She loved him. Before he had been a dream, an unreal adventure for her, but the stakes in her game had changed. He was better than a dream; he was real. Nobody is as perfect as a dream, but a person's true love is perfect for them. Flaws and all, she accepted him. She trusted him, not because her abilities initially told her he was being honest, not because she could read his feelings and tell what he felt, not even because she was sucking sexual energy out of him that was clouding her judgment. She trusted him like any woman trusts any man they are passionately in love with, blindly and unconditionally, with no paranormal net underneath her. He may not ever want her, she was only a human, and possibly she had been a willing plaything for him. But for the first time in her life she trusted another person; he was a good man. Warm, smooth, safe, dreamy, trustworthy, corporeal, and forever unobtainable.

If he was leaving her she wanted this last night, not to convince him of anything, but to be in his arms one last time.

Jade pushed open the door of his bedroom. All the destruction he had done to it before they left the house had been repaired. It was back to the room he had transcended her into the first night they arrived.

Nias looked down to her and suddenly all his arrogance faded and the light inside his body died as he saw the woman he loved. But he also saw a woman with expectations. A woman who was only going to be more hurt if he let her closer, or made love to her again and then left her. Even if he managed to find his way above ground again he would never risk her human life; plain and simple, he loved her enough to let her go, forever.

"There is nothing I want more than that, Jade, but," he knew a flash of indecision ran like a streak across his face, a reluctant smile, brow furrowed, pain in his eyes, "I'm sorry, I can't."

Chapter 30

"Yeah, I get it," she sighed, looking down his long legs to the same slat of walnut flooring he was staring at. Then she stopped to stare at his muddy boots. He was going to leave her, she was certain now it was coming, and in that moment she just didn't want to think about it. *Lalalalalala.* She put mental hands over her ears and silently began to chant her favorite "I am ignoring the world" song. When a man says "he can't" to sex, what he really means is "he shouldn't," which of course meant she shouldn't, but …she was going to. The madness of her thoughts swirled, but she just didn't care.

Jade took two steps forward, which helped her arrive within three inches of his warm, dirty body, and any doubts she had about overriding his conflicted brain were over. The scent of dirt, masculinity, and sandalwood and a faint flavor of lust still remained on him. His worn t-shirt hung from his hard pectorals, leaving half an inch between it and the rock-hard abs she knew were underneath.

Jade slipped two fingers into this space and moved them back and forth, slow and firm over the skin just above his belt. She looked up and a sheet of blackened hair threatened to envelop her. She caught his eyes and they stuck to hers, and the confusion in them turned a little wild.

"Really, Jade, you're going to do this? I have clearly stated that…"

Jade grabbed that dirty sheet of hair and used it to pull his amazing lips down on top of hers. The hand she had been tentatively grazing his belly with scraped up his chest and her nails dug in.

Nias wrapped his hands around her waist and picked her up to his midsection and pulled her in tight. As if it had been practiced a thousand times, her legs wrapped themselves around his waist and seemed to scream, *please don't ever let me go.*

The kiss consumed her. She may have initiated, but this man was unmistakably in charge here. She was clearly overly excited and he pulled back, then slowly grazed the four fingers of the back of his left hand across her cheek and grasped a large chunk of her hair. He pulled her back in and nipped at her top lip.

"Ahhh," she whimpered.

A smile spread easy and hungry across his face, culminating with a sparkle in his focused, now-luminous, golden eyes.

Nias walked toward the bathroom with Jade wrapped around him. He didn't look where he was going; his mouth remained with her nibbling her lips, and then she felt teeth grazing and then biting at her neck and shoulder.

He brought them over to the giant tub and with one hand remaining firmly on her exposed ass, reached to turn on the faucet of the bath tub.

The water rushed behind them as he unwrapped her feet from his waist and she unenthusiastically placed them on the floor. But then his hands moved to the top center of her tank top and he ripped and shredded the flimsy fabric, tossing it to the floor. Two of his fingers went inside her bra and she moaned out loud as he slid the cup down, grazing her nipple and replacing it with his tongue. He pulled her bud into his full lips and the end of his tongue began to flutter over its tip. Chills ran their way down her belly and spread out through her arms and then she could feel the wetness begin to well. Licking and sucking her into his mouth, she could feel the tingle and sensation of his rough hands remove each of the straps from her shoulders and then unfasten it completely.

He unclasped the button and undid the tiny zipper on her shorts and let them fall to the ground. "Remove your boots, Jade," he whispered gently. She made a motion to bend her knees and work on the laces, when he said "No, bend at your waist. Bend straight over and remove your boots."

"But …"

"Exactly."

He turned her around, his massive arousal pressed into her and he put one of his hands around her waist and applied pressure to her back, bending her. Her eyes and hands began to work on the laces of the first boot as she heard the tearing of her panties and his knees hit the floor.

Nias placed his tongue directly between her lips and atop of her most sensitive core and then ran it all the way up and back again. The sweet purr he loved released from her mouth as the sweet taste of her arousal met his tongue. Back and forth he ran his tongue absorbing her, consuming her. He heard her hands clutch the edge of the tub and her nails clack as she began to lose balance.

She moaned louder and he stopped and rose to his feet.

"No," she moaned.

"You will not use that word with me again; 'please' will get you what you want much more quickly."

He picked her up, turned her around, sat her sweet rear down on the edging of the tub, and spread her boots three feet apart. Nias tasted her neck, lowered to suck and then bite her nipple, licked downward to her navel, circled it with his tongue, and then let it run down into her moist folds. But he wanted more. He pulled her bottom forward, tilting her at an angle with her hands braced behind her, and he moved her lips completely out of his path.

"Uh, huh, okay, please…" she sighed breathlessly.

She heard him chuckle softly as he replaced his mouth and she came completely undone. Euphoria filled her entire body and she raged with a fire of passion; it swarmed through her loins as his tongue rocked and owned her.

"Please …" Jade's moan became more of a wailing song as the heat within her threatened to turn her insides to a boiling liquid. And then she erupted and screamed as her body shuddered and climaxed over and over and over … until she felt her body begin to give way and her arms folded completely, which is when she began to plummet backwards, head-first, into the steaming water, boots and all.

When she pulled her drenched head out of the water, Nias was laughing, but not at her; he looked to be in a state of absolute joy. His eyes gleamed when he looked to her and said, "By the gods, woman, I love you. You truly delight me."

Jade raised her brows. She couldn't believe the words she had just heard emanate from his grinning mouth. And then he looked into her ecstatic smile, apparently realized what he had just said, and then he frowned, turned, and walked out.

When she was dressed she found him still a dirty mess in the library, elbow resting on the mantle of the fireplace, staring into the flames. He walked across the room to her and took her by the hand.

A light wind swirled around them and they appeared in Jade's flat, back in Manhattan. The air in the room was stale, and everything was exactly where she left it.

She knew it was over. He had returned her to her life. Her boring, uneventful, daydreaming life. But this didn't feel like her life any more. He did. They did together; that was a life.

Nias was facing her, both their hands holding on to hers, forming a circle between them.

His exotic black-lashed eyes consumed her. A resigned sorrow emanated from them and seemed to wrap around her throat and her chest. She didn't feel like she was even breathing anymore at all.

Silence … neither of them said a word, for there was nothing left to say. It was over. Everyone was safe and home, but she could not fathom how she would live without this man in her life.

She felt the backs of his nails run the length of her arms. There were no chills this time. They felt like razors running pain into her skin. Wrapping these fingers around her biceps, he pulled her toward him. With the softest brush of full, soft lips, their tongues connected and made love to each other. She was not filled with lust. Her pounding heart was shrinking, slowly imploding into nothing. Their kiss continued … and continued … and then it was done. They separated completely and his eyes only flashed down into hers. Her now-tiny heart felt stabbed.

Nias was heading toward her door. His shiny black hair swung slightly on the back of his black t-shirt as he walked; faded jeans, perfect shoulders, waist, butt, he opened the door … and closed it behind him.

Jade went to the window. He should have transcended, been completely gone, but he was walking away. A steady, determined stride continued block after block, until he faded out of sight. And the rain began to pour down in the streets. Lightning crashed out of nowhere.

A cracked whisper escaped her lips.

"Come back …"

Behind her eyes a pressure to cry pulsed, constricting her throat tighter. Jade didn't know how long she stood there. But the sun had gone down and finally she sat down in that spot, on the floor, and fell asleep.

Jade's entire being, her body, her soul, felt like it had oozed into the floor. Like there weren't even pieces she could pick up and put back together. Waking up was the worst thing that had happened. She wasn't even in the middle of watching him go. She was alone.

The back of her head throbbed from the pressure of the wooded slats her head rested on. Tears welled and slid from the corners of her eyes, down her cheeks. She hadn't even known she was crying until she felt the wet streaks pool next to her ears and fall into her hair. She was staring at the white ceiling, not sure how much time had passed. Finally she pushed herself to her hands and knees. She tried to scold herself into movement. She tried telling herself this had always been the inevitable end. Dinner and movies and books and sex. It had been the fantasy; it wasn't going to happen. He fought and killed monsters. She was a human bookstore owner. He was gone.

Nias transcended straight back to the desert once he was out of sight of Jade's apartment. There was no reason for him to stay any longer. Joss, Rachel, and Jade were all safe. And the hole in his heart was the only evidence he had left of her … the only thing he could bring with him.

He had actually appeared a few miles from the entrance into Sheol. He wanted to walk for a while. To breathe in the fresh air of this world one more time. His walk was a slow, methodical one, and his thoughts hovered around one thing. Jade Shear. She was all he could think about.

He thought of the first time he saw her, how she twirled her flaming red, calamitous tangle of hair absentmindedly. How she could barely take two steps without tripping over her own feet. How her lips pouted at him, her quirky smile and sense of humor made him chuckle. How his Kitten had grown up right before his eyes. And finally, how she looked at him in shock and anger and pain when he left.

He was a bastard.

But he had done what he had to do. He was committed to seeing this through; to return to Iblis as he had promised and eventually, he was sure, let him kill him. Because he would never do what Iblis wanted. He would never try to convince the other Djinn to return to Sheol, especially his own family.

He had left them a message implying he had gone into seclusion for a time. By the time they realized what he had done, it would likely be too late for them to do anything about it.

An unusual fog had settled over the desert as he walked. As he looked around at the thick soup surrounding him, he grunted. Iblis was ever overdramatic. Show-off. He came near to the entrance to Sheol and saw figures through the cloud. One was dark and huge, with wings fanning out from it. Iblis himself had come to see him into Sheol, standing a few yards inside the threshold between worlds. As Nias walked, he saw the Shaitan who had stood to outline a path for Nias right to the entrance. They sneered and snickered as he walked past them.

As he stepped closer, he also made out Hamartia's form and grimaced. No doubt she was thrilled about this turn of events. He wondered if she would take a crack at him once again.

Nias paused right outside the threshold where Earth ended and Sheol technically began, and nodded. "Iblis, I'm here to fulfill my part of the bargain."

Iblis beamed evilly, clearly pleased with himself. There were several Protectors here with him as well, and a number of Ifrit to ferry them all down into the depths. It was obvious he was pleased with himself, and confident, otherwise he would never have ventured this close to the surface. "Nias, my boy, I want to welcome you home. It will be just like old times."

Nias grimaced, looking over, and automatically took stock of the situation, as he was trained to do. Ten Protectors, Hamartia, Iblis, and twelve Ifrit. All here for him, and he wasn't even planning on fighting. In other circumstances, he would have been proud to be held in such high regard.

He shoved his hands in his pockets to keep them from presenting themselves in a threatening manner. A posture of resignation. "This is the deal, Father." Nias spat out the word with contempt. "Joss, Rachel, Jade are all safe from any reprisal by you."

Iblis rolled his eyes, looking bored with this conversation. "Yes, yes, the deal was you return to Sheol willingly and they will be safe. Shall we go now?"

Nias looked at his father, then down at the invisible transition between Earth and Sheol. One more step, and he would be theirs. His thoughts filled with all those he was making this sacrifice for – his family, Joss, Rachel … and most of all, Jade – and he took that step.

"God's nightgown! Look at what the cat dragged in! And I do mean dragged, girl," Matt said, as Jade straggled into the front doors of her business for the first time in two weeks. Matt took her hands in his and spread her arms to take her all in. He was attempting to cheer her, but Jade practically ripped her arms from his grasp. It was the exact same way Nias had held her hands the last time she'd seen him.

Coming back to the store was her attempt at moving forward, or at least trying to reenter her own life. She now saw the echoes of him everywhere. The bookcase where she had first seen his cocky, perfect body leaning and glaring at her. The books he had read to her. There would be no getting around it.

"You need a hug worse than anyone I've ever seen." Matt smothered her in an embrace. He spoke softly when he released her. "I don't know where you've been, but you're back now, Mama." Jade pushed back at the tears threatening to well in her eyes. "I am here for you." He insisted on hugging her again, whether she wanted him to or not. People passed by behind them and the day's activities moved on; the world wouldn't stop for her heartache.

The week back at work rolled by in a haze, and she didn't try to shake herself free of it. It was safer there. She wasn't hungry, trying to be cute didn't cross her mind, being clean became an annoyance. She worked, then felt hollow, and went back to work. She did things that were not even her job.

She continued to see signs of him everywhere. It was ridiculous; books, soup, knives, even videos. They had not even watched one together, but she had imagined it. She had seen it so clearly; curled into his warmth, Nias's arms would encase her. Jade had envisioned there would have been a love story on. And ice cream, which he would feed her and himself with one cold spoon. He would inevitably, possibly unconsciously, pull at the ends of her hair with his fingertips. Feeding her the occasional frosted spoonful of Vanilla Bean, maybe even drizzled with hot fudge. Slowly placing the cold metal to her tongue and letting it linger and burn a little and then sliding it out. "Ummmm", is the sound that would come from her aroused mouth. Knowing Nias, it wouldn't have taken him long to replace the spoon with his tongue. He would manage to intertwine and delve into the chilly cavern and heat it within seconds. Nias would, in fact, have had far more of that ice cream eaten off her nude body parts than a ridiculous utensil such as a spoon. Oh yes, she would have been sticky. But she was one hundred per cent sure by the time he had covered the insides of her thighs and then the uppermost part of said thighs she would … and at that thought she began to sob. Even ice cream was her enemy.

Jade put on sweats, even though the city was in the middle of one of those muggy New York heat waves. *Heat be damned,* she thought, *this city doesn't even know "hot."*

A full week had passed. Dirty curls piled on top of her head, empty ache down to her bones, she stomped into her kitchen and was determined to eat sugar, not ice cream; she had to start slowly and watch a movie from her couch, not a love story. Westerns – surely if there was any safe genre it was Westerns. *High Noon* and hard candy it was. Practically a deprivation for a romance-and-chocolate junkie; it was like being stranded on a desert island where it constantly rained with nothing but lemons for nourishment.

Jade turned the air conditioning up to high. She wanted it so cold that frozen ice stalactites came from her ceiling. She wanted to be practically covered, in whole, not part of the space around her. Cozied up with three blankets, Ugg boots, and a wool beanie, she let her tears fall and put the TV on.

Casablanca was on and she got sucked in before she could

change the channel. She knew how wrong it was for her to watch a movie about a man and woman who fall in love in the middle of a tumultuous war and then that love is unrequited in the end. She knew how *Casablanca* ended; most romance addicts do. But it captivated her. Rick, the bar owner, is tortured and angry over the circumstances of the love he had lost. Hum. In *Casablanca* it was one and the same woman who he lost and loses again. But Jade cried anyway. In the end it was the fact that the man who everyone took for a grumpy, crass, uncaring jerk turns out to be a moral man who fought for a cause and lost his love and his sense of duty to the world. And then she saw the end. And clicked it off and started to fall asleep, thinking about lost love.

The feeling started as an annoying itch, then a nag, like a whisper in the back of her mind. She was uncomfortable and restless on her couch under all those blankets. Then this voice began to scratch until it was like nails scraping down on a chalkboard. Casablanca is the story of a man bitter because of a love once lost and to all those around him he looks to be a man out for himself alone. But here, Jade thought, was the part that bothered her. Casablanca ends up not only as a story of love, but a story of self-sacrifice; "Fucker" she mumbled. Humphrey Bogart sacrificed his one true desire, to be with Elsa, for the greater good of the war. The struggle was at the heart of the movie.

Son of a bitch – that self-sacrificing son of a bitch. That is what Nias did. His last act with her finally made sense. He was denying his love for her and invalidating her love for him, in some misguided attempt to make it easier on her. Selfish prick! It was to make it easier on him too. *Why do men always have to be the hero, have to be the martyr?* Now, here she was, alone again, with no hope of ever reaching the one man she truly loved.

Her sadness turned into anger. Anger at him for what he said. Anger at Iblis for what he had done to them. And anger at the world for not having a solution for her.

But then she had a thought. She would go back to Phaeton's

to assemble an army, consequences be damned.

Jade threw off the blankets, unbound her feet and head from the snow gear, went to her always swollen and stuck wooden window, and jammed it open. She yelled to a man across the street, sitting outside at the café.

"Hey, Djinn!" The exceptionally large, exceedingly attractive, man turned to look up at her. They had always been watching her. Either they thought she didn't notice or they just didn't care. She suspected the latter. But they had been guarding her ever since Nias left. They had reminded her too much of Nias, so she never engaged with them, until now.

"Can you come up here please? I need you!"

He was there in a gust of wind, his eyes darting about the room like he expected Hell itself to leap out at them both.

"Easy there, big fella. I want you to take me to Phaeton right now."

The man looked her up and down. "My orders are to guard you here. Not to be a taxi service."

Goddammit, do they ALL have to be so infuriatingly obstinate? Her anger rose and she growled in response. "I don't have time to argue with you. Take me to Phaeton." Something inside her shifted, and she could actually feel her will shoving the Djinn's aside. His eyes glazed for just a second before he shook his head and refocused.

"Of course, wherever you want to go. Are you going to go dressed like that?"

She looked down at her rather disheveled self, then looked back up into his face. "Give me five minutes."

Chapter 31

Jade had dressed in a much more functional black outfit and grabbed the pack of weapons she had worn into Sheol, and the Sentry transcended her to Club Djinn, where she then argued for a few more minutes with Wrain before being taken to see Phaeton.

Phaeton then stood, staring at a frantic Jade. She explained her revelation, *Casablanca*, and her desire to get Nias out of Sheol. He looked at her as if she had lost her mind, with the way she too quickly rambled out the facts, the battle-ready gear, and clothing she wore. But when she was done talking, he ordered the Sentry into action.

After a thorough search of Nias's home, stomping grounds, and any other possibilities he could think of to try to confirm Jade's suspicions, Phaeton had an enormous team of Sentry assembled. Jade could see he was completely ready to move in and slaughter his way to Iblis and his brother.

"Jade, I truly appreciate your help in retrieving Joss and in coming to me with this information, but I can't allow you to go with us. We won't be going in quietly like Nias and yourself. Besides the fact Nias wouldn't want you anywhere near this. This is going to get ugly. You would have to be protected, which would end up being a huge liability to us."

Before Pheaton had a chance to go on or issue an order to

233

transcend to the desert, she closed her eyes and pushed at the Sentry's minds. Many of them she found could be swayed. Jade forced out their annoyance, doubt, and impatience toward her continued presence and replaced it with a desperate longing for her help. Several then voiced their new found desire for her assistance.

"She will be a huge help, Phaeton," a blond Sentry stated matter-of-factly.

"I agree, we could definitely use her. She could be invaluable," another offered, trying to persuade Phaeton.

Jade smirked and lifted her brows at Phaeton and he rolled his eyes. "No, Jade, not going to happen, but that is very impressive." He chuckled. "Kohle, Wrain – move your group to the desert." His direction was aimed at two of the guards, apparently unaffected by her persuasive abilities.

"I will be going with you!" she said angrily.

Then she threw two balls of energy at Phaeton, knocking him back onto the dirt of the courtyard where the Sentry had assembled. He gave her an incredulous glare. She lunged toward him and as he attempted to get to his feet, she gave him her best side kick straight to his chest. As she quickly moved to stand on his chest and pin him to the ground, to demonstrate her ability to break the neck of a Shaitan with her foot, he transcended up and grabbed her, pinning her arms to her waist.

Jade kicked and thrashed, but Phaeton was far too strong for her to struggle away from.

"Okay, fine, you've got me!" she shouted, but when he set her down she went for him again. And again he grabbed her.

"I get it!" He set her down and stepped back with his palms held up facing her, a sign for her to stop. "I took down Protectors when I was there, Phaeton, I can defend myself."

"Nias is going to have a fit," he looked down at the ground and shook his head, "but, fine, you can come." He grinned at her. "You have gotten stronger, Jade, much, much stronger. I am truly impressed. From what I was told, you didn't have the ability to move matter, only thoughts."

"Yeah, I am way stronger, stronger with my mind, with my energy, and even my body strength. I have to say, I am loving it, it feels really good." She smiled at him again, and then … she was back in the blasted desert.

This time, however, she had Phaeton, Joss, Ella, Locke, and upwards of twenty-five Sentry anxious to end as many of the underground-dwelling Daemon as they could.

The fighting began the moment they reached the stairs. As they moved through the dark terrain, a bloody wake lay like a dried river of the dead behind them. Jade hardly had a chance to attack anything. Phaeton was keeping her in the center of the group, and this group had come for blood. The Sentry were trained and anxious to use every skill they had ever learned in their many long years of preparation. They moved quickly and never stopped to rest. Phaeton offered to have her carried, but Jade felt strong and trudged forward, easily keeping up with the rest of the group, strangely never even feeling fatigue.

At some point they started torturing Shaitan to find Nias. If the monsters wouldn't talk, they found ends far worse than the others. They eventually took multiple Shaitan at once, torturing and ending one in front of the other. Jade looked away while some of the information was obtained.

The group moved through a cavern-like tunnel, which opened into more of the deep-blue, swirling underground sky. As they trudged forward Jade saw a gray stone medieval-looking castle. Its energy was pure evil; it felt almost like it had a pulse of its own, becoming stronger the closer they moved toward its structure.

"We will go straight in. They know we are coming, so we have no choice but to move through the front gates. Jade, stay near myself or Ella." *No problemo*, Jade thought to herself. This had all seemed like it would be easier and less bloody when she had envisioned it from her apartment. But the thought of Nias inside kept her moving forward. He may not want to have her be a prolonged member of his life, but her feelings for him wouldn't allow her to leave him in the hands of that terrifying Dark Angel.

As they approached the Gates of Insanity, Jade thought she actually heard Nias screaming.

Nias let out a massive war cry, which echoed throughout the castle, and then looked down at himself, at his blood-soaked clothes. And couldn't believe how he felt. Good, he felt good. He had managed to end a hundred or more of the various Shaitan and now he was going to end Iblis too, or die trying. The Dark Father had let his guard down too much. Nias had only to turn a few of the Protectors against Iblis and, surreptitiously, control of the castle had become his. The Protectors he had under his command had been easy to convince. They were a disgruntled lot, who hated Iblis for his treatment of them as his underlings. Iblis was beyond reason, more powerful than any of the other creatures in Sheol. The Protectors worked for him because they had to, or die. But given an option, one where they could possibly overturn Iblis's control of them, they were anxious to take it. Nias knew why; they wanted to be in charge, and there were so many of them. If they could rid themselves and Sheol of Iblis they believed they could realize that goal. Without Iblis or the Djinn they would reign here.

Nias laughed inwardly to himself, knowing they were an out-of-control group whose downfall would always be that every one of them would want to be ruler. They would eventually destroy each other without a clear leader. They needed Iblis; he was a necessary evil for them, but they would never understand the complexity of this problem themselves, and he wasn't about to explain.

"Move up the stairs; we will go into his chambers through the back entrance," he yelled. But when they turned the corner to move up the stairwell, Hamartia stood guarding Iblis's door.

"Hello, pretty. Finally we are without the human. Just let me deal with this group of traitorous slime you have with you and we are free to explore the possibilities between us. I have been waiting far too long for your attentions." He could tell she was doing her best to purr this at him, but it had come out more as a broken, whiny grumble.

"Hamartia, perfect; I am so glad to see you, love, during an ending spree. This will be the one and only time you hear this from me … come to me, sweetness, come." Nias put his hand in the air and motioned her toward himself. *So I can end you once and for all, you vicious, malevolent atrocity.* Then for a moment he felt pity for her. For the existence she had endured … and then his thoughts circled back around and he lifted the giant axe to place it at the perfect height to take her neck.

The clomp of boots behind Hamartia was loud and the pace being set by their wearer was rapid. Whoever, or whatever, it was, it was determined. Deep male voices shouted, trailing behind the quick strides, and hollered for whomever the wearer was to stop. Nias saw a short sword come up behind Hamartia's dreadlocked hair. He knew Jade's weapon; there had only been one like it.

The thought of Jade being injured, as always, sent his entire being into a panic. This time it caused him to hurtle forward. His movement was that of any predatory animal going for its kill: sharp, fierce, and beyond deadly. It seemed a mere flash and he was beside them, ready to pull Jade out of the way before, he thought, Hamartia would turn and end her life.

But suddenly, before Nias could swing, the head of the Ghoul smacked to the ground and began a bloody trail, bumping its way down the stairs. Hamartia's body buckled and collapsed as it too fell forward and planted itself hard on the stairway behind him and he had to slide beside its tumbling weight.

Jade looked at him, sweating and breathing hard from her brief exposure to the overwhelming heat as she had run from Phaeton's group towards Nias, her skin having turned red, and smiled.

Nias looked up, still in "save Jade" mode, and reached his arms toward her. What he found was a beautiful, capable, trained warrior, dressed in leather, smiling, and as her sword clanked to the floor…she began kissing him.

His brain screamed for him not to reciprocate; regardless of the kill it was dangerous here and she needed to leave, but there wasn't a single piece of his body listening. Like a spoiled child, it wanted what it wanted and would have it. Their bodies meshed, not a sliver of air remaining between them. His arms wrapped themselves into the place they had wanted to be ever since he had walked into her life.

Nias tilted his head and pressed his mouth to hers. The moment she had initiated the bond, his body screamed out in pleasure and stole control of the situation. His tongue instinctually slid across her natural pouting lips and pushed its way through. His embrace was desperate for her. He felt her energy run through him, warming his chest, slipping across his belly, and coming to a throb in his groin. He grinned and placed his hands on either side of her jaw, pressing his thumb to her lower lip and smearing it to the side, his teeth flashed a wicked smile and his tongue licked at her tongue as he began to chuckle softly and then kissed her again.

"Hello again, my Kitten," he said into her open mouth as he pulled back to see the beautiful face he loved.

With her eyes still closed and her lips slightly parted she purred up at him, "Hello, Nias." He couldn't help himself; he brushed his lips to hers again and his hands began to slide down her back, gripping her firmly on her butt.

"Yeah … um, hello Nias," Phaeton said sarcastically as his giant form came up from behind her. "I am quite glad to see you as well, but keep your filthy paws off me, and if it's alright with you, I'm gonna pass on the making out, too." Nias looked over Jade's head and smiled at his brother, as the carnage continued beyond him.

Not willing to break the contact he had with her, he leaned in and gave her one more brush to her beautiful lips. He moved his hands around her hips, turning her back to himself and fitting her like a piece to a puzzle perfectly against his chest and stomach, pulled her snugly, and she set perfectly into his embrace.

"That's so wrong. Not even funny," Nias tried to growl. But he was simultaneously enormously glad to see them and pissed off they had come.

Nias then stepped back from Jade and as the latter emotion took hold, "What are you doing here? You shouldn't have done this, Phaeton. Damn it, you shouldn't have come. And what the fuck were you thinking, bringing Jade," he shouted now.

"Hey," Jade turned to Nias. "This was my idea; I wouldn't allow Pheaton to leave me behind."

"Stubborn woman, when will you learn to …"

Jade cut him off midsentence with a hiss. "Listen to me," she said as she pointed a finger at him. "If you hadn't come back down here, we would not have had to come for you…"

He cut her off. "I came down to protect the rest of you and Phaeton's stupid decision to come get me negates the entire pact I made with Iblis, not to mention how dare he bring …"

"How dare he nothing, you ass!" Jade actually jabbed him in the chest several times. "Coming to Sheol for you was my idea; I finally came to my senses, which you never seemed to have in the first place. How dare YOU make decisions for the rest of us, for me? I would have never let you do this if I'd known the truth! I am strong, Nias!" She stabbed him in the chest again, this time with a jagged, broken fingernail. "If you would open your eyes and stop trying to protect me, you would see I am perfectly capable of defending myself now! Look, for God's, or whatever, sake!" She shook her head and clenched her teeth in frustration. He tried to cut her off again, but she held up that jagged fingernail and the look she gave did its best to threaten his very life. "Hamartia is dead! I killed her! Me! I have gotten stronger and stronger ever since I met you. I can throw energy, my body is strong. I can push more than just feeling, I can coerce the weaker Daemon to my will." Again he opened his mouth to say something. "If you fight with me any more, I am kicking your ass just to prove my point!"

Jade looked to the ground and the anger drained out of her. One moment she could feel it boiling and threatening to burst out of her skull, and the next it rolled out and down her body and seeped out her toes. It left her with nothing but exhaustion and all the sadness that had been welling inside her these weeks he had been gone.

Nias looked to his brother and the troop of Sentry behind him. "Phaeton, can you give us a few minutes, please?"

"Of course, but are you aware of the Protectors loitering behind you?" Phaeton glared with serious consternation behind Nias.

"Yes, I am aware. These have had a change of heart, for now." Nias looked back to the threatening-looking mob of dark-hearted men. "Go with Phaeton. Do as he says and Iblis will be put out of power."

Phaeton motioned for the Protectors to move past him and down the back stairwell with a grimace, which clearly conveyed his mistrust, then turned to follow the group out. Wrain shouted out the command and slowly all could be heard backing off and down the corridor they had come through to give the two some privacy.

"Ignorant, selfish, beautiful man, I love you." She spoke the last piece of it to the dirt, unable to lift her head. "I love you, and I know now you love me. And when you went away, part of me felt like it died." Jade exhaled again, and then willed herself to look up into his eyes. "When I realized what you did, when I watched *Casablanca* … okay, long story." She couldn't help but laugh, as he looked at her like he often did, like she was crazy. "When I figured out what you had done, I am the one who came up with this plan; I talked your brother into it. I love you and I forced your brother to let me come, because I had to."

Jade looked to the ground again and thought another piece of her might die then and there. Until she felt his warm hand under her chin, and raise it until she was forced to meet his gaze.

"I do love you, Jade." His other hand pulled the end of a curl, causing goose bumps to run a lust-filled wave up and down her body, despite the heat. "I just wanted to keep you safe… because I love you."

A long moment passed as they looked into each other's eyes.

"Please don't leave me again," she said to him.

"Please, at least let me try to keep you alive, then." He smiled. "Fine."

"Fine." Jade purred when he again grabbed her butt and pulled her in for a kiss, this time with no hesitations.

When she finally came up for air she took his hand and said, "Okay, let's go kill the bad guy."

"Ugh, woman were you not even listening?"

"Oh no, I heard you. Go ahead, keep me alive please!" She practically giggled. "Or you could just stay close so I don't incinerate and watch me kick some ass."

"Stubborn woman," he mumbled as he followed her to where the Sentry had assembled.

Chapter 32

Phaeton had his back toward Nias and Jade as they turned and walked to the top of the ancient castle's grand staircase and joined him. They took a position on either side of the Sovereign. They faced his warriors, upwards of twenty Djinn dressed in their usual random assortment of black camouflage, combat boots, and every metal-forged weapon imaginable, including the Roman spear point from the fourth century, a camp axe head spear, and the Celtic axe Fforde had found on a recent fight while in Gaul. Collecting these ancient weapons they now used to behead and gut the Shaitan had become a popular hobby with the Djinn.

They were all tall and muscular men, a fierce group any leader would be proud to have behind him. They stood at various levels of the staircase and the floor below, ready and waiting for instruction. Phaeton had a command of the Sentry that made Nias proud to call him brother and Sovereign. Thank the gods he was so able and willing to take charge when Nias stepped aside.

"You're sure about your abilities, Jade?" Nias said to her for the fifth time, feeling a bit of fear for her safety as they looked over the battle-ready warriors.

"Phaeton, look away for a minute, I'm gonna punch him," Jade stated sardonically in an exasperated deadpan.

"Please, if he asks again I'll join you." Phaeton beamed at Jade and then turned his smirk into one of pure sarcasm as he looked to his brother.

"Okay, I'm ready, little brother, let's do this," Nias replied.

"Little brother?" Jade looked at the two hulking men; Nias dark and exotic, and Phaeton with the long, dark, shaggy mass of waves and that always-present devilish, sexy smile, which could knock any girl off her feet. Phaeton certainly didn't look like anyone's little anything. In fact, Jade thought he looked more like a Spartan than a Daemon. He emanated a strong, completely-in-charge, Greek-warrior vibe; but also from hearing about his behavior and his wild parties she knew he was always likely to partake in the affections of the female variety.

Jade looked over to the Sentry as they readied and began to move in rows of two back through the halls of the castle, with the gang of willing Marid behind sneering and looking like the angry group of oversized hellion they were. They traveled the fire-lit corridors of the castle and after several turns they were directly in front of the double doors, which the Protectors had told them would lead directly to Iblis himself.

Before any of them had the opportunity to even touch the black metal handles, much less smash through the fifteen-foot, black metal doors, they began to dissolve. The surrounding walls came apart as if melting and disintegrating into tinier molecules and then ceased to exist.

The room, if it had ever in fact been a room, was wide open in front of them now. They were outside; sparse fires burned and outlined the mounds of rock around them. Jade noticed immediately the darkened purple sky above. A dirty pink-and-yellow-tinged moon was glowing and hanging in the air. It wasn't a typical-looking moon; the shape wasn't round, but jagged and fierce-looking, an angry, misshapen throwing star placed behind Iblis like a spotlight, grimly illuminating the dank night.

Several corpses lay piled in the dirt and the smell of burned and boiled flesh accompanied them. It seemed right Iblis should surround himself with death and decay. What else would there be here?

The creature they were looking to destroy sat lazily picking at his teeth with what looked like a sliver of bone. A dismembered, unrecognizable body lay directly to the side of the enormous black-gilded throne he sat in. As she stared, one of its fingers twitched and then an arm moved. It was reanimating. She wondered if, like the suicides, these continued to come back to life only to be picked apart and eaten again. She didn't have the chance or the desire to ask.

"Welcome home, my children, my most beautiful, traitorous deserters." Iblis raised a pointed brow, discarding the bone to the side, leaning back and resting his elbows on the large arm rests, his knees spread. He looked almost bored. "Come to end me, have you?" The beast chuckled. "You are in violation of our deal, Nias, but if you would acquiesce to have all your Djinn here stay with me in Sheol now, we can still redress our agreement."

Jade stepped forward towards Iblis and spoke, and even Nias seemed shocked by the defiance in her voice. "He will do nothing of the kind, you twisted monster. His deal is over! Although we appreciate the gesture, we have decided to take our chances. You cannot have him – or any of them."

Iblis started, almost twitched, shocked at Jade's boldness. But instead of moving to crush her, Iblis let his rage waft, emanating from where he sat. He became completely motionless, as if an ebony statue of himself. She watched as his eyes turned a solid black. It only added to the eerie stillness. A sheer dark fog came from nowhere; it crept along the stone floor, threatening to seep into her through her feet, like a sentient thorny vine crawling up her legs and into her soul. Jade felt chilled goose bumps rise on her skin as the fog reached her. But outwardly she stood her ground, keeping her body tall and rigid, her face stern. Only silently did she talk to herself, *Just fake it, Jade. Just fake it, do not turn around and run.*

Nias could see a slight twitch in the hand Jade had hidden behind her back and knew what was going through her mind. He took a step forward, placing himself in between Jade and Iblis, blocking Jade from Iblis's direct line of sight, his body casting a shadow on her.

Nias wasn't intimidated by his father's theatrics, even as he too felt the growing powers of Iblis's rage building.

"Iblis, you need to consider whether you are ready to risk all-out, unbridled war, over your desire to regain control of the Djinn. Conflicts that will arise between the Shaitan and the Djinn will only be the beginning. It will throw the worlds out of balance and, to be sure, it will send those uptight Goddesses into a rage. Just let us go. I am not going to do what you want me to, you can see that. And my Jade can take care of herself."

A deep rumble seeped from Iblis's throat as he continued to remain unmoving. The rolling wave of energy pulsed toward them as he spoke. "How about I simply kill you all … right now."

Jade's energy began to build inside her. Nias could feel the power coursing through her body when he gripped her hand, hoping to calm her a bit. But she shook her hand loose from his and stepped out from behind him and into the red-and-orange light. And then, damn his unruly woman, she talked back to the enraged black devil.

"You can try," she sneered.

Jade rubbed her raised hands together, accumulating a ball of energy and preparing to thrust it at the enormous horned monster.

But prepare was all she would do. The stillness and general wafting evil coming from Iblis turned. It was immediate, creating an instantaneous implosion of all the black energy in the room. It pulled at their bodies and down the surrounding rock. The energy whooshed in at the same moment he stood and his mammoth wingspan spread out and into the open air, casting the entire group in his shadow. The flames in the distance grew to fifty feet and roared their excitement, making the juxtaposition of light versus dark even more pervasive.

His wings began coursing a powerful push and pull. The muscles in his torso flexed as his body used their strength to shoot him easily into the air. Like a hawk swooping in on a minuscule rodent, with no chance of escape, his horns aimed themselves directly at Jade as his feet drew toward the sky and he came sharply down at her.

The claws on his hands struck, puncturing her neck, and she could no longer breathe.

Nias saw Iblis going for Jade even before Jade had. Most likely because he knew Iblis had reached his limit of patience and Jade had thrown him over into the depths of insanity. No one spoke to Iblis like that when his energy began to radiate and take on a life of its own. He knew exactly what was coming.

As Iblis's hands attached to Jade and his feet reached the ground, Nias grabbed him from behind, reaching between his enfolded wings and wrapping his arm around Iblis's neck, pulling him into a headlock. Iblis released Jade and turned on Nias. Jade's body collapsed to the ground and she gasped to take in that next gulp of air.

Iblis spread his wings and grabbed Nias by the back of his t-shirt and lifted him from the ground. A loud thud, swish, thud, swish, wafted into his ears as he flew higher into the sky and threw Nias into a large, jagged rock without much effort. Nias's form crashed and rolled down to the gravel, scraping off the skin on his bare forearms as he hit.

"Surely that's not the best you can do!" Nias said acerbically as he picked his aching body up from the ground and brushed the dirt from his jeans, turning to Iblis. Looking around, he saw the Sentry and their new allies were occupied by a force of Iblis's loyal army that had cut them off from Nias and Jade. They were on their own.

"Not even close, Son," Iblis said, flapping his wings back and forth, stirring the mist and heat along with them as he descended down, talons extended toward Nias's chest, ready to pick him up again or possibly rip out his throat. *No use giving that any more thought*, Nias supposed. Instead he ran as quickly as he could for the side of a large rock formation and ran his feet up the side and flipped his body. Nias's feet flew over his head, twisting in the air, and came down on the back of Iblis's intensely muscular flapping wings.

Using the momentum his body had gained, Nias wrapped his arms around Iblis's neck, then swung his own legs down to the ground and pulled Iblis with him. The two Daemons both came crashing down and Nias slammed Iblis's horned skull into the earth with a pounding thud.

Instead of injuring him, the impact only seemed to make Iblis angrier. The flames behind him in the massive chaos licked toward the darkening, now blue-tinged, moon, and the fog thickened around them. Nias ignored the weather changes being effected by Iblis's continually escalating emotion and used an increased strength brought on by sheer rage to push Iblis's face to the dirt.

With one hand on Iblis's neck and a boot pressing into his back, Nias raised his hand and shouted in Jade's visually unobtainable direction, knowing her whereabouts only by the tiniest sounds she made, which were carrying through the thickness.

"Jade, your sword! Throw it to me!"

Jade, having barely gotten her breath back and staunched the flow of blood with her hand, reached behind her back with the other and lifted the sword diagonally, unsheathing it from its holster and tossing it into the air toward Nias, where he caught it by the handle with his raised hand. Nias's boot pressed harder into Iblis's back and he raised the sword and began to bring it down in a slicing motion to separate the head from the body of the father, who had, for centuries, only brought pain and destruction to everyone around him.

As Nias used every bit of strength in his being, he moved the sword with incredible speed toward his target.

But just as the sword should have connected, his boot dropped to the ground, the sword chopped at the dirt, and he stumbled forward. There was nothing beneath him.

The winds around them kicked up and swirled violently, the black fog prevalent everywhere. A horrendous roar emanated from the skies above them. The flapping of massive wings pushed and pulled the fog, creating a hole in the ceiling of the night, revealing Iblis's bared teeth and pleasured grin pointed down at his favorite son. Nias knew Iblis had transcended himself away and remembered why Iblis would always have the upper hand in Sheol.

"Damn it," Nias grunted, looking up to Iblis, his thoughts immediately forming a new plan. He would have to outsmart the Angel. He couldn't win a physical battle with an opponent that could disappear at will. Nias could see, in the pleased and evil look plastered to his father's angular sadistic face, that he thought this fight was all but over. Iblis's muscles tensed and flexed as his powerful wings hovered above him while he relished in his victory.

Jade saw Iblis begin to shift, the claws of his feet turning birdlike. No, they were turning into oversized talons. His skin morphed from the bruise-colored flesh to thick ebony scales. His eyes, once a solid black, now glowed piercing red. And the beast was growing. In the space Iblis had once occupied flapped an immense ebony dragon.

Jade fell to her knees and closed her eyes. She had no idea if she could pull off what she was attempting, but with the realization of Iblis's ability to transcend, she had to try. Jade opened her mind and tried to summon some emotion that would block Iblis's powers.

As she did, all the emotion of the full-blown war between Phaeton's Djinn and Iblis's crew of loyal Protectors battered her:

the clank of metal against metal, the slices of flesh, the grunts of those being wounded, and those winning their individual fight. She would have to cut though the testosterone-filled and overly masculine rage flying about her. She actually managed a small smile.

She pressed the sides of her head with her hands and closed her eyes, blocking them out. "Focus, Jade, come on stupid powers, you have tortured me my whole life, work for me now!" she said out loud to herself.

She searched the room with her mind and quickly found who she was looking for. The fact he was radiating sheer evil and was currently an animal made her task a bit easier.

Now for the hard part. She heard Nias make several painful grunts and knew the dragon had descended upon him and was tearing him apart. *Let's just hope I can summon a feeling that will stop him.*

Jade's knees ground into the dirt, tiny rocks stabbing sharply into her skin. Her head felt like it would split right open as a knife-like pain attacked her. The bastard was pushing back. The fury that had been flowing out of Iblis since she had first talked back to him this evening could apparently be directed, and he was directing it at her.

This beast, Dark Father, Angel of Hate, whatever he wanted to be called, had powers she had never imagined, her powers. This could have been the reason she had been chosen for the mission of retrieving Joss in the first place. It had seemed strange to her. Nias and a few Djinn appeared capable of moving through the various levels of Sheol on their own. Although she had been helpful, sure, she now saw her real purpose.

So the Goddesses had thought me capable of this; here's hoping they were right.

Nias saw the giant Dragon coming down at him and couldn't help but say, "Oh, shit!"

Iblis was now three times his previous size and the claw-like nails of the Angel's feet were now talons a foot wide and two feet long, with razor-sharp nails to match. They gripped his t-shirt-covered torso and began to tear through him. He winced and groaned as they entered his flesh. But as long as the thing attacked him directly, he at least had a fighting chance. He gripped Jade's sword again and brought it sideways, creating a gash in its leg, and then pointed it upwards to stab into its underbelly. As the point of the sword drove in with a beautiful chunky slide he felt the winds kick up as Iblis prepared to transcend.

But the wind died suddenly. And Iblis remained. The tip, and then the entirety of the sword, entered his guts. Surprised, Nias pulled the sword out and slammed it back in, full length. The beast roared and began flapping its giant wings as Nias moved out from under it, attaching himself to its neck and again thrust the sword, this time beginning to slice one of the wings from its body.

The dragon screeched and shook him off. But Nias landed on his feet and immediately went back in to strike before it regained its equilibrium.

Nias brandished his weapon and moved like lightning toward Iblis. But the Dark Angel moved even more quickly than Nias. Iblis's injured wings spread behind him, lifting his form into the sky, and then further and further, where he stopped to hover above them. Iblis let loose a growl, piercing the night like a sonic boom.

The ground was littered with the bodies of wounded and dead. The men who remained standing and fighting froze and looked up to the giant beast.

Jade released the sides of her head and shook out her brain, "This is the part where a gun would have come in real handy," she said loud enough for everyone to hear, including Iblis himself, who was morphing back into his Dark Angel form.

"Stupid little human, thinking of stupid little human weapons. They don't hurt the Shaitan – they certainly won't hurt me." The anger in his voice fell on them, pressing in its intensity. "You will not be taking my existence from me on this day. And, in fact, by coming to take Nias and undertake this attack, all you have managed to do is begin the war you have been trying to stave off for these hundreds of years since the abandonment of your home. You have just destroyed the only chance you had of coming peacefully back to me."

"Pretty cocky for a dude who was just on the verge of getting his ass kicked," Nias called up at Iblis, who had completed his shift. But Iblis ignored his taunting and continued with his diatribe.

"The Djinn will not continue to blight my efforts with the humans, and they shall from this day forward no longer have the freedom to move about above ground without being targets themselves. Surely, Phaeton, new Djinn leader that you are, you know of the risks you were taking coming in here and killing so many of mine. Nias stole my finest creatures from me and now, Phaeton, you are personally responsible for killing hundreds of my Protectors, Guardians, and Watchers. Shaitan whom I use to preserve Sheol in the manner I prefer it."

Phaeton glared at the floating apparition of evil above them. "If you mean to continue with the torture, affliction, consumption of human flesh, repeating the acts of suicide, then I will gladly take you on. Fuck the balance! It's time to tip the scales, old man."

"Sounds like music to me, Phaeton. As does the new way I will have you hunted – all of you. You are a lost race. You may have somehow stopped me, for now, but I will bring my Shaitan back to full strength and come for you."

Iblis began to laugh again as his wings spread to their full width and he ascended into the dark night's sky. And, just like that, the battle was over.

Chapter 33

The journey back through Sheol was quick. Having ended the majority of the higher class of Shaitan on their way in through the dark zones, these normally stringently run areas were left in chaos.

The Sentry regrouped within the immense stone walls of the courtyard of the compound when they transcended from the desert. The dirt kicked up around them as they settled in, but Nias was done.

As Phaeton began speaking with him about new tactics the Sentry would need to initiate in order to combat the Shaitan once Iblis had rebuilt a new army, Nias looked into the eyes of Jade, who was already locked on him. Her eyes wandered down his hair to meet his and then began a descent to the lower regions of his body. She had her neck bandaged by Ella on the way back up, and although it was sore, she didn't feel like paying it any mind at the moment.

"I can see the return of the glare, my Kitten; the glare which has quietly followed my every move since I first saw you."

She tried to contain the hungry look in her eyes and only managed to create a smirk, which reconfirmed her yearning. Nias turned from his brother and gathered her in his arms and began to kiss her. Phaeton's protest was lost to the air as he transcended them to his bedroom.

"I was not glaring!" She didn't even give a solid effort when she tried to stifle the giggle which came to her when the false statement escaped her inviting lips.

His hands began on her hips and he scraped the tips of his slightly outgrown nails up her perfectly formed sides, removing her tank top out of their way. Nias's lips invaded the seam of her bra, where it met her cleavage and kissed his way over to her lightly fabric-covered nipple, pinching it with his teeth. The sound of her moan caused the already-present hardness between his legs to swell further and he began to walk her backwards toward the bed, where he pushed her body down, never relinquishing the firm contact between them.

"I am considering a previous thought I've had," Nias said, as he pinned her down underneath his body. "In addition to keeping you in this bed with me for at least a month, chaining you to it would have the added benefit of actually keeping you safe."

She looked up at him drowsy with lust. "Why are you talking? I have so many other things planned for your mouth."

Nias began to laugh and kissed her again with every bit of passion and the inconceivable love he had for her. He felt her hand move down his body and slip inside his jeans, and it was his turn to moan.

He rose to his knees, his legs still straddling her, and began removing the rest of her clothes, "You are so beautiful, Jade. I will never get my fill of you looking at you." And then he stripped himself down as well. They spent hours in his bed making love in every way they could conceive and then a few they hadn't until now.

When she curled into his arms, spent and exhausted, he finally found the courage to tell her what was at the forefront of his mind. "There is no place I feel more comfortable than with you curled and lying in my arms. I love you more than I ever thought it was possible to love a woman. You are my one true mate, Jade." He paused and turned to stare directly into her eyes. Nias let go of Jade and slid onto the floor, propped on his knees and with his hands holding hers, he continued. "This is too difficult," he exhaled and forced himself to continue. "I would like for you to spend eternity with me. I want you to become blood-bonded to me. In human terms, Jade, I am wondering if you would consent to becoming my wife. I want you with me always, and I never want to have to let you go again."

Nias didn't get a response. In fact, what he got was silence, a complete, utterly void wasteland of silence. Then he felt Jade begin to shake. And her breathing became sporadic.

Jade began to shake and tears welled in her eyes as she looked at this man, this Daemon, and her emotion began to overwhelm her.

"Jade, give me an answer. If you don't want to bond with a Daemon, it would make perfect sense to me. Why are you crying?"

"Shut up!"

"Excuse me?"

"Did you not hear me say I love you?" She took his face in her hands and brushed a sweet kiss across his lips. "I love you and I would love to be bonded with you. I would love nothing more than to spend eternity in your arms, and raise little bossy Daemons just like you! I love you. But you know, that's impossible. I'm a mortal human. I'll get all old and wrinkly and you will still be ..." She paused and sighed deeply as she looked at him. "... well, you!"

Nias smiled. "I intend to rectify that situation."

Epilogue

A light cloud of fog permeated the area Nias entered. Surrounded by a powdery whiteness, enveloped in its ethereal beauty…

What the fuck ever, Nias thought to himself. The Goddesses may be on the other side of this war from Iblis, but they were no less dramatic with their insistence for an overdone scene.

Coughing slightly, he waved the fog away from his face and looked up to take in the immense white doors. Their tops disappeared into the increasingly dense misty, cloudy, powdery, whatever it was that always hung on tightly to the entrance of the realm of Arcadia.

He had every intention of blasting his way through these gates and telling the Goddesses how it would be. But now, standing here, about to enter, the enormity of what he was about to ask for, of what he would lose if he were denied, hung with such importance to his heart, that he couldn't move.

He thought about the love he had for Jade and the reciprocal, unabashed glee with which she looked into his eyes these days, and reaffirmed his decision. Being a pussy right now wasn't going to be his course of action. His Kitten had walked into situations beyond reason for a human, conquered them, laughed while kicking ass, and become nothing but stronger through her journey. *She is truly dazzling. These women are just going to have to accept the way things are going to be. I am keeping her, forever.*

He placed his hand on the large crystal knocker. The doors swung open and, as before, the three Goddesses Jibreel, Eeia, and Aquila stood, the edges of their clothing, skin, and hair appearing in a wavering shimmer, positioned upon their pedestal at the end of the long, bright, otherworldly pathway.

"Nias, please step forward." The temples of Arcadia loomed, the intricate weaving art that was their façade creating a towering beauty, which spread as far as the eye could see behind the radiant females. His strides created a puff and separation of misty vapor with each step, until he was before them.

Nias was not in the mood for the formality with which they liked these meetings to progress. He fisted his hands and placed them into the back pockets of his jeans, exhaling and trying to calm himself a bit.

Jibreel spoke. "It is a pleasure to see you back before us. Joss home safely, the balance seems restored." Yeah, that blew the calm thing right out of the water.

"Restored?" Nias all but roared his disbelief. "I cannot believe I just heard you say that. Either you like to make happy chatter or you Goddesses have misplaced your crystal ball! Restored is the furthest thing from where things stand, Jibreel!" The glowing silver-haired beauty all but physically twitched as her mouth fell open.

"NIAS!" A crashing boom of a voice came from Eeia at Jibreel's side. "You have been warned about talking to Jibreel, or any Goddess, in such a way. I thank you for your service and bid you a long-overdue goodbye." Eeia began to lift her hand to the air and strike him with a wave of her hand that would end his existence, or at least try to.

His eyes darted towards hers and squinted his threat before the words began to leave his lips in a measured growl. "Don't … even…think about it."

She froze at the challenge and he continued. "Either Arcadia has completely lost touch with what is going on out there or you just want Sodom and Gomorrah. Open your eyes to the big picture, ladies. Nothing is restored. Shit has hit the fan and it is deteriorating quickly."

Aquila spoke calmly, as if she had all in control and Nias had simply been misinformed. The third Goddess had remained silent during Nias's last visit and rarely spoke at all.

"The way we see it, Iblis's armies have been contained, the numbers he once had decimated when the Djinn went in to retrieve you. We had thought to simply keep the status quo, but Phaeton's movement into Sheol with the Sentry destroyed Iblis's numbers. We couldn't be more pleased, and look." She swirled thin, feminine fingers through the mist as if stirring the air and a vision of Joss and Rachel in the great room back at the compound appeared before them. "Your brother and even this female you are so fond of are back safely above ground."

Nias was stunned. He had rarely heard such a long speech from the quiet, redheaded Goddess and as such was taken aback. Plus there was the simple fact of how out of touch they were. They seemed to have no idea what was about to be unleashed. But he was getting derailed from the real reason he was here. He took a deep breath and plunged in. "There is still the matter of Jade Shear. I wish to discuss her future."

Jibreel held up her hand. "Enough. Nias, you sometimes … what is the human expression … 'wear your heart on your sleeve.' You would come here and ask something of us after the way you continue to berate us? Your insolence knows no bounds." Then she allowed herself a slight half-smile. "Besides, you do not need to ask what has already been granted."

Nias tilted his head. Was she saying what he thought she was saying? "You mean … ?"

Eeia rolled her eyes. "The instant she received the gifts, immortality came with them. Now we can always try to take them back …" She observed Nias's tense reaction and got some satisfaction from it … "but I don't think that will be necessary."

Nias blinked a few times in disbelief, filled with a sudden, nearly uncontrollable, urge to get back to Jade and at least attempt to make love to her for the rest of eternity. "If that's the case … then I suppose there is nothing more to discuss." He tilted his head slightly in their direction and transcended home almost immediately.

Eeia sighed and looked to her sister Jibreel. "I still don't know what you see in the Djinn. They are arrogant, condescending, haughty, impudent, reckless …"

Aquila interrupted her. "And our best hope in the coming storm – and you know it."

Jibreel looked at her auburn-haired sister. "How do you think Nias will react when he learns the truth about his brother?"

Aquila's eyes swirled the same bright red as her hair. "We should be more worried about how his brother will react when he learns the truth about himself …"

Acknowledgements

Dawn:

To Meredith Hanna who picked me up a thousand times dusted me off and set me back on my way.

To Aaron Speca without whom the jumble of words that was Dark Dreams would not have been shaped into the magnificent adventure it has become.

Aaron:

Wendy, Leisha, and Jammie, for dragging me into this world of creative writing in the first place. Patricia, for always having a word of encouragement and having my back on every project I've ever taken. Torie, for being out there and showing me it really can be done and for paying it forward like nobody's business. Dawn M., for being my first fan and following me all this time. And of course, Dawn T., for having the vision to create this world in the first place and for inviting me to be part of this adventure.

To everyone I did not mention, I hope you know who you are,

and how much you have meant to this entire process. I can never thank you enough.